MOONLIGHT IN MAGNOLIA BLOOM

A MAGNOLIA BLOOM NOVEL BOOK 4

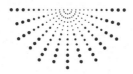

PAULA ADLER

DRAGON DREAMS PRESS, LLC

The Magnolia Bloom series:

Magnolia Bloom: Beginnings – three origin novellas - eBook BOX SET

Magnolia Bloom: Beginnings – audio BOX SET – coming soon

Return to Magnolia Bloom, a Magnolia Bloom Novel, Book 1 (also available in audio)

Mistletoe and Magnolia, a Magnolia Bloom Novel, Book 2 (audio coming soon)

Springtime in Magnolia Bloom, a Magnolia Bloom Novel, Book 3 (audio coming soon)

Moonlight in Magnolia Bloom, a Magnolia Bloom Novel, Book 4 (audio coming soon)

If you enjoyed *Moonlight in Magnolia Bloom*, please leave a review on your favorite sites (Amazon, Goodreads, BookBub). It's the most amazing thing you can do to help an author! THANK YOU!!

Please sign up for Paula's newsletter at https://www.PaulaAdler.com to receive her next free novella, updates, and information on all future publications. You can find her on Facebook at https://www.facebook.com/PaulaAdlerAuthor, and by email at Paula@PaulaAdler.com. She answers all emails personally.

PRAISE FOR MAGNOLIA BLOOM

Grab your copy and get ready to fall in love with Magnolia Bloom and Castle MacInnes.

Adler is a fresh voice who really knows how to tell a story.

I LOVE the saga and was super stoked to read more.

You feel the characters she write, in your heart and soul, you cry with them, you laugh with them. I highly recommend reading the previous books to this and I pray the author has more to the series.

All the books in this series are wonderfully written.

It swept me off my feet and was hard to put down. This is just a fantastic story to lose yourself in. I am ready for the next episode in this great story!

I would love for PBS to make a mini-series of this series so I could binge watch it!

All the characters have so much depth and personality. The author tells a great story. I highly recommend this book and the series.

I have read all 3 and so love them!! These are feel good stories but also at times require a tissue. Must read series!!

Absolutely adore this series! Ms. Adler brings these characters to life and makes you care about them. Even Lulu, the ever escaping, adorable sheep. Wonderful read to be savored.

I absolutely love this book and can't wait to read the next one. I love the magic within this family to overcome their obstacles and find true happiness. This is definitely a series I will read multiple times.

This is one of my favorite series now and I can't wait to read more from Paula Adler. I can't recommend this entire series enough. By the end, you'll be wanting to visit Magnolia Bloom and rub Penny the Dragon's nose and cuddle with the adorable sheep, Lulu.

Deeply emotional and richly imagined, the world of Magnolia Bloom is a universe that captured me and wouldn't let go, long after I turned the final page. ~ *NYT* and *USA Today* bestselling author Jean Brashear

Return to Magnolia Bloom is a gorgeous story of love, magic and second chances. I loved every second of it and can't wait to see what Paula Adler does next! ~ *NYT* and *USA Today* bestselling author Tracy Wolff

I wrapped my reading arms around RETURN TO MAGNOLIA BLOOM and didn't want to let it go. A big, big story alive with love, longing, and the wonder of family. ~ *NYT* and *USA Today* bestselling author Cathy Maxwell

Paula Adler has a gift for drawing the reader into a story. With wonderful prose, a heroine to root for, a heartwarming romance, and a sexy Scot, Adler has scored a direct with this story! ~ *NYT* bestselling author J. Kenner

Three women struggle to find themselves as they push through the mistakes of their past and the entanglements of the present to find the future they deserve. Wonderful writing. I couldn't put it down. Highly recommended! ~Bestselling author Dee Davis

Paula Adler gifts us with a multi-generational family saga that combines romance, heartbreak, an honest-to-goodness Texas castle, travels to exotic locales and a cast of characters who'll grab your heart and not let go. The love gluing the MacInnes family together shines through on every page, even when they're dealing with the pain all families experience. So pour a cup or a glass, snuggle into your favorite chair and prepare to become an instant member of the clan! ~Bestselling author Merline Lovelace

Return to Magnolia Bloom is the comfort read you've been waiting for, but you don't go to Magnolia Bloom just for comfort. It's where you go to finally challenge and face yourself, to grow up in ways you haven't dared to, knowing that even if you fall apart there, you can always pick yourself back up again! *Return to Magnolia Bloom* will have you believe in love and magic, but most importantly, it will have you believe in yourself. ~ *USA Today* bestselling author Sherry Thomas

I got so engrossed in the story that I didn't want to put it down. I highly recommend this book. I can't wait for the next installment to continue the saga of the MacInnes family.

A refreshing book about family, love but more importantly finding true happiness in loving yourself first. Will definitely be looking out for future books from this author.

This novella captivated me from the beginning. It's been a long time since anyone but Margaret Atwood has been able to keep my attention for a fictional book. I can't wait to read more.

I love the unique way of using a young girl as a narrator in women's fiction. This story checks many boxes, contemporary, romance, historical, family saga, southern Literature, and women's fiction. ALL OF MY favorites I will seek out Paula Adler from here on out.

Get nice and comfortable, (you) won't want to put the book down.

I didn't want it to end, so that should tell you how good it was. Grab your copy and get ready to be drawn in, like I was.

It pulls you in and keeps you wanting more. I would recommend this book. It is a very good read.

Great intro to the new series. Loved this book and wished it kept going so I could see what happened next!

CHAPTER ONE

LEXI

As God is my witness, I'm never flying overseas again. As soon as I find the strength, I'm texting my American cousin that I plan to live at Castle MacInnes for the rest of my life.

A dozen or so hours ago, I locked the front door of my beautiful home in Bearsden, which is a stone's throw from Glasgow, excited to begin my new adventure. I've never been to America. The farthest I've traveled is once to London and once to Paris, but those are a lot closer than Texas. Now I'm half afraid my hindquarters are permanently adhered to an airline seat, so the patina of travel has worn off.

"Ma'am? When we get parked, you sit tight. I'll get your bag down from the overhead."

To my delight, my companion from Heathrow to DFW is a bona fide Texan. As we traded bits and pieces about our lives, I discovered DeWayne Tomlinson is forty-one, has recently been promoted to lieutenant colonel, and is stationed at RAF Lakenheath. He's headed home from England to celebrate his promotion with his family in Dallas. To my delight, he's even been to the Highland Games at Castle MacInnes a few times, giving us plenty to talk about.

"You're a true gentleman, DeWayne. Thanks for making the hours fly by, no pun intended."

"My grandma'd have my hide if I didn't treat a lady like a lady, especially a beautiful one."

It's easy to dismiss his flirtation, and he's done quite a bit of it during our long voyage across the Atlantic. I even teased back a little, although I'm hardly known for my skill in that arena. It's easy because it's all in fun. He can't possibly be serious, so I appreciate the distraction.

Despite my companion's efforts, though, I'm so ready to be off the plane, I could weep.

Rest assured, I'm not the weepy type. I'm a born-and-bred Scot. Weepy isn't allowed unless you're full-out steamin', and then only for a moment before your mates toss you into a bed to pass out. Soon as you sober up, it's back to stoic. Still, if I don't get my feet on solid land soon, I might throw a flakie that would impress the most exhausted wean. Much like a fatigued five-year-old, I'm dangerously close to lobbing my too-long-empty stainless-steel mug at the bulkhead. Not at the flight attendants, mind you. They all deserve medals for putting up with cranky people.

Truth be told, I've never behaved badly in public, but it's fun to think about.

Having my handsome, self-appointed guide stick by me all the way to baggage claim mitigates my Negative Nellie inner monologue, and by the time he pulls my two big suitcases off the carousel and grabs his duffel, I'm back to my more genial nature.

He straightens to his full, military-trained posture. "It's been a pleasure, Lexi. I expect a call when you get settled. Dallas is only a short drive from Magnolia Bloom, and I'd love to show you around my beautiful state."

"Two hours is a short drive?"

"Depends on which side of the city you start from, but in Texas, that's a quick jaunt. Hardly long enough to get down a whole soda and pack of peanuts."

"Regardless, I'm sure your family will keep you far too busy for you to be traipsing over half the state with a stranger, but I do thank you for making this a lovely trip."

"Half the state?" He coughs a laugh as he hands me back my phone. He's entered his contact information, seemingly not trusting me to get the details correct. "Lexi, half the state is a good seven hours with stops, so you can do the math if you have a hankering to go from Louisiana all the way to New Mexico. Heck, DFW alone is the size of Manhattan."

"You're bammin' me."

He raises his right hand in the on-my-honor position. "No, ma'am. I swear on a case of cane sugar Dr Pepper."

Goodness, he is serious. I tasted this elixir he waxed poetic about on the plane, but I'm not sure it's the mead of the gods he claims it is. I refrain from sharing my opinion of the sacred drink of Texas, though, as the service cart had no Irn-Bru for me to challenge with. Too bad, that.

I see he's stalling and decide it's time to stop this nonsense, fun as it is. "Thank you for everything you've done, from keeping me occupied to playing my personal valet, but you need to get going."

"I'd rather not leave you until your folks get here."

"Traycee and Bethanie will be here shortly. They said to wait inside, and they'd fetch me. I believe that's the term they used."

"I'll stay, just the same. My grandma—"

"Would skin you alive. Sounds painful."

"She might lower my punishment to a whuppin'. You don't know wounded pride until you have to go cut your own willow switch to get your hide tanned with."

I firmly believe DeWayne is playing up his Southern roots a tad, but I do appreciate his unflagging amusement. "I'm sure you're past corporal punishment, but I dinnae want a newly minted lieutenant colonel getting a thrashing on my behalf."

"I appreciate you having mercy on me."

Before he can come up with another ridiculous Texanism, I hear my name and turn to see a lass with her dark hair piled in a high, messy bun, wearing a loose cotton top and shorts. Her summer wear should've been a clue, but I'm distracted by her companion in a dressier sleeveless royal blue cowl neck and cropped chinos. Her hair is pulled back as well, but fanning out behind her head is a short afro framing her beautiful face and high cheekbones.

I give a last wave goodbye to DeWayne and lift a hand to indicate they've found me, taking a look around to notice the range of dress, from pajama bottoms and fuzzy slippers to coordinated outfits seeming straight off a runway. I wish I could chalk up my stretchy pants and top and my needs-a-good-wash hair to normal travel wear. Unfortunately, as my chic welcome delegation stands before me, their smiles wide and warm hospitality practically shooting from their bright gazes, I feel an exhaustion more than jet lag.

My abnormal lack of concern comes from the lonely hollow I've been living in, created by the absence of my husband. I can imagine Douglas, his voice booming as he charms these two lovely women who've come to collect me, and to be honest, I miss having his strong arms to haul around all this luggage.

I have no regrets about my life choices. I'm happy with the way I look, in general terms. I'm not one for limelight, so you'll never catch me in a hot pink tracksuit, and I'll never be caught in an airport in bunny slippers, but what I see in front of me is effort. Optimism. Hope in turquoise and pale yellow and denim.

My current gray-and-basic-black theme is probably worth a session with a therapist.

I'm not the moody sort, but I zero in on their lipstick and how the pop of color brightens their smiles, which reminds me I haven't put on makeup since the funeral.

It's been a long time since I was lit up from the inside, much less shined from the outside. At Heathrow, which I am certain is the training site for the devil's minions, people had been too exhausted, angry, or both, to care about fashion. It seems the rules in America—or Texas, at least—are different.

"I recognize that look. Dehydration and too much airplane food. I'm Traycee Everson, the woman who's going to get you to the Bloom in one piece because I'm the better driver. Welcome to Texas."

Bethanie rolls her eyes and gives me a smile, one even warmer than I saw on our video chat, and herds us all toward an escalator. "Let's get to the tram and out of the airport twice as big as Magnolia Bloom."

"Okay, right, first DeWayne saying it's bigger than Manhattan, now you."

"Crazy, but true."

"My poor brain's beyond this, but I can at least tell you that while I appreciate the name badges, remembering names is my superpower." I'll easily recall Traycee's because I've never seen it spelled so uniquely.

Both ladies glance at the lanyards hanging around their necks, share a look, and Bethanie points a thumb at her compatriot. "Traycee owns the Emporium, which I promise will be your favorite shop by Friday. She presented at a Women in Business marketing conference in Dallas, and I'm her lucky sidekick. Since we were close, we were tagged to grab you. Hope you don't mind."

"Och, nae, although I'm looking forward to meeting Kiki. We traded a hundred emails as I finalized my itinerary."

The girls relieve me of my bags, which certainly makes things easier, but despite DeWayne's delightful company, fatigue is creeping in, making me feel crabbit and old. I promise my better angels I'll be back to my usual self soon. I might be within a wink and a nod of fifty, but I've always felt like a bit of a poster child for the positively peri-menopausal, full of energy and determination. Just not today.

I guess losing your husband of almost thirty years long before you're supposed to would take the wind out of anyone's sails. I'll chalk it up to exhaustion, but right now, I agree with my brothers-in-law, who called my Douglas a fekkin' bawbag for having a heart attack and leaving me out of the blue. I'll pull up my knickers and get on with getting on later. For right now, I'm tired, sad, lonely, mad, lost, and about thirteen other things I'm sure my brain would supply if I could get a strong cup of tea in me, and maybe a scone with clotted cream.

Do they even have clotted cream over here? I might pitch another imaginary flakie if they don't. I force my mind away from childish meltdowns and content myself to listen as Traycee takes up the conversation.

"Kiki would've been here if she wasn't under doctor's orders to slow down. To keep her from being the world's crankiest pregnant lady if she's ordered to go on bed rest, we're your temporary B-team. We're delighted, though, and are happy to get you caught up on all things Magnolia Bloom."

Fear shoots through me, burning off some of my fatigue. I feel I already know Kiki from our chats, so even though I've never met her in person, concern overwhelms my self-pity. As a mother, I remember the terror even the thought of losing a baby causes, much less being in any real danger. "Please tell me Kiki's all right."

"She is, and little Kiki junior is plugging along on schedule. Don't worry. Doc says if she takes it easy, they'll both be right as rain. Not much besides a scare of this magnitude could manage such a feat."

With what I've gleaned from my conversations with Kiki, I can safely agree. "She does seem something of a dynamo."

Bethanie directs us down yet another wide, bright white walkway. "She's done amazing things for the estate, and I'm thrilled she let me add the castle as one of my marketing clients, but the fundraising gala for our new regional hospital is taking all the available oxygen right now. Which is how I—and by association, Traycee—was tasked with picking you up. We try for a conservation of energy, and folks coming into the big city often grab everything from bags of feed to lovely cousins arriving from exotic foreign lands."

Even tired as I am, I have to laugh. "Of all the things Scotland gets called, I'm not sure 'exotic' is one of them."

Traycee lifts a perfectly penciled brow over captivating gray-green eyes. "Regardless, I want to visit. I haven't been to Europe yet."

"Well, both of you have an open invitation to Bearsden—and by extension, Glasgow—any time. Right now, I'm so tired I might start greetin' and I think I'm out of tissues."

"No crying allowed on our watch, so just hang tough for a little longer."

After gesturing with a perfectly painted purple nail toward the sign saying Skylink, Traycee gives me a compassionate pat on my bicep. "It'll take a hot minute to get out of here, but I promise we'll have you home and settled as fast as we can."

They make good on their claim, navigating through the airport and into the car park with admirable ease. Before I can really take it all in, we're on the road, and I learn Bethanie and Traycee aren't related to my crazy brood of relatives, but Magnolia Bloom is a close-knit community and stays connected in many other ways, both through history and the fact that the MacInnes estate is the second-largest employer in the area. The Broder Factory, I'm told, holds the top title, but everyone's connected somehow, mostly with the insane growth of the smaller shops making the quaint city a tourist destination, and the castle is the crown.

When Traycee tells me she hopes their little town of under five thousand won't disappoint me, I chuckle. "I was born in a place called Pitlochry, which boasts a grand total of less than three thousand, so I adore small places."

We settle into a comfortable silence as the miles fly past, and finally, Traycee points toward an enormous iron gate with turrets visible to the east. "We're almost there. We'll drop you straight into Eunice Greene's capable hands to get you a bite to eat and settled. All I ask is you promise you'll say hi to Penny in the morning."

"Penny?"

Bethanie gives me a horrified glance. "Kiki hasn't told you about Penny the Dragon?"

"Och, aye, she did. My head's mince right now. Sorry."

"No sorries allowed." Traycee's voice is stern, but her eyes are dancing. "Kiki'll take away my honorary MacInnes badge if we don't give you platinum service."

I'm not the overly touchy type, but I can't stop myself from putting a hand on Traycee's arm and giving it a quick squeeze. "You're a lean-nan, Traycee, you are."

She lifts one of those perfect eyebrows. "I assume that's a good thing?"

"Indeed. You're a sweetheart in any language."

"Back at you, Lexi. We can see you're wrecked, so we'll have you on solid ground in no time. So you know, we're sorry we're dumping you right into the middle of the gala, but we're sure glad you're here."

"I'm happy to take the little things off Kiki's list to help her out."

Bethanie gives me a confused frown. "Um, little things?"

"Sure. I've run a business with a thousand moving parts, so I know it's the small jobs eating up your time. I'm happy to free her of them so she can take care of the important ones."

Bethanie's expression goes perplexed and worried. "Lexi, we don't need you to take the margins on this. We need you to take over."

I blink suddenly dry eyes. "Take over?"

She nods. "The gala. The whole kit and kaboodle, except for major contracts. For the most part, those are done."

My headshake is frantic. "You're off your trolley, lass! I've never planned anything bigger than a birthday party. Piping and fittings, I know. Toilets and faucets, sure. Chandeliers and seating for five hundred, not so much."

Bethanie's quiet for a long moment. If she's hoping to make me feel better, it doesn't work. I almost didn't make this trip to Texas, but in the end, the chance to fly away from the malaise I've been in danger of adopting too thoroughly was irresistible. It's normal to feel lost and bereft, considering I thought Douglas and I were all set to enjoy retirement, although what the darn fool and I would have done to fill our days is a mystery.

But I was willing to give it a go.

Facing a future alone was never in the plans I made, yet it seems the cards I was dealt were reshuffled, including my image of what the next couple of months were going to entail.

They say the universe will deliver the same lesson to you over and over until you learn it. For the life of me, I have no idea why the powers that be determined a past-her-prime widow needed to flirt with a serviceman. Or why they planted the idea of adding something tangerine to my boring, sensible wardrobe.

Or why they believed a woman whose life revolves around P traps, backwater valves, and closet flanges can pull off a high-profile gala.

CHAPTER TWO

BETHANIE

SEEING the deer-in-the-headlights terror on Lexi's face leaves me with raging heartburn. After dropping Traycee off at her shop, I finished the trip to the castle with Lexi, but despite her promise she'll get herself sorted in no time, I'm afraid I've screwed up her well-deserved vacation. I might be giving her an ulcer to boot. How had I misread the situation? I talk with Kiki every day, and both of us were giddy with relief to have Lexi take over the heavy lifting on the gala.

Or so we'd thought.

I'm not even halfway around my desk when I see a shadow in my doorway and pause to smile at Eunice, who's glancing behind her at Lexi's door.

"She all settled?"

Instead of putting my desk between us, I perch my hip on the edge and give my hand the so-so wobble. "Getting there. She wanted a hot bath and then to come down for tea. I think that means dinner to us."

"Well, if it's literal, I'll have the kettle boiling when she's ready. If it's supper she's needing, I've got that covered, too. I'm anxious to meet her."

"She's a sweetie for sure, but I kinda blindsided her with the gala. She had the idea she was going to be backup quarterback, more of a list checker than throwing Hail Marys. Her eyes got four sizes bigger when I explained, and I feel horrible about it."

In typical Eunice fashion, she closes the empty space between us to pull me into a patent-worthy hug. In fact, I'm convinced Eunice's hugs could broker world peace, but there's no chance in hell she's leaving Texas. She considers New York a dystopian nightmare, so I'm afraid the United Nations is out of luck.

She might not cure the world's ills, but Eunice has a damn fine track record of easing most human troubles. She'll even take on a passel of border collies and blacknose sheep...as long as they stay out of her kitchen.

As for me, being wrapped in the surprisingly strong arms of a woman edging into her nineties is inches shy of heaven. She releases me and steps back, and I feel like Atlas after shrugging off the world.

"Child, you're taking on guilt you don't own. We've talked about this."

Indeed we have, or more precisely, Eunice has scolded me to stop being so serious and working so hard. My part of the conversation is managing to get in an occasional *yes, ma'am.*

I nab my pencil and roll it between my palms. "I'm trying. I really am, but I can't screw up this gala. I can't let Kiki down, and I can't fail the castle." My throat closes so tightly I struggle to finish. "I especially can't disappoint my dad. He never gave up on me, even when I deserved it ten times over."

"Oh, pish. Your daddy's the happiest man on planet Earth right now, and it's not 'cause he's Magnolia Bloom's newest newlywed. Well, he might be tied with Harville in the blissful department. Oh, wait, and Zach since he wised up and won Paige back." She flaps a hand at me. "Anyway, there's nothing you could do to change how proud your daddy is."

Oh, but she's wrong. There's plenty I could do, but honestly, relapsing isn't my worry. The thing keeping me awake isn't crawling back into the bottle. It's a return of the deep, bruised hurt in his eyes I caused for a decade. That I'll see his shoulders slump and his head bow. The smile on his broad, sweet face every time I see him is a major part of what keeps me steadfast and focused on proving his faith in me isn't misplaced.

"Lord, child, we'll get it all figured out. Your biggest worry about the upcomin' hootenanny should be who you're gonna bring. Have you asked anyone yet?"

I look at her as if she's grown another head. "My clipboard's accepted my invitation, and to make it a threesome, I'm bringing my favorite pen."

"I need to disabuse you of this notion you're a comedienne. This is going to be the event of the year, next to the games, or maybe Christmas at the castle, or—"

"I get it. It's going to be amazing, but I don't need a date. I have too much to do."

Besides, everyone within a ten-mile radius is intimately familiar with every bit of my business, and no one is interested in being seen on the arm of the former town drunk.

"Nonsense. By the time the big day rolls around, it'll all be done but the singing, so you need to put on your dancing shoes with the rest of us. It's not like you lack for handsome men to choose from, or maybe you need a refresher. There's always Omar, the new assistant librarian. He's got tall, dark, and handsome wrapped up. And JJ Everson's become quite the entrepreneur with the gas station. Before you know it, he'll be opening his own Buc-ee's. And can't forget dashing Colt, Cammie and Trey's new law associate. Of course, no list is complete without the double-trouble, super-sexy twins. Not every town's lucky enough to have Nathanial the fire chief and Roy the super stud police chief at their service."

I ignore the skipped beat of my heart and give her points for trying to be subtle. "Like I have to tell you I've already had a date with the super stud. It was a memorable night of handcuffs and personal delivery to the city jail where he read me a lovely poem. From there, he's showed me to a private room with an ensuite bathroom as he processed my papers for my second, and thankfully last, DUI."

"Aw, honey, that's all in the past. You've remade yourself tip to toenails." She stops and gives me her trademark nail-you-to-the-floor look. "*You* did it and should be damned proud. I am."

Warmth floods me at her unfailing support, a phenomenon I'm not quite used to yet. I snagged a double dose of love when her daughter married my dad. He and Mina are happier than any twenty-year-old honeymooners, and it seems I got a stepmother and a stepgrandmother out of the deal. I'm completely okay with my jackpot win.

"You're overly partial to me because of Mina."

"Pishposh. My girl was smart enough to let CT past her guard, and while it sure as shootin' doesn't hurt she loves you like you're her own, that's hardly the reason behind what I'm saying. You changed your life. No one else. And I don't have on rose-colored glasses."

"Be that as it may, you need to worry about your own love life. Which posits the question, who are you bringing?"

"I'm not sure. Ben's getting a little too pushy, thinking I have time to go off with him in his new motor home at the drop of a hat. Like I don't have obligations and things to do." She sniffs, as if highly offended. "I have a notion, since Bailey and Doc have Lem Broder on such a good road, he might enjoy going with someone he recognizes. He was a recluse for so long, I want to help our new medical wonder-workers on their mission."

"Their new dementia center has done wonders, and we sure need it. It'll be an amazing addition to the hospital, too. But whoever you bring, they'll have the best time there."

"We'll see." She gives me another *look.* "You may be smart as a whip, but don't try to change the subject."

"Eunice, I love you, but you've got to let this go. I don't even have a full year of sobriety under my belt. Everyone in the program says don't make any major decisions or get into new relationships until you pass that big milestone."

"I wouldn't dream of telling you to do anything to risk all you've gained, but going to the gala isn't getting married." She holds up a hand. "I'll stop, but think about it."

"I will." I won't, but it's a white lie I'm willing to tell one of the sweetest women on the planet. She can be acerbic when it suits her, for sure, but underneath any bluster is pure cotton candy.

"All right, then. I'm going to head back downstairs and get the water hot. Send Lexi my way when she's freshened up. You come, too, if you want."

"Thanks, but I've got a lot to catch up on after spending two days in Dallas with Traycee."

"How is she? She hit a bump in the road on her own program, but she seems back to rights."

I'm delighted to reassure her. "Her relapse scared the hell out of Kiki and me, but she came through rehab recommitted. Some of us have to bounce a few times before we get settled. I pray I'm not one, but you never can tell."

I resist the urge to reinforce the threat of falling back into the bottle is why her matchmaking plans need to go on hiatus. I'm a hundred times thrilled for my friend, but watching her journey reminds me none of us travel the same path. I'm sorry she went down a side trail, but I appreciate the cautionary tale.

"All right, all right. I'll pull my nose out of your business. For now. But don't work too long. You get home and take time for yourself, hear?"

"Yes, ma'am. After I send Lexi your way, I promise to be a good girl."

Eunice comes closer and puts a veined hand against my ear, then strokes my hair back from my face. "You've always been a good girl, Bethanie. You just don't believe it."

I watch the octogenarian with more energy than me and Traycee and three others put together head to her uncontested domain. I'll keep my promise and direct Lexi downstairs, then drive straight to my little apartment off downtown in one of the renovated Victorians so quintessentially Magnolia Bloom.

And I'll lock away any thoughts about going to a ball with a certain handsome police chief. There's no sense torturing myself with dreams of what can never be.

CHAPTER THREE

LEXI

I EXPECTED my long bath in a gloriously oversized tub to put me straight to sleep, but being clean and the ache eased from my back makes me a new woman. My plan, as I tuck the blow dryer in the cabinet and pull my hair back in a simple braid, is to visit the intriguing Penny, then meet the famous—or maybe infamous—Eunice Greene.

With one step outside my new, temporary abode, my feet slow to a crawl. How could anyone rush through this stunning castle? As I descend the left side of the majestic curved stairway, the railings of dark wood polished to a blinding shine, I feel a tad silly imagining myself in a costume straight out of one of the portraits in the gallery. But I see myself dressed in fine cotton trimmed with yards of Alyssa's lace, each piece of soft blue superfine fitted perfectly to my form over my equally beautiful corset done in luxurious satin. One gloved hand delicately trails the balustrade, a kerchief, also trimmed in the famous lace, tucked into my cuff. My other hand holds a parasol, and my skirts swish as they trail behind me down the vibrant red runner covering the marble steps.

It may be time to admit my *Downton Abbey* addiction, but as there's no one to hear my confession, I pronounce myself forgiven without a single minute's penance required.

Reaching the entryway, I stop dead. If I were wearing the imaginary large-brimmed hat matching my outfit, I'd have to use one hand to hold it on as I arch my neck back. The articles I read in two or three architectural journals and various internet searches haven't remotely prepared me for this experience. The greatest photographer of the age couldn't do justice to the scene as I take in the chandelier more than two stories above me. I breathe in a long gasp, knowing from my research the elaborate crystal fixture was given to Alisdair and Evajean by her stepmother and father and cost a fortune in the late 1800s. It must be utterly priceless now, but no dollar figure could capture its stunning beauty.

"Oh my." My voice is barely audible. Every synapse in my brain is overloaded with the details in this front room alone that could keep me entertained for days.

"It's amazing, isn't it?" Bethanie comes toward me, but I'm too awestruck to do more than give her a cursory wave.

"I have no words, other than awe."

"It's magical in here, especially as the light changes throughout the day. The first time I came to the castle sober, I wandered around for eight hours, and it still wasn't enough."

I give her a wink. "Would you be surprised if I told you I've never been in a castle? Not even Edenborough and I live a few handfuls of kilometers away."

She gives a delightful laugh. "No more than you being surprised I've never been on a horse."

"I suppose stereotypes abound on both sides of the pond. Horses scare me, so I avoid them, but it's going to take my entire stay to satisfy my raging curiosity about everything else Texas."

"Wait until you meet the sheep. I'm in love with every one of their little black faces, and I drive Rory and Juliette crazy coming to see Lulu when I'm stressed out. But you'll meet our resident sheep ambassadors and new MacInnes mascot another day. It's a good thing we've got you captured until November, isn't it?"

"I wouldn't dream of arguing, but I feel I'm keeping you. And why aren't you off the clock?"

"I am, officially, but since you're already down here, let me introduce you to Penny, then when you're done, head back through. You'll find Eunice in the main kitchen. Do you mind?"

"Sounds grand. Lead on."

The early evening sunshine isn't as brutal as my introduction at the airport, and the fluttering trees provide a lovely ambience shading the circular drive at the bottom of the impressive stone stairway. A brisk breeze makes the temperature glorious, far warmer than home, but a pleasant change.

Bethanie guides me around the enormous fountain with water spraying high into the air, but instead of joining me, she pats my arm and heads on her way.

If I thought the girls' description of Penny was something out of a wild imagining, and the foyer out of the grandest of dreams, the reality is far beyond expectation. I'm awed all this came about from the dream of a woman I'm tangentially related to. Evajean Whitson MacInnes made this happen in what was then the Wild West, in an age when it was considered impossible for a woman to be an architect.

Meeting Penny, backlit by the setting sun, overwhelms me nearly as much as the entryway where I stood moments ago. "Saints preserve us, you're beautiful."

The urge to rush over and touch the huge stone dragon is impossible to resist.

"Hallo, beauty. You're much prettier than your pictures." My greeting comes out in a whisper, but it would be useless to deny I'm already in love with the pink granite transformed into a breathtaking mythological creature. Her head rests on her front foreleg, and her wings are spread. I swear they're about to be furled against her sides, and for half a second, I wish I could nestle next to her and let those wings encase me in darkness.

Maybe, for a moment, I'd feel safe again. Maybe the world would feel less empty, where the one person I've loved my whole life wasn't stripped from me. Maybe for a second, I wouldn't be too young to be a widow but too old to be worrying about finding another partner to join me on this crazy journey called life.

I shake away my ruminations, give Penny one final stroke on her long snout, and retrace my steps back through the castle to the huge, brightly lit kitchen. Before I can take in the juxtaposition of the breath-taking antiques to the state-of-the-art cooking space that would turn any Michelin star chef green with jealousy, I'm drawn into a lung-crushing hug from the one and only, muscle-bound Eunice. I'm not given a chance to opt out before she points to a chair with a wooden spoon.

"Sit while I get this stew simmerin', and we'll chat. I've got you some chicken salad and lemonade to tide you over. Glad to have you here, Lexi."

"I appreciate the kindness, and I'm thrilled to be here." I watch, curious, as she bustles to an enormous stainless-steel refrigerator and retrieves a plate of sandwiches and a ceramic pitcher.

For me, this trip is about branching out, shedding my cocoon, and it hits me my homebody self isn't as uncomfortable with all the newness as I was afraid I'd be.

I take a sandwich from the plate and bite into tart, freshly baked sourdough and the famed chicken salad Kiki described as nirvana. The crisp, cold lemonade hits the spot, too, and I don't need to be a county fair judge to know Eunice deserves every one of her blue ribbons.

"Am I tasting tarragon?" Maggie, my great-gran, would be proud I didn't speak with my mouth full, although it's hard to stop myself from shoveling in so much deliciousness.

"Yes, indeedy."

"It's magnificent. Truly." Okay, Maggie wouldn't be proud any longer, but being surrounded by fabulous food and drink in such a warm, homey environment soothes the spot I've long neglected.

"Thank you, child."

I smile around a swallow of the sunshine-infused elixir I've been nigh onto guzzling. It's been a flurry of years since I've been called a child, but I have neither the inclination nor the energy to argue. After stirring what I'm suspecting is chili in an enormous pot, she puts the lid on, glances into the oven which is emanating the exquisite scent of chocolate and vanilla, and joins me at the table I imagine has hosted generations of hungry MacInneses.

Eunice points to my plate with a hand showing she's no spring chicken, but with a bicep I wish I had, and I'm at least thirty years her junior.

"Would you care for more?"

I push the plate away and give a satisfied sigh. "Och, nae, but that was pure dead brilliant. I feel a million times better."

"Then I'll count my new batch a success."

"New? This isn't the famous secret recipe people have been trying to copy for decades?"

"I've turned a new leaf. I'm revamping all my cooking to be more macro-friendly."

Then she flexes her bicep at me and laughs, a deep, throaty sound out of proportion for someone so tiny. Since I'm in America, I do a quick calculation from centimeters, and if I'm correct, I'm five-nine, so I tower over the head cook by eight inches at least, and I easily outweigh her by a good three stone…er, thirty-ish pounds. She has her steel-gray hair cut in what I call Jamie Lee Curtis stunning, and I wish I had the guts to copy her.

She looks amazing. I'm afraid I'd look laughable.

I'm far from being silver-haired, but I have no intention of discontinuing dying my long-but-nondescript style to cover the spikes trying to take over. Since I lost Douglas, I can't bear to look in the mirror and see the red he loved so much, so I chose a deep chestnut brown this last year. I'm not fifty yet, but it's not too far over the horizon, and I'm darn sure not going gently into that good night. I'm no vixen, but I'm not ready for a walker and orthotic shoes, either.

"Don't take a solo trip down memory lane. Let me join you." Eunice sets down two glasses of water with thin slices of cucumber wedged between the ice. "Flyin's got you dried out, but we'll get you fixed up. Besides, it'd be nice to get to chat a bit before all the gala craziness kicks into gear."

She pulls up a chair and settles in, apparently intent on invading my thoughts whether I want her to or not. I refuse to think about planning an event I have no experience with until I get a good night's rest, but I'm not one to air my business. Still, if Eunice wants to talk, we'll talk.

"I was thinking how I'd been planning on riding out my old age in a rocking chair, one for me and one for Douglas, but that's not what my future holds. Maybe I'm finally starting to accept it."

I didn't plan on being quite so honest, but Eunice doesn't seem the type to shy away from candor.

"I know your pain, dear. I lost my Neville many a decade ago, but I still get lost in my memories once in a while. You wouldn't be human if you didn't, and yours is fresh."

"We used to talk about a lot of nothing, which often migrated into the shite our two children put us through. We'd eventually pat each other on the back and remind ourselves they'd grown into fine adults. Then we'd clink our pints, and lament how time passes so quickly."

"That's what couples do, and it's healthy. When you're in the shite, as you so accurately call it, you have to hold your nose and wade through, but hopefully you're holding hands with the person you love beside you along the way. There's a reason folks say kids will be the death of you, because raising them isn't easy, and they take a toll on a marriage no one tells you about."

I start to cringe for revealing something so personal, but Eunice is easy, like talking to a friend you've had since primary. The person you want to have right old blether with, someone who knows the real you.

"My daughter, Sadie, has blessed us with our first grandchild, and although I love my son-in-law, I have to remember to keep my angry face in the closet during the rare times I can manage a visit. He moved them all to Spain to be closer to his family. I wouldn't be human if I didn't admit I'm frustrated by it at times."

"I have twin girls. Fina and Mina, my hellcat and my mouse. Well, not anymore. Mina's happily married to one of the best catches in Magnolia Bloom, and she might as well be reliving her twenties, thirties, and forties with CT. You'll meet them soon. My Mina's an inspiration on how to do a U-turn and make up for lost time, and Fina's... well, Fina. She married her teen crush, a tall, striking Dane, but I'm glad Anders has no intention of trying to tame her. Those two are setting the world on fire everywhere they go."

I try to imagine U-turns and do-overs, but I can't picture a new beginning since I have both feet firmly rooted in my old life.

"My son, Travis, has done us proud by excelling at university. He's here in the States doing his doctoral work in engineering at the Caltech. He's texted he'll try to figure out how we can meet up, although I'm how will manage that is a mystery when there's nearly two and a half *thousand* kilometers between us. I love my son, but it would take a king's ransom ten times over to get on a plane right now, even for my sweet boy."

"Does he look like his father?"

I grab my water glass so fast liquid sloshes over the top. The cool hits my throat, and I pray the iciness stills my quivering chin.

"Aye, he's a living testament to his da."

Does it make me a horrible human being to say it wrecks me to be around my own son? He's painfully handsome, far more handsome than Douglas was, but they share the same dark hair and crystal-blue eyes. They even share the bushy eyebrows I beg him to let me trim when he's home. His shy smile and soft laugh have melted me since he was a baby.

"My Travis is my most adventurous. He's apparently rather popular with tanned California girls, although he swears he's not interested in anything serious until he gets done with his coursework. His Instagram account shows a different story, containing a curious number of blond and brunette beauties in scanty bikinis."

"Could be he doesn't want his mama to worry."

"Probably. I'll confess I stalk both my weans a tiny bit, although I don't helicopter them."

"Stalking's baked into the mom gene."

"Aye, right, but I'm grateful I couldn't have the entire cricket team Douglas wanted. I'd be exhausted."

"My Neville wanted a baker's dozen, too, but even if I'd been willing, my lady parts were uncooperative." Eunice refills our water glasses, like she plans to chat all night.

The lengthening shadows over the surgery-room-clean floors remind me how long we've been visiting. I can't remember the last time I sat down with a friend and talked until we had nothing else to say. I haven't felt the slightest urge to check my phone, and it feels good to be free to focus on the simple pleasures of conversation and the green slivers of cucumber in my water.

"I had to evict my uterus. It was the bad neighbor in Lady Partsville."

Eunice's laugh is delicious. "Saves having to worry about birth control, though."

If I'd taken a sip of water, Eunice would have been wearing one of said cucumbers.

"Douglas appreciated the perk. I did, too, truth be told. You'd think that would have waned since he'd been by my side since I was a lass of sixteen, and we married a month after I graduated high school. He was a warm, steady, dependable presence my whole life."

And he left me. Alone. Lost. Hurt. Angry.

Eunice's face pinches like she sucked on a lemon. "An electric blanket's warm, too."

"Aye, but there's only so much I can process at once. It's all left me adrift."

Definitely unmoored. Since I sold Douglas's portion of the business to my brothers-in-law, I'm no longer tied to the family dock.

"Adrift's right where you want to be. It means you're floating toward something better." Eunice bustles away from the table, taking my dishes despite my protest, then takes a tray of cookies from the oven, transferring them to a wire rack with more-than-practiced efficiency.

"Did you remarry?" An hour ago, my question would have been intrusive, but we've covered everything from kids to broken reproductive systems, and there's something about Eunice that makes time irrelevant.

"I never felt the need." She gives me a wink. "Not sayin' I've spent all my evenings alone shelling peas, mind you, but I've liked going home to my things and my ways, without having to clean up after anyone ever again. Not that Neville was a bad man, mind you. The opposite, in fact. But he was a creature of the times, and between cooking at home and here at the castle, then all the driving with two girls to get to practices and such, I barely had time to breathe. Now, I enjoy being courted, but I'm clear where rings and forever are concerned."

"To many a disappointed heart, I'm sure."

"I'm okay with it. These days, it's usually me and a weight bench and whoever's hovering to make sure I don't drop the bar on myself."

I look at her with new respect and can't help but tease. "I have the feeling there's a waiting list to be your spotter. Your workout routine has served you well."

And I'm inspired. Not only by how full of life she looks, but how she grew from a past similar to mine and created something to her own liking completely different from what she knew.

Pride radiates from her face. "I have the best time messin' with the boys down at the gym. Each one of 'em's a darlin', and it keeps me healthy." Her self-assured smile slides into a sly one. "And I have a few gentlemen callers who I let take me dancing every now and then."

"Dancing? I'm jealous. Douglas surprised me two years back...." My throat closes. It's been three years now. How is that possible? I cough to clear the block and forge on. "He surprised me with ballroom lessons for our anniversary, and we loved it. We were never going to win any competitions, but we had a grand time."

"You won't get a lot of straight ballroom around here, but at the Magnolia Moon, they'll play waltz, cha-cha, East Coast swing. A few of the slower songs you can rumba to, but the songs will mostly be country."

I can't help but smile as I realize one of the things Eunice doesn't have for me is pity. She doesn't see me as a widow with nothing left to live for, but as a woman going through some shite is all. It's possible I'm hallucinating from being on a plane for so long, but the smile she gives me contains nothing more than reassurance I'll be fine.

"I love the genre. In fact, there's an annual British Country Music

Festival in Blackpool we used to go to every few years. Ally would have stolen the show."

Eunice gives an approving nod. "I'm so glad that girl got away and spent time with your side, and I'm dang proud of her for forging a new path for herself. Speaking of, we need to put some items on your dance card, as it were. We'll get you to the Moon soon, but Iron Core's top of the list, after you're rested up, of course." She does another circuit around her kitchen, an unstoppable force of stirring and tasting.

With all the honesty fogging this kitchen, a scoff escapes I don't try to hide. "I've never been the gym type."

"Says everyone before they fall in love with iron. Come with me one time to the Core, and you'll be hooked. Trust me."

Oddly enough, I find myself hoping to trust Eunice with a lot of things during my time in Magnolia Bloom. I feel springier than lamb's wool.

I take a cookie from the plate she's put on the table and moan as the warm chocolate and brown sugar melts in my mouth. "If you tell me this is diet-friendly, I'll kiss you."

"I've made a few tweaks, but no, you can't call that a low-cal cookie. But if you're careful, you can make it work in your—"

"Macros?" I've learned a little of the lingo.

"That's right. Getting fit isn't about torture, girl. It's common sense and consistency."

I feel every extra stone I've put on over the decades, but damn if a woman almost twice my age makes me feel like a bag of marshmallows belted in the middle. Maybe I'm fashin' myself a bit, but my thinking's clear now that I'm refreshed by Eunice's amazing cooking. It forces me to be honest about how easily I let Douglas's declarations that he loved all of my curves be my excuse to put off getting serious about eating healthy and exercising until another week turned into a month, then a year.

I may not feel this way after I've had some sleep, but I make an impulsive decision. "Eunice, you're right. While I couldn't lift anything heavier than this napkin right now, I'll take you up on your invitation. I'd love to visit your gym while I'm here."

"Hot diggity. I'll call Mina. She has a whole line of athletic wear she keeps stocked at Traycee's Emporium that'll look adorable on you."

"I'm sure I packed some shorts—"

Eunice's finger shot up. "Don't argue with me. If you're going to be my protégé, you're going in with style."

I'm not sure I agreed to be her work in progress, but she adds a stern frown not entirely playful.

"Okay, right, then." My voice is equal parts amused and obedient. "Who doesn't love new workout clothes?"

"Good. We've got that settled. Now, you go get some rest. I hope you'll sleep until the mornin', but if not, you can wander to the family kitchen upstairs. Help yourself to anything you find, or mosey down here. There's wine in both places, too. I'm an early bird, so come see me for coffee."

She shoos me to my room, and with my burst of energy after my bath deserting me, I offer my thanks and head out. Even though the internet says jet lag going west is considered easier than going east, my back and my thighs are inclined to argue. I've enough oomph to climb into a ridiculously comfortable bed between gloriously soft sheets smelling like sunshine.

And the last thing I remember is dozing off with thoughts of U-turns, do-overs, and barbells.

CHAPTER FOUR

BUNNY

I STRAIGHTEN the nameplate my team had made for me when we opened, but *Bunny West, Proprietor* still makes me smile. My little office in the back of the Due West Saloon has been my refuge for the last five years, but this evening, it feels crowded and stifling.

I wish I could shake the unease parked on my shoulders for ages now. I may have gotten this business as my sole portion of a bitter divorce settlement, but I've built it into a major player in Magnolia Bloom's downtown district. I've shown the world, but mostly to myself, I'm not just a pretty face. The problem is, for all the things in my personal win column, it's included the caveat that success isn't the cure for all one's ills.

Especially if one's ills are of the heart and not the wallet.

As if my hands are working of their own accord, I pick up my phone and speed-dial Emmett. While it rings, I march across the taproom and stand by my entrance so I can look diagonally across the square to where he spends as much time as I do here. Seeing the Magnolia Bloom Art Gallery, even from this distance, makes me smile despite the acid climbing my esophagus like English ivy on a brick wall.

The phone finally connects. "Hey, Bun, wassup?" I imagine I can see him waving from behind his own enormous window-paned storefront.

Emmett was the first person, as well as the first merchant, to welcome me to town. Many more had told me they were glad I was here, but I'll always be grateful for Emmett's open, easy greeting turned instant friendship.

"I need an emergency shrub meeting."

The hesitation in the dead silence speaks volumes. "Come again?"

"I have a meeting with Gene, and I'm worried my last tweaks may have been a mistake, spoiling my best batch. Can you come over?"

"I'm assuming this is your mocktail venture and not a new species of rhododendron."

"You, Emmett Everson, are no Chris Rock."

"Or course not. I'm much better looking."

I huff. Loudly. "Are you coming or not?"

"I'm not sure I can get away, with the crowd and all."

I give an obligatory chuckle. Tuesdays are slow most any time of year, but this month has been especially lackluster, for reasons the Magnolia Bloom Merchants Association and the chamber of commerce combined can't explain. We're not worried. Magnolia Bloom's well on its way to becoming quite the rival to Fredericksburg and Wimberley, and once we get the regional hospital up and running, we'll be even more attractive to new businesses.

"Yeah, yeah. Get your butt over here."

"I live to serve, mistress. I'll mosey right on over."

He may not be able to hear my aggrieved sigh, but I'm sure he feels it. Emmett Everson is one of the most erudite people I've ever known, but he loves to play up his twang as part of his nonstop teasing me about my Dallas roots and accent. I may have given up the Aqua Net and teasing comb a long time ago, but he refuses to give it a rest.

I have confidence he's about to roll up dressed in a flawlessly tailored suit, his shoes without a scratch, his handsome face serene. Which means he has no room to tease me about my past sartorial extravagances, but it's our long-standing play, along with me gibing him about the skin care routine keeping him the envy of the entire female population of Magnolia Bloom…and half the men. He's given me a list of his favorite brands, but my bank account can no longer afford those luxuries.

The word *luxuries* makes me think of the gala, which makes me think of Bethanie, so I type her a quick text thanking her for letting me know Lexi has arrived safely. I'll be working with her until the big day, and although I haven't met the MacInnes relative who's come over from Scotland to help out. Like most others in this town, I breathed a sigh of relief Kiki has finally relaxed her insane control issues. Our collective goal is to make sure she doesn't take the reins back so she'll concentrate on the baby we're all waiting on pins and needles to coo over.

I hurry to the industrial refrigerator in the back and grab the bottles I want Emmett to taste. I'm behind the bar when he throws the door open with a dramatic flourish.

"It is I, your resident gay, Black art dealer, here to save my poor white lady friend from imminent doom."

"Seriously? You stomped on about twelve now-forbidden subjects in one sentence, and for posterity, I remind you—you're no Chris Rock, Dave Chappelle, Eddie—"

"Yeah, yeah, so you said. But *I* remind *you*, all the aforementioned have made their fortunes making fun of political correctness."

"But that platform's generally reserved for stand-up routines, not someone hawking paintings for a living."

"Did you say 'hawk'?" He pretends to head back to the entrance.

"For the love of God, can you sit your gay, Black, art dealer butt down and help me?"

"While you've asked so nicely, I can't. I mean, I can help, but sitting will crease my new sla—"

"Sit!"

With a sniff, he takes the stool directly in front of me.

I hide my smirk as I uncork the sample I'm sure I've overtweaked, along with the control bottle I've kept untouched.

I slide the two small servings across, and he dutifully drinks the first, rolls it over his tongue a couple of times, then swallows. After a sip of water, he repeats the routine, knowing he's killing me with his overdone delays.

"Well?"

"Well, Miss Impatient, I'd have to say...."

I grit my teeth until I can't take it, and cave. I lean across the bar into his personal space. "Say what, damn it?"

"They taste exactly the same."

I pull back in surprise. "They...can't."

"But they do."

"I'm telling you I put twice the mint in the new batch. It's impossible for them to taste the same."

"I will have you know, I can tell the year and the vintner of every bottle of vino in my cellar with one taste and eyes closed. I can tell the difference between two flavored simple syrups."

"Fine, Mr. Wine Snob." I turn away, muttering, "But you're wrong. And it wasn't simple getting the proportions perfect."

I guess there was more hurt in my voice than I intended, because when I face him again, he reaches across the bar and takes my hand. "I'm sorry, Bun. I'm being a dick with the teasing, but honestly, I really can't tell much of a difference. Okay, so there's a bit more mint? It's not over the top, which means if you doubled it, it sure mellowed out."

Not something mint is known to do.

"I suppose this means you're going to nominate me for Worst Actress in a Drama for next year's Razzies."

His squeeze tightens on my fingers. "I won't if you'll stop dithering and tell me what's really up."

"Besides me wasting five years of my life, the life I swore I was going to reclaim all Helen Reddy, hear me roar?"

Emmett gives a dramatic, slow perusal of the saloon and nails me with hiked brows over the trademark gray-green Everson eyes. "I'm sorry, was there another Bunny West busting her ass to remake this old building into a landmark? The woman who used to have to shine her windows with vinegar and elbow grease because she couldn't afford the blue stuff? The one who, when she had two nickels to rub together, hired Tom Jenkins and his worthless son to make these tables and chairs? Oh, and who gave Cooter Gilroy fifty percent off for life on his tab because he had a flatbed and hauled this monstrosity of a bar up from Gruene? She must be your doppelgänger."

I squeeze his hand and let go before I drain all the blood from his fingers in a small attempt to show my appreciation for his unflagging support. "Apples and oranges, my friend. My apple cart's full of beautiful bottles of custom beer and ale, and I've no false modesty about the success of the saloon. To torture the analogy, though, the problem is my orange trees are lackluster and not bearing fruit."

"Climbing out on a limb here. I'm guessing Buddy…sorry, Gene… is still the winner of the Captain Oblivious medal of honor."

"Yup, but I'm pretty sure he's Colonel Oblivious now."

"You may be right, but we'll check with Kiki to see if we have our ranks correct." He finishes his shrub and hands me the glass. "So what are you going to do about it? It's not the 1950s anymore. You can take the lead. You won't get run out of town with a scarlet A on your shirt."

"True, especially considering he's not married." I swat at him with my bar towel, but easily miss. "It's not that easy, though. Not for me."

My fingers reach for the scar under my jaw. The nearly transparent line of white there, plus the ones behind each ear, are the only evidence I carry with me of the accident that changed my life. The burning hatred of my ex may have abated into a tiny pocket of rage that only flares now and then, but I will always be grateful to the schmuck for having the skill to put my face back together. The five surgeries were worth it, but they took a toll on me mentally as well as physically.

"Honey, those scars are damn near invisible."

"It's not the physical ones, Emmett. These honestly don't bother me. They're reminders I'm actually glad to have."

"Interesting. I don't think you've ever said that."

"I don't talk about the accident much. I'm mostly grateful my arrogant stupidity didn't cause anyone else to lose their face, or their life. The oak tree might have a thing or two to say about me, but otherwise, I'm the only one who paid for my hubris."

"You'd be a great thirty-second public service announcement for texting and driving. All that aside, you're still not telling me why you don't put on your faux Jimmy Choos—"

I gasp. "You're a monster."

"And you still love me, but before I was rudely interrupted—march your beautiful butt down to the Moon and wake that man up."

"I broke the heel on my one-hundred-percent-authentic Jimmy Choos, which we will ignore I got at Trader Days in Atlanta last year and are only three seasons out of date. They're in the repair shop."

The enormous mirror spanning the wall behind me reflects Emmett's Oscar-worthy huff strong enough to make my ponytail flutter. "While I'm known to be the honorary Buddha of Magnolia Bloom, a veritable font of patience—"

It's a good thing I direct my snort in his direction, and away from my jaw-droppingly expensive mirror. It might be insured, but my deductible is pretty high, and I'm not certain "business owner's response to customer's dramatic sigh" would count under the natural-disaster clause if I crack the sucker.

"—you are about to drain the well bone-dry."

I use a thumbnail to scratch at a nonexistent spot on the bar. "I guess I figure if he hasn't gotten the hint by now, it would hurt too much to put it in the open and find out for sure he isn't interested in me."

"Girl, let me tell you one thing. If I wasn't gay, and the happiest man on the planet when I got lucky enough to find Wyatt, I'd be after you like a greyhound after the fake bunny. No pun intended. And with my exquisite taste, that says something."

The pressure eases behind my eyelids, and I throw him an air kiss. If nothing else, and there are a thousand *elses* between Emmett and me, he's wonderful for my ego.

"Thank you, my friend."

"One more thing, and it's not because you should've been a model, even though those days are *loooong* past you."

I glare at him through eyes so squinted I can barely see him. "I formally rescind all the nice things I was about to say to you."

"These are my last words of advice, and then I've got to get back to the shop before the madding crowds mow Wyatt over. You said Gene's coming in for his own taste-test, so woman up and ask him on a date. Hell, take him to the gala. It's a nice, safe, people-filled option."

"I'm not going to the gala. I don't want to see any of those people from Dallas. There's a few from the past I'm sorry I lost in the divorce, but not many."

Emmett slaps the top of the bar. "Remember the Wonder Woman coffee cup I gave you last Valentine's Day?"

I frown at the non sequitur. "Yeah?"

"Give it back. You don't deserve it."

"Hey, I'm not being that pathetic."

"You're waffling worse than a three-stack down at Vivann's at Sunday brunch. Where's the spine of steel you forged under your no-longer-designer duds?"

"It's got some rust on it." I use the bar towel to polish the already-blinding wood between us. "What if I give you a note, and you can pass it to Gene after class?"

"Do you love me? Check yes or no."

"Maybe."

"Could work, but he might misunderstand, and then Wyatt would use him for fertilizer in his new garden."

"We wouldn't want that to happen."

"No, we wouldn't. Wyatt doesn't look good in orange."

"No one looks good in orange." I flip the rag back over my shoulder. "I guess I have to do this myself, then, since you have no intention of helping me. And I thought you were my friend."

Emmett slides from his stool with his natural grace and comes around to my side of the bar to pull me into a warm, sweet, wounded-heart-melting hug. He's the best at those.

I squeeze back for all I'm worth. "Couldn't you try to be straight?

For me?" My words are muffled by his shirt, but the rumble of his laugh vibrates against my nose.

"Girl, my mama asked for a year before she finally came to terms, so don't think your wimpy sniffles are going to get you anywhere. And don't get snot on my shirt."

Pulling back, I pat his chest and move away, tightening up his perfect Eldredge-knotted tie before I start crying and actually do get snot on his blue pinstripe Luigi Borrelli shirt.

"Couldn't hurt to ask. It'd save me a lot of trouble, but if you want to be selfish, I guess I can't change you."

He kisses my forehead and strolls over to the door, but there's no teasing in his voice or on his face when he catches my eye. "Do it, Bun. Give it a try. And I'll let you in on a little secret. The magic of Magnolia Bloom isn't reserved for the MacInneses. It might've started in the castle, but it comes to all of us. You can share it, if you'll let yourself."

Then he's gone, and I grab my keys to lock up so I can head down to the Core for a desperately needed massage. I'll come back, clean up, and hopefully, Logan can save me from looking like I'm one step from rigor mortis during the real taste-test.

I'm afraid, though, Emmett's dose of courage and even Logan's patent-worthy muscle pounding will desert me before the moment of truth rolls around.

CHAPTER FIVE

LEXI

AFTER SLEEPING HALF the morning away, which is distinctly unlike me, I'm on the second-floor balcony spanning the castle between the back turrets, dressed in adorable leggings and a racer-back top that fit like they were made for me. They were sitting outside my door in a Magnolia Bloom Emporium bag, and I feel like Christmas came early. The exquisite shades of purple and a pattern of Monet-like flowers made me gasp in delight, and I didn't hesitate to slip them on.

In a move completely out of character, I hurry to the balcony and snap a selfie in the glorious morning sunshine. I'm normally not comfortable taking pictures of myself, but Douglas will—

My breath leaves me in a rush, and I scrabble over to a chair, fall into it, and pull my knees up. I wrap my arms around my shins and hang on for dear life, but nothing will save me from the flood of tears coming hot and full and fast. These are the lightning strikes of grief, moments I can't prepare for attacking hit me without warning.

I hear the public door accessing the balcony open, but I still have my head buried between my knees when I feel Eunice's hand on my back. "Hey there. Deep breaths now."

I obey and raise my head to see her holding out a tissue. "Thank you."

"Good thing I decided to come check on you about coming down to breakfast."

"Definitely good for me, but you're probably already sick of my moping."

"Pish, girl. It's all part of the process. Tell me what set off the waterworks."

I give her a weak smile, then wave toward the turret. "I came out to see the famous balcony in my fine new clothes, and my thoughts went straight to Douglas and how I knew he'd love to see this schist stone, all those greens and blues alive in the sunlight. So I took a selfie." A watery hiccup stops me for a second. "And then I remembered he's not here anymore, and I can't send it to him."

Eunice sits in the rocker beside mine, letting me breathe in the soft breeze coming from the west, laden with the scents of grass and wisteria, jasmine, and verbena. Of course, it's impossible to miss the rich, earthy aroma of the dirt from the banks of the water and the warming stone surrounding me. I'm usually not so good at picking out specific smells, but the air is so perfectly perfumed and the wind so gentle, I think I'm in the ballpark.

Eunice seems as lost as me. "I remember those moments. Like how, for about two seconds before I opened my eyes, I'd reach across the bed, expecting to feel Neville."

"Me, too. I can pretend Douglas will have finally stopped snoring, because I'd have prodded him to roll over. I teased him a million times that he was a thermonuclear device, radiating warmth like the sun itself, which made him the perfect companion on cold Scottish nights."

My gray-haired companion nods in complete understanding. "Except instead, we find fluffy pillows, undented by a head-shaped hollow."

"And we can't pretend they've gotten up to go to the loo and will be back to climb under the covers. In Douglas's case, he'd pull me into the curve of his body, his large hand wrapped around my breast as he snuggles in for 'just five minutes, love.'"

"Those were the best mornings."

The heaviness is back around my heart and my throat, and the sorrow lingers. The air's so thick with it I can't escape. There's no shelter from this pain. No bandage to mend the hole left when someone's ripped from your life. The same someone I awoke to for almost thirty years.

My internal storm changes, and it's not the lightning now as much as the thunderclaps of remorse. It pains me to air the truth, but I confess the apology I'll never get to make to Douglas.

"I wish I could go back to those times I pushed from the bed and headed for the shower, insisting we didn't have time to waste. I'd never pretend again I didn't feel him run his fingers through my hair to expose my neck for a kiss, knowing where that would lead."

"Me, too, darlin'. So many wasted chances."

What I would give, pay, beg, or bargain to have one more *just five minutes, love.*

Eunice gives me another pat, then stands. "You take your time, honey, but come on down to the kitchen when you're ready."

In her usual fashion, she doesn't wait for arguments and heads inside, leaving me clutching the jumper I grabbed out of habit when I came outside. I ease my death grip and stroke the soft wool. This sweater was his favorite, the robin's-egg hue perfect for my complexion. He was never a poetic man, and I've never considered myself especially beautiful, but he was never ashamed to be seen with me. For a tall girl who went from gangly to feeling a bit cloddish as I gained weight, the love in his eyes was a balm.

Pushing my morbid thoughts away, I follow Eunice inside. The lure of the smell of caramelizing onions and something baking—bread, I'm fairly sure—beckons me like a ghostly crooked finger of irresistible yumminess.

When I reach the arched doorway, I take a step back into the dim hallway. The room is so quiet, I didn't expect to see the huge table surrounded by ladies, all clad in athletic wear, each one glued to a laptop, a tablet, or a phone. They all look over sixty, but with each of them decked out in designer gear and all in better shape than I am, I have no way to guess exact ages.

A woman who looks more or less my age glances up and smiles at me. "Good morning. Joining us for brunch?"

Eunice turns from her massive ten-burner stove and points with the spoon I now believe is a genetic component of her fingers. I wonder if she's a mutant-chef superhero, and it pops into existence whenever she needs it.

"Sit. More coffee?"

"That'd be brilliant."

She turns off burners and scrapes cloud-soft eggs into a bowl. "You let me pour you a mug while you get us started. I've got all the fixin's for breakfast tacos, and then I'll introduce you to the gang."

I'm a little unnerved by six sets of eyes waiting for me to fix a plate, so I hand my travel mug over to Eunice as I stall in front of the small buffet of choices, flustered by my ignorance.

"I've never had a breakfast taco. What do I do?"

The lady behind me urges me a step forward. "Get ready to have your world tilt on its axis. Take a tortilla and fill it with whatever you'd like. Eggs, potatoes, bacon, onions, cheese. Add salsa or sour cream, or both, and roll it up and let your taste buds experience heaven."

Ready for the culinary adventure, I do as I'm told and am quickly swept into the maelstrom of gossip flung around the table. I settle into the only free chair and let the energy roll over me. My taste buds are initially confused, but I decide the instructions were correct. Breakfast tacos are now another reason why I'm never getting on another plane. Who would want to if they have to leave this bliss behind?

Eunice gives everyone a chance to eat, then raps her knuckles on the table. "All right, everybody, settle down. Lexi, I'm going to do roll call, but we don't expect you to remember everyone."

I can hear the delight in my own laugh. "I already told Bethanie and Traycee at the airport that remembering names is my superpower, so no worries."

I receive a raised eyebrow. "Is it now? Color me impressed."

"Comes from running my husband's family's plumbing business for almost three decades. You'd be amazed what people will tell a service tech. The boys'd come back with tales, and I started using folks' names when they call, asking about the dog dropping something in the commode, and commiserate about vet bills or the like. Made people customers for life."

"That's genius."

I nod, proud of how successful a simple investment in time and a bit of mental energy paid off, not only in profit, but also in connection. "Thing is, it wasn't a marketing ploy. I really got to know our regulars, and honestly? I miss them."

Eunice nods in understanding. "I've had my fair share of midnight confessions over chocolate mousse in the passel of years I've been here. Never fails there's someone from the wedding party or birthday bash who makes it down here, escaping the hoopla going on, so I understand."

She pulls back and gives a wave to the lady on my left as if she's lit up like a vowel on the puzzle board.

"All right, then, this is Emma Everson. She's our captain and does her best to keep us in line. She's Traycee's grandmother. Then there's Lorraine Pepperdine, and the young'un next to her on the end over there is her great-granddaughter Gabby. She's a travel agent and helping us plan our next cruise, which is why we're all here this morning."

Gabby gives me a little wave but doesn't interrupt Eunice's flow.

"Next to her is Sarah Broder. She's responsible for the Broder clan, and you'll get to know a bunch of them as we get to work on the new hospital. Last there is Mabel Goodson. Her granddaughter runs the Rise and Bloom Inn."

"It's a pleasure. I'm sorry to interrupt your meeting."

"Nonsense." Mabel's grin is decidedly wicked but welcoming. "It's not like we're planning our next naked dance under the moon in the magnolia grove."

If she's testing me, she fails, because I'm far from scandalized. "Okay, right, if you do, can I join?"

The universal bobbing of heads and round of cackles make me delighted with the whole lot of them.

Eunice's lips twitch. "That's on the agenda for next week, but we'll send you a text. For now, we're fighting about SCUBA diving in Roatan or a ten-day Christmas-shopping excursion along the Elbe. Starts in Berlin, ends in Prague."

A delightful ping-pong of opinions bounces across the table as each person offers her two pence about which one's better. Eventually, Emma Everson taps her glass with her spoon.

"All right, enough. We've got to get this kitchen cleaned up and head over to the gym, so let's vote and get going. Remember what happened the last time we were late?"

As if choreographed, all five of the women collectively called the Grannies wince and groan.

Sarah Broder glares around the table, leaving Gabby and me out of the laser beam of warning. "I'm not doing an extra leg day because of you bunch, so pay attention. If you want to book an extra class to ogle Logan, you do it on your own time."

Sarah tips her head toward me. "We've decided Logan Jameson and Dwayne Johnson are twins separated at birth. And if that isn't enough, he's super smart and funny to boot."

Wow. This Logan must be one heck of a trainer if he has to live up to those reputations.

Dire warnings are unnecessary as the group offers concise reasons for their choices, but the clear winner is SCUBA diving. Apparently, there's time for them to do nothing but shop when they're old and feeble.

I refrain from asking what the benchmark is for that condition with this crew, because I'm fairly certain they've found the fountain of youth and are hiding it from everyone else.

"Wait a second." Lorraine Pepperdine makes everything come to a stop. "I want to hear about the gala."

Eunice's frown is fierce. "Lexi only got here yesterday, for the love of Pete. Give her a minute before you start telling her about the disaster of '87 and scare her off."

Lorraine waves a dismissive hand. "I wasn't going to start with anything before '90. I'm trying to caution her against calla lilies, is all."

I stand and clutch the back of the chair for support. They're actually going to regale me with tales of disaster galas? And I'm supposed to jump in and *not* re-create '87 or whatever year clearly is in Lorraine's mind?

"No dithering, ladies." Mabel raps on the doorframe, where she stands waiting. "Lexi, you look marvelous, by the way. Mina's gonna put Magnolia Bloom on the map all by herself with her beautiful creations."

I'm not sure I look anything more than marginally well put together, but I'm grateful the cut of the top is kind to my less-than-toned physique. One of the benefits of being tall is my weight is at least distributed over a bit more real estate, so I can pretend I don't look as heavy as the scale attests, but still, I avoided the mirror when I scraped my hair back into an elastic and put on socks and trainers. I'm darn glad I won't keep the combined motivating force of Magnolia Bloom waiting. I don't know who this Logan is, but even if he is ogle-worthy, I'm not so sure I want to meet the man who can put the fear of Bulgarian split squats into these women.

The Grannies, however, couldn't care less about my concern and hustle me out the door.

CHAPTER SIX

BETHANIE

I'M tongue-in-teeth concentrating when my mischievous inner klutz leaps to life and I knock my favorite pen to the floor. Before I can stop it, the silly thing rolls to the farthest part of the darkest corner of my desk's kneehole. I've been actively trying to train myself out of my inherent clumsiness, but to little avail. I'm not tripping-over-the-ottoman clumsy, but still....

I need another cup of coffee, but I'd caught Eunice and the Grannies, with Lexi in tow, as they were leaving for their workout and don't feel like making a fresh pot for only me. Eunice's kitchen is spot-less, of course, and she considers "those single-brew contraptions" an abomination.

My sigh may or may not be a cover for several expletives as I push my chair back and crawl in, using the flashlight app on my phone in the space suddenly feeling both as vast as a black hole and as tiny as the cardboard box the delivery guy set on my credenza a few hours ago. With my booty in the air, I'm in my best downward-dog pose, trying to nab the runaway fountain pen before it leaks on the carpet, when two male voices fire up right outside my door.

I offer a rusty prayer my office appears empty.

Those someones are Roy Hilton, Magnolia Bloom's entirely too sexy police chief, talking to his twin brother, Nathanial, our fire chief. They're standing less than ten feet away. And they're both basketball tall, which means my office yoga is in full, not-so-fabulous view.

To most, they're so identical they depend on their respective uniforms to delineate them. Nathanial's a goofball, and I'm lucky my patience hasn't detonated in his presence. He needs to stick to fighting fires instead of lighting up my last nerve.

I close my eyes and give a quick listen to the smooth baritone my ears would automatically attune to in a crowded room. I've never understood why people can't see the shadow of sadness haunting Roy's eyes or realize his trademark growl covers a wounded, sensitive soul. I can tell the brothers apart in a split second, because Roy is the hottest, most handsome man I've ever met, exclamation point, end of story.

My trouble is my active imagination. Over the years, I've cooked up one super-sexy fairy tale starring the alluring police chief, and I add a page, or twenty, in my dreams every night.

But there's trouble in Sexytown, and the dreams usually end with a record scratch. I have zero chance of ever having any kind of relationship with Roy, other than being a fellow proud Magnolia Bloomian. And I'm hoping one day my common sense will finally deliver the knockout punch my imagination sorely needs.

Today, it seems, I've lucked out, as it appears I haven't been spotted by the Hilton brothers. I grab my pen, douse the app, and stay still, hoping they'll mosey on past.

"No. Nathanial, damn it, I'm not trading uniforms with you so you can avoid Eunice Greene."

"Come on, man. We've done this a thousand times."

I'm not used to hearing Nathanial sounding desperate.

Roy and Nathanial bicker with each other constantly. Our two emergency-services departments have a combined forty-something paid employees, if you count admin staff, but the volunteers are just as valuable. Still, Roy and Nathanial argue like they're public-safety

Goliaths charged with protecting the population of Chicago and not the 5,859 residents of the greater Magnolia Bloom area.

"Not a chance in hell, Bro. I'll go back to taking down meth labs in Jersey before I take her on." Roy's response leaves no room for argument.

So of course Nathanial is going to argue. "It's a routine inspection. She's never failed one." He tries for a no-big-deal tone, but even from across the room, it's clear something's up.

"Then I fail to see the problem. She's eightysomething years old and all of five-foot-nothin'."

"Like that matters. She could bench-press you and me both now."

I can see Roy's exasperated head shake in my mind. "Eunice may be determined to take the powerlifting medal in her weight division next spring, but come on. Did she debone your spine at the last fish fry?"

"No, but I had to give her a markdown."

"Oh, so she took your balls and left your backbone broken."

"I'm hurt, man. Where's your family loyalty?"

"You're the boss. You have staff. Delegate."

"They all said they'd quit."

I could barely make out Nathanial's words, and it seems Roy couldn't, either. "Come again?"

"They'll quit, all right?"

I wince at the dramatic change in Nathanial's volume.

I hear a clapping sound and assume Roy has gripped his brother's shoulder. "Looks like you're SOL, buddy. Good luck."

"Fine, but Tawny told me this morning she loves me more than you."

"Dream on. Now go away."

Tawny's the secretary for the combined emergency-services offices of Magnolia Bloom, and it's been a running joke she tells each of them she loves them most every day. I admire her unflagging ability to keep her two overworked bosses in line.

Silence finally returns. I back out of my hidey-hole—and promptly whack the back of my head.

"Ow!"

A rustle sounds at my door, and I wish the knee space was indeed a black hole to another universe, and I could fall in.

"Bethanie?"

Of course it's Roy. Of. Course.

Caught, with no good way out, I feel my pulse shoot to full-on panic. He's moved into the room. And his view is nothing but my butt.

I finish wiggling my way backward, as there's no graceful means to extricate myself. "Hi, Roy. Hey, Nathanial."

"You okay?" Roy appears honestly concerned. Nathanial's laughing without even pretending to hide it.

"Dropped my pen."

"Need some help?"

Yes, I need you to take me out of the friend zone.

With that miracle never going to happen, I hold aloft the Mont Blanc fountain pen, a birthday present from my dad and Mina, like I won the gold in the three-hundred-meter freestyle. "I'm good."

But I'd be a lot better with you.

Clearly, I require psychological help, but his degree is in criminology, which I no longer need assistance with. An uncomfortable silence descends as I clamber to my feet and stand there like my brain's taking a siesta.

Nathanial decides it's time to chime in. "You certainly look good. Been working out, have you? Lots of squats?"

I shoot him the glare perfected from years of being an angry drunk. I might be sober now, but I've retained my signature squint. "Don't you have somewhere you need to be? Like Eunice's kitchen?"

He opens his eyes in too-wide innocence. "What? I was trying to give you a compliment. I'm woke now. Old me would have said, 'Hey, Bethanie, nice ass.' New me has evolved well past my expectations. Of course, I've always been an overachiever."

Roy rounds on his brother in slow motion. "Go."

"But—"

"Now."

With a wink at me, Nathanial leaves, having the audacity to whistle

"Brick House" as he walks away. Nathanial and I have become good friends over the months I've been in recovery, but after one disastrous date and an embarrassingly awkward kiss, friends is all we'll ever be. And we're good with that.

With a little effort, I find my lost voice. "Is there something you need?"

Roy clears his throat. "Uh, yeah, I was here to talk to you about security for the gala and the groundbreaking. I got a text saying Kiki's out, and you're taking over?"

"I was. I mean, I am, but only partly. Kiki's cousin Lexi is here, and she's going to be the go-to for logistics, but she needs a day or two to get up to speed. Can it wait?"

I get a characteristic Roy grunt, and my nerves settle. This Roy is familiar. The pragmatic police chief who's thinking through the details.

"Sure. We've got time, but we can't wait too long."

"I'm certain Lexi will be up and running before Eunice removes Nathanial's testicles."

Roy cups the back of his neck, and it's one more thing unsettling my equilibrium. Many words in the English language describe Magnolia Bloom's relatively new chief of police, such as tall, dark, broody, and for the hyphenated portion of the program, dream-making, whip-smart, and self-assured. Of the plethora of adjectives available, however, *awkward* isn't one I've ever associated with the out-of-my-league and absolutely out-of-reach officer of the law.

"Heard all that, huh?"

"I didn't mean to eavesdrop. I was really hoping you'd walk on by and not catch me doing my wombat imitation."

I don't get a grunt, but I do get a confused frown.

"You know, wombats use their hind ends to…. Never mind. Let's fast-forward to where you say, 'Have a nice day, Bethanie,' and I say, 'Thank you,' and you text Lexi to set up an appointment, and we pretend none of this happened and never mention it. Ever."

Evidently, my plan is satisfactory because I get a half nod and a half grunt, and he about-faces toward my door.

Equally evidently, my mouth hasn't listened to my brain, because it says, "So, you switch uniforms and prank people, huh?"

He stops, does that slow turn actors do in the movies, and my heart's pitter-patter rockets to rib-cracking thumps. He's every bit as attractive and every bit as heart-stopping as the sheriff of Sexytown in my dreams.

"What the brain-deficient prat meant was, in high school we'd switch football uniforms to fu—uhhh, *mess* with the coach. I've never, ever disrespected my badge."

Internal you've-done-it-now klaxons blare at hearing-damaging decibels. Or maybe that's the screech of metal-on-metal brakes for my dreadful sense of humor. Crazy factoid: I thought I was pretty funny when I was a raging drunk. At least in the early hours of the evening. I don't have many memories of the late ones.

In a split second, I go for honesty instead of doubling down on failed jokes. "I'm sorry, Roy. I didn't mean to get silly."

"No worries." To my complete delight, his expression goes a bit sheepish. "Sorry I bit at you. Nathanial sets me off sometimes."

"Brothers." I add a wry grin, as though I have a clue what I'm talking about.

"Trust me. Don't ever have one."

"My dad may be blissfully exploring his second marriage, but as he and Mina are both sixty, I don't think I'm in any danger."

"Lucky you."

"I have a sister, but we've been estranged for years, because of my…you know." My chest heats like I've lit an internal blowtorch, but it's hardly news to Roy how much I've screwed up my life. He had the honor of typing up my arrest record.

"I hope you can work it out someday."

"I hope so, too."

Then he transforms the frown usually pasted on his rugged, devastatingly handsome face into a smile I scramble to commit to memory. "Have a nice day, Bethanie."

Forget my boobs. My whole body feels like it's on fire, especially the real estate just south of my belt buckle, and I'm absolutely sure I'm too young for menopause. "Thanks. Have a great day, Chief."

He touches two fingers to his temple and gives me a salute, leaving my office but giving me a lust-inducing view of his slender hips. Sadly, his long legs, which I have had the pleasure of watching during leg day at Iron Core a few times, are hidden beneath black slacks. He's got a nice backside, though. Round, firm. No flatbuttitis for the sheriff of Sexytown. No, sir.

I dismiss my silly notions of me and Roy and dreams. I'm more than familiar with how this town works, and have no illusions about how many people know a hundred percent of my business.

When it comes to me, the thing flashing in Roy's mind will always be the click of him reciting my Miranda rights as he locked handcuffs on my wrists, and the harsh, crass string of words I can't recall, though the burn of the tone I used remains.

He'll always be polite to me, always be as genial as he can be when not grunting, but he'll never allow someone like me inside the walls he's built to protect himself and his child. I can't blame him. I'm well aware of the damage I've wrought in the past, and the damage his ex, my fellow sister of the liquor bottle, inflicted on his child. I've never met Chloe's mother, but Roy's still in ongoing battles with her. I sit in meetings with women like her every week. And the truth is as pointed as the fountain pen in my hand.

A drunk is a drunk to Roy Hilton.

And the closest he'll ever get to one is when he cuffs them. Just as the first and last time he touched me was when he put his hand on my head so I didn't bump it on the back door after I was *invited* into his patrol car for a trip down to the station for a booking.

He also knows we're liars. Good ones. Who make Academy Award-worthy promises and then break them like cheap pencils. His ex is locked in the it's-different-this-time years, and my heart breaks for young Chloe.

I might have a stretch of months where he hasn't had to barrel up to my car with blue lights strobing, but I can't ask him to believe in me now or down the road.

How can I when I still struggle to believe in myself?

CHAPTER SEVEN

LEXI

I'M in love with each one of the Grannies by the time we circle the town square and are forced all the way down to the corner of Purple Thistle and First Avenue to find a parking place.

"The Iron Core's where the Steele family had their original tractor-supply business." Lorraine Pepperdine has managed to get her turn as tour guide. "They got too big and moved outside of the city limits decades ago, but as happens in small towns, the space will forever be known as the 'old Steele building.'"

We're practically jogging now, but Sarah Broder zooms past us on the left. "Less jawing and more walking, Lorraine. Don't think I won't leave you behind."

I have zero doubt she'll do exactly as threatened, so I put some oomph into my steps.

We arrive at the much-lauded Iron Core. Huge rolling doors are open to the street, and a glance back into town shows we're on the farthest corner of the square. I can't wait to explore, but my curiosity's forced into submission as we all come to a unified halt.

And I'm less than two meters away from the most gorgeous man I've ever seen.

I'm desperately glad the Grannies are all ahead of me, because the man who looks exactly as Sarah described is standing at the check-in counter. In truth, he's slightly shorter and not quite as muscle-bound as The Rock, but my pulse has sailed well beyond those details.

I haven't bought a pair of heels in decades, because Douglas was barely ten centimeters taller than me, and while he swore he didn't mind if I wore them, I never believed him. Besides, I never had the fortitude to "rock my inner Xena, Warrior Princess," as my best mate, Gina, urged me. Since it was easier to wear ballet flats to work, and we rarely went out, my shoe tree tends toward comfort, not fashion.

Which is why my meandering thoughts conclude I could wear a reasonable heel with this man. A stiletto even, but I'm far and away from a high-heel kind of girl. A nice, comfy wedge or a sexy, strappy sandal would do to put my lips within kissing distance of his. I could easily wrap my arms around his muscular neck and run my hands over his perfectly shaped head.

I've always had a thing for bald men, and Logan is a mouthwatering one step removed. His hair is dark, pure black, and my fingers tingle at the mere thought of stroking his not-quite-shaved fringe.

I press the back of my hand to my forehead to check for a fever. It could be delayed jet lag.

Or the easier answer is I've lost my damned mind.

Emma Everson leans close enough to not be overheard. "Told you he was gorgeous."

"You've a gift for understatement. I'm going to have a third-degree burn from the blush I feel heating my face."

"You won't be the first or the last. That man's inspired many confession-worthy dreams in Magnolia Boom."

"Emma!"

"What? I'm married, not dead, and my husband Quinton's his partner in the gym, so I get to see him even more than this lot does."

The teasing's cut short when he meets my eyes, and a who's-this smile creases his full lips.

I've always wanted full lips. I have unremarkable medium lips. Neither excessively thin nor plump and sexy. Exactly like the rest of me. Boring. Average. Just…medium.

Before my new tribe can introduce me, a woman who's everything I've ever wished I could be walks up, nods to the Grannies, and gives a thousand-watt smile to Hollywood's loss and Magnolia Bloom's gain. If I had a list of all the things I'm not, this lady would tick off each box. As tall as me, but svelte and toned. Hair pulled back in a simple ponytail, but the softly highlighted blond looks elegant and commercial-worthy. Face with enough lines to say, *Hey, I'm a woman of a certain age, but I can rock your world.* Eyes so blue they're the definition of piercing, an expression used in a thousand books. Now I understand it.

I'm so jealous my stomach seizes.

"Thanks, Logan. You got that knot out, at least for now."

Great. Even her voice is a mixture of deep and husky. She's like a sunshine-haired Jessica Rabbit in a bit more clothing.

I want to hate her.

Lorraine Pepperdine leans toward me, speaking sotto voce. "Logan has magic hands. Best massage therapist in three counties. I'd put him up against anyone in Dallas or Houston."

Her words make my gaze go to the long fingers wrapped around the ones the Jessica Rabbit wannabe offered moments ago. Of course, her nails are perfect, not ragged and in desperate need of a manicure, like mine.

Emma Everson takes a small step forward, and I can see why she's the captain of the group. "Good morning, Bunny. Hi, Logan."

Bunny? The woman's name is Bunny? Surely that's a nickname.

Jessica Bunny turns her bright smile on me and steps over, offering her now-free hand. "Hi. You must be Lexi."

Dang it, her eyes are so open and sincere, guilt floods me. First off, I was practically swooning like a historical heroine in a bad movie over a complete stranger, then I was harshly judging a woman who doesn't deserve it. Neither reaction makes sense, and I don't like anything about my lack of mental functioning during the last three minutes.

Forcing myself to crank the dial on my bitch mode down to zero, I smile back, making blasted sure it's real. "I am."

"Welcome to Magnolia Bloom. I'm Bunny West, by the way. I didn't know I'd get to meet you so soon, but since fate has stepped in, please come by the saloon when you're done letting Logan torture you. It's too early for beer, but I make a mean glass of iced tea."

"Sounds lovely. Thank you."

"Great. The Grannies will tell you how to find me. See you in a bit."

To my shock, I didn't merely mouth the words. My initial reaction to Bunny has dissipated like I snapped my fingers, and before I can dissect the moment any deeper, she's greeted all the Grannies and left the building. Logan steps into the now-open space, and my hand is claimed again. This time, the fingers enclosing mine are warm and callused enough to give the most delicious scrape against my skin. His grip is firm and sincere, but I have a sense Logan knows exactly how strong he is and makes sure to keep his ability to crush small bones in check.

"Eunice said she was going to get you down here, but I didn't think it'd be the day after you landed. Why I'm surprised, though, is the question as she's Magnolia Bloom's force of nature. I'm Logan Jameson."

My brain meant to say, *Nice to meet you.* I swear those are the words I intended to come out of my mouth.

Instead, I say, "Nice muscles."

Aaand now I'm going to die. Right here on the concrete, I'm going to immolate and leave a tiny pile of ash all over the floor.

Laughter titters around the Grannies flanking me, and there's no doubt Logan's trying not to join in. "Thank you."

"Oh, God." My voice is a harsh, raspy whisper. "Let me die now."

I start backing up, but Sarah pats my arm and pulls me back in. "Now, now, don't fret. Logan's used to women falling at his feet. Good thing is, he hasn't let it go to his head."

Logan gives her a mock frown. "Stop it, Sarah. You bunch go get stretched out."

The Grannies abandon me, leaving me feeling like my skin is the shade of strawberry not actually appearing in nature. I realize there's hardly been a handful of days in the last several decades I haven't been surrounded by men. Sure, most were related to me by blood, marriage, or part of the plumbing trade, but none of that explains my ridiculous reaction to Logan Jameson.

I also owe an apology to my long-standing secret crushes on both Idris Elba and Dwayne Johnson, but they'll always be fantasies. Logan Jameson's real—and decidedly more handsome and oxygen-consuming. Let's say I didn't watch *Fast & Furious 6* and *Furious 7*, much less *Hobbs & Shaw*, for the scintillating scriptwriting.

Thankfully, Logan appears blithely unaware he's responsible for my current hypoxia and imminent danger of brain damage.

"Are you going to join the class today?"

My ears hear the words, but it takes a full five seconds for me to process them and respond. "I'm, uh, not sure. I haven't been to an exercise class in a long time, so…maybe?"

Logan gestures toward the Grannies stretching on padded flooring. "You're welcome to jump in, but I don't want you lifting anything more than five-pound dumbbells or the smallest medicine ball, okay? Do as much as you feel you can, but we don't want you getting hurt your first time in the door. We start small and build here."

Great. The world's sexiest gym owner thinks I can't keep up with women my mum's age and more. Sadly, he's probably correct.

By the end of the class, I'm mollified I didn't embarrass myself, but it's clear I have a long way to go before I earn my new workout duds. I can't wait to meet Mina and compliment her on her fashion and comfort. Not one single squat risked me having my own version of plumber's crack. I've seen enough of those over my lifetime, thank you very much.

To my relief, class ends, and the Grannies head out for their traditional after-workout coffee. They invite me along, but I decline, feeling I've interrupted their routine enough for one day.

I head back to the dressing room, using the hair dryer to get the sticky strands off my neck and feeling a little more refreshed before I set out on my new adventure. It'd be impossible to get lost, as my destination is literally two blocks away. If I walk a straight line one I get to the square, I'll run into the front door of the Due West Saloon. I'm not sure I want to parade around town in my athletic duds, but the urge to have tea with the woman I so wrongfully judged is even stronger. Eunice assured me Bunny will get me back to the castle, or barring that, I'm to call, and someone will come fetch me.

My plan to slip out and be on my way is foiled when I spot Logan manning the front desk again. If there's a back door I could escape through, I'd take it, but having set foot in the facility a mere hour ago, it's not unreasonable to have no idea where an alternate exit might be.

Sucking in a breath for some courage, and reminding myself at least my hair's dry and I don't look like a sweat-soaked rat anymore, I brave the walk to the entrance.

I try for nonchalance as I reach the desk. "Thanks for the workout. It was fun."

That's a right lie, but what else am I supposed to say? *Thanks for making me realize what an out-of-shape sack of mashed tatties I am?*

"I'm glad you came in, and I hope you'll come back. I've got openings for private lessons to get you trained in proper lifting techniques. I've got time now, if you'd like me to show you around the gym and give you some basics to work on."

"I'll think about it, thanks, but I've got a date with Bunny." I manage not to stutter and certainly don't add my thoughts will be more than filled with images of him, his snug T-shirt, and proper, but dream-inducing, shorts. I've already embarrassed myself enough for one morning without the additional visual aid of his muscles bunching and straining as he lifts heavy things turning me into a tongue-tied girl afraid to talk to the cutest boy in the room.

And I can even deal with the words *private lessons*.

"If I can't convince you to take a look around the gym, can I talk you into dinner? I know you've barely had a chance to take a breath, but I'd be happy to be your tour guide."

I do a slow blink. Wait. Did Magnolia Bloom's resident muscle man just ask me out on a date? I feel the damned heat rising again, and he's probably confused about why I'm doing my best public imitation of a hot flash, but given my genealogy, I can't help it. What an utterly absurd thought for me to have. He's being nice is all, as every single person I've met so far has been.

Upon reconsideration, to think a man as Hollywood-worthy as Logan Jameson would ask me on a date after my disastrous first impression is painful.

"You're kind to offer, but I'm sure your duties don't include having to shepherd visitors around town."

"True, since I'm not the local Welcome Wagon, but that has nothing to do with wanting to take you to dinner."

Much like earlier, my brain short-circuits and I blurt my thoughts. "But why?"

He tilts his head, his high forehead wrinkling. "Is that a trick question?"

Since I've already proven myself to be a right eejit, there's no sense trying to back out now. "No, it's a serious one. Why would you ask me out?"

"Because you're a beautiful woman, and I've enjoyed having you in my class, and I'd love to ask you about Scotland? Maybe, I don't know, five or ten other reasons?"

My embarrassment turns to full rage in a snap. *Beautiful woman*, my arse. I have no clue why he's bammin' me, but it takes me off-center, and I've had enough. "It's unkind of you to tease a woman, Mr. Jameson. I'll be on my way."

I race out of the gym, ignoring his, "Lexi! Wait!"

I'm not about to stop. My pride's shredded, but I hold my head high and come as close to a run as these bones can manage and race down the sidewalk.

CHAPTER EIGHT

BUNNY

I GLANCE outside and catch Lexi heading in my direction, but her posture's all wrong. Most stroll past the quaint shops lining the square, pausing at the window displays, yet she's all but stalking, and I wonder what's happened. I turn, pretending not to see her as she stops in front of my door, and a hint of a smile flashes. She takes in the mug of beer adorned with a frothy head and a mariner's compass with a needle pointing west, my custom-made sign for Due West.

The name I picked because Bunny West was long past due for some happiness.

Never in my wildest dreams did I imagine a saloon would save my life, but this place—each board overhauled to my satisfaction, the people who grace the barstools and tables with kindness and loyalty, the exchanges I have with my customers—are food for my soul.

Lexi's deep breaths are lessening. The old-fashioned bell above the door finally rings, and I look up as though I've just noticed her.

"Hey there. Glad you came."

"Thanks for the invitation, although I'm wee duffed it's too early for a pint of one of your brews." She shoots a glance at the display of taps behind me.

I wave to a barstool and reach for a glass. "It's five o'clock somewhere. You sure?"

She sighs and nods. "I'm acting like a broody hen, pecking at everyone around me, and I feel like a fool. I don't dare start drinking now, though my da would give a thumbs-up at the idea. No telling how I'd act the rest of the day."

I settle forward on my wrists in the move I've seen Gene perfect. I call it attentive tavern-keeper mode. "I've been in this job long enough to recognize stress when I see it. What's up?"

I might not be a bartender extraordinaire like Gene, but I have my own share of success getting people to confide in me. I can't help but think half of Lexi's discombobulation might be from feeling she's landed on an alien planet. I love Magnolia Bloom, but there's an adjustment period for everyone.

"Logan Jameson asked me to dinner."

That certainly isn't the revelation I was expecting, but I smile because, if true, my business is about to get even better as every single woman from here to Atlanta comes in to drown their sorrows. "Good for you. Logan's super hot, and he's the nicest guy. Which I don't say lightly. He's kind. Truly, deeply kind."

Lexi looks at me like I've asked her to tap-dance naked across the bar.

"It's nae wonderful. It's embarrassing."

I've clearly missed something. "I don't understand. What's embarrassing about being asked out by the man most eligible women—and truthfully, a few married ones—in this town dream of nabbing?"

"No man who's, as you say, super-hot, is going to ask me out unless he's totally steamin' or his mates have put him to a dare."

Definitely missing something. "Let me get us some tea, and we'll sort this out." I hold up an empty glass. "Sweet or unsweet?"

"I'm sorry?"

"Your tea."

"Oh, um, I'm not sure. This tea's served cold, aye?"

"Yes, but no worries. I'll give you one of each." I head for the ice well and return in short order.

I put three coasters on the bar, then three glasses—one for me, two for her—and await her decision.

Her grimace tells me the sweet version's too much, and a small shrug reveals the unsweet lacks something, but she mulls her appraisal like the fate of nations depends on it. "Can I try half of one and half the other?"

"That's good enough to keep your honorary Southerner card." With a deft hand learned from hours behind this very bar, I give her a half-and-half and join her on the customer side of the gleaming wood. I'll wait until we meet again before I introduce her to an Arnold Palmer.

We clink glasses, and I lean closer. Not far enough to invade her space, but definitely a distance to invite some camaraderie. "Now, tell me what's got you so kerfluffled."

As she gives me a quick recap, I try to maintain my poker face but fail and realize my forehead's scrunched in a deep frown. "I'm sorry, but you're going to have to give me a little more. In the five years I've known him, I've never heard of Logan being rude. Are you sure he was teasing you?"

"What other explanation could there be? 'Beautiful woman,' my arse. If anyone's beautiful, it's him, all dark skin and solid muscles. I'm so pale I used to tell Douglas I bought blue sheets so he'd be able to find me. And then there's the several stone I've needed to lose for decades."

I'm always amazed at the difference between how people see themselves versus how others view them. She sees something unsavory when she looks in the mirror, but I doubt she's ever seen ugly like I have. You understand the many shades of beautiful real fast when you nearly have your face torn off in a car accident and spend months and numerous surgeries putting yourself back together again.

"You're a gorgeous woman, Lexi. I know it's hard to believe anything but the versions of ourselves we've created, but trust me."

"Don't you do it, too. You Texas people have a reputation for fleechin', but I'm a bit raw and don't appreciate it."

"Fleechin'?"

"It means flattery, but in this case, it's insincere." She uses a napkin to capture the condensation on the side of her glass, then presses the cool dampness to the back of her neck. "I might not make small children run away in fright, but I'm well aware I'm no head-turner like you."

I shouldn't let the comment rile me, but it appears I'm in my own mood today and feel she's in need of some perspective.

"Let me show you something." I pull out my phone and open my photos to the album I labeled Do-Over. At the time, I thought it appropriate, because a near-death experience will have you praying and begging for a second chance. "There's no tiptoeing into what I'm about to show you, but this face cost me time, money, and damn near my sanity. Feel free to scroll."

I hand her the phone, and barely a second passes before she gasps.

"That's you?"

"Yes, and while I acknowledge I have enviable genes in the weight department and started with features described as classic, none of that deserves accolades, as I had nothing to do with it." I point to my phone. "After my accident, which was entirely my own ego-induced fault, I married the man who fixed me, realizing too late he'd made himself pretty on the outside, but was empty on the inside. Beauty's only real if there's kindness and decency to properly illuminate it."

"Aye, that's fair certain."

"You, my dear, have incredible hair, perfect skin, and a smile that lights up a room, and you likely snagged Logan's interest in about five nanoseconds. But if you were even a hint of fake, like so many of the women who chase after him, he wouldn't have so much as blinked in your direction. He's a great guy. Super grounded. And I've never seen him drawn to the phony and flashy."

I wince, knowing I've overdone it, but a person's exterior isn't the sum of who they are, though I've been judged for mine one time too many.

"You're right, and I'm being a twit." She takes a long drink, and her lips wobble as she tries for a smile.

"If Logan asked me out, I'd have doubts, too. He's so pretty he sometimes doesn't seem real, but I promise he is."

"I'm glad, but now I feel extra foolish."

"Don't. We've all been guilty of it." I take my phone back and turn it off. "My face is mostly mine, but isn't it funny how I still remember the bump in my nose I had my ex fix? One thing, now gone, that if I look too hard, I can still see. I guess we're just human in the end."

She drains her glass and sets it down, the jury clearly still out on her final verdict. "Aye, I've been accused of being overly analytical, and it bites me sometimes."

Considering my tendency to think about the one man I've analyzed to death, who I wish would ask me out for so much as a hot dog at the food trucks over off Main Street, I can hardly throw stones.

"Go to dinner with Logan. If you don't have a good time, you can leave mid-date or not accept another invitation."

"Okay, fine. I'll consider going, and if I do, and he's not all you say, I'm coming back and saying I told you so." She eyeing her empty glass like it may be growing on her, and returns her napkin to the bar. "I guess I was too harsh on Logan, but I don't react well to surprises, good or bad ones. More so since I lost Douglas. Let's blame jet lag and a sore heart. On top of that, I'm having a stare-down with fifty I'm going to lose soon."

"I'm not too far behind you, sister. My marriage immolated like a vampire caught in the noonday sun. I was pretty touchy for too long. Sometimes I still am."

"How long were you married?"

"A bit over fifteen years. You?"

"Douglas and I were planning for our thirtieth, year after next. He decided to have a heart attack and die on me instead."

"I'm so, so sorry, Lexi."

Lord, why can't I keep my mouth shut?

"Forgive my horrible attempt at levity. Joking's never been my strong suit. I left that up to my husband and his numbskull brothers. The thing is, the gut-wrenching devastation everyone tells me will hit me hasn't yet, but that doesn't mean I didn't love the big lug."

"I don't want to risk bad karma by saying I wish my ex had chosen the option yours did, so I'll leave it that he got most of the money, but I got the brewery. That and a guarantee I never have to see his hundred-thousand-dollar face again. Trust me, I got the better end of the deal."

"I know my marriage wasn't perfect. None is, but we had a good run, even if it wasn't all fireworks and roses."

My stomach turns. I got reeled in by fancy light shows and hothouse flowers, and boy, I was epically foolish to believe they were real. I figured out too late I'm an occasional candles-and-wildflowers kinda gal.

Hating the sadness haunting Lexi's eyes, I slip around the bar to refill our glasses as well as change the subject. "Tell me how you're connected to the castle."

"I'm a MacInnes from Alyssa's branch."

"Alisdair's sister."

"Aye, the patriarch of this crazy brood, and while my direct lineage is from Alyssa's marriage to Niall MacMillan, it's a heritage I'm happy to claim."

"I've seen paintings and even a picture of Alyssa as a young woman. There's even an article about her, Alisdair, and Evajean from one of the local papers when the city chartered back in 1872. She was a woman far ahead of her time."

"That she was."

"I'll admit I'm a bit starstruck by the castle, and I've parlayed my friendship with Bethanie into sneaking hours alone in their gallery. Every time, I'm utterly captivated by people who lived ten, fifteen decades before I was born. The children. The couples. The families, all growing and changing over so many years."

There's a lot of love in that room, almost too much, but those canvases call to me. I can't explain it, but sometimes I need to stand there, transfixed by the texture of the oils or the framing of the photographs, appreciating the artists and the people who inspired them.

I'd trade my face and figure in a heartbeat to have one second of the love I feel between the couples in those paintings.

"Soak up every second you can inside the castle." I plunk a few ice cubes into our warming tea, the bemused shake of her head as she studies the national drink of the South making me smile. "Since we've fresh friends, I'd feel a lot better about shoving my surgery pictures in your face if you'd tell me more about you and Douglas."

She plays with a drop of sweat beading down the side of her glass. I wait, not wanting to push, but I recognize the expression of someone in need of a sympathetic ear.

"I've gotten so much advice over this last year, I could have my own column in the Glasgow Times. Most of it's some version of people telling me they understand how I feel, that they know I'm all twisted up. The thing is, I'm not. I've been sad, of course, and cried a river of tears. Douglas was a walrus, like his brothers, but he was a good man. A good da to our weans, who are now far away from being babies, but I guess you never break that habit."

I start to tear my napkin, strip by strip, at the mention of her kids.

Lexi stops and reaches across the bar. "I'm sorry, did I say something wrong?"

"Not at all. I always wanted children, but that wasn't in my cards." And turns out, my ex didn't want me to have them. Damaging waistlines, fluffy tummies, other catastrophes. "Keep going. Tell me more about you."

"There's not much to go on about. I worked in our family plumbing and carpentry business for decades—office manager and general flunky—but instead of being debilitated by losing Douglas, it's like I told Eunice. I'm more adrift. Not because I'm uncoupled—an expression I heard on the telly—but because I don't know what to do now that I'm not working at the shop anymore."

Uncoupled. All these fancy new words for being alone.

"After the divorce, I felt the same. I fled Dallas and the country clubs and high teas, and poured myself into my little brewery here. This place saved my sanity." I can't tell her something's still missing, that when I lock up some days, I not only feel adrift, but I'm the only boat in the sea.

"I tried, likewise. Poured myself into the business twice as hard, but the truth is, it was never mine. It was always Douglas and his brothers' dream. Without him there, I felt more and more of an outsider, which is all my own doing. His brothers are sweeties, but my heart left when I lost Douglas. When Ally put the bug in my ear to come help Kiki with the gala, I jumped on it so fast I scared everyone, including myself. It was an excuse to get away. Kiki could have found a hundred people to help her, I'm sure, but I'm really glad to escape and have something to do while I'm here."

The bell tinkles, and we both look over. For a split second, I'm scared my expression fires up klieg-light bright, but I give the friendly smile I always give Gene, thankful he can't see the thundering of my heart.

Lexi looks between Gene and me, evidently noting something I haven't managed to conceal. She gives me a sly but sweet smile and doesn't say a word as he crosses the room. I wonder if she finds his close-cropped salt-and-pepper hair and eyes that have those spends-a-lot-of-time-in-the-sun crow's feet as sexy as I do.

"Gene, this is Lexi Stewart, the MacInnes visitor from Scotland."

"Gene Autry." He offers her his hand and his usual welcoming expression. "It's a pleasure. You'll hear some folks call me Buddy, so you can choose either. Bunny here thinks Bunny the Bartender and Buddy the Bartender is too much, and on top of her determination to steal all my customers from the Magnolia Moon, she decided she's calling me Gene. I can't break her."

Lexi's smile turns downright devilish, and I wonder if Gene's teasing has her about to unleash the Scottish version of a leprechaun. "Sounds like an interesting story, but to keep things simple, I'll go with Gene. It's nice to meet you."

"Ignore him, Lexi. He's here to give me a hard time and sample something I'm trying out. If the shrubs take off, I'll let him buy them for the Moon at twice-retail so he can lure back all the customers I've stolen."

"Shrubs?" She looks around, and I swear she's searching for greenery.

Gene and I both laugh, but I can tell we haven't insulted our new friend. "Shrubs are the newest iteration of an old-school idea. They're simple syrups, basically, that you add to seltzer for a nonalcoholic selection, or to a neutral base like vodka for a leaded version. Gene keeps a lot of options at the Moon for folks who don't drink, and he's got me hooked now. I like the idea of having something fun to offer my designated drivers, or folks who don't want alcohol, but since I only have a beer-and-wine license, I can't serve cocktails. These are a nice alternative."

"Sounds dead brilliant."

"Would you like to stay and be a taste-tester?" I offer because my mama's bad-manners alert works even from the grave. Part of me's being a chicken, trying to keep her here, but the other part's back in high school, wondering if she's going to out the secret crush she's managed to read like it's printed across my shirt.

Lexi slides off her stool. "Thank you, but I'm going to run over and see if I can catch Eunice at the coffee shop and head back to the castle with her. I'm meeting Bethanie to get to work on the gala schedule, and then she and I are treating Eunice to dinner out. You have no idea how hard we've had to work to talk her into ordering a meal instead of making it."

"All right, but if you miss her, come back, and I'll hook up the mice to the pumpkins to whisk you back to the castle."

"I'll do that."

Gene bids her goodbye, and she's gone in a blink, leaving my leg muscles firing with the desperate need to run away so I don't reveal what a fool I am. As I feared, my shot of courage from Emmett and my muscle-pounding from Logan fail me as fast as an ice cream cone on the Fourth of July.

I am a fool for Buddy Gene Autry, and I'm seconds away from showing it.

CHAPTER NINE

LEXI

I FIND Eunice in plenty of time, enjoying more of the ping-pong of the Grannies' repartee as the ones riding back to the castle to claim their cars keep me in stitches. After popping into my suite for a leisurely shower and comfortable clothes, I'm ready for my meeting with Bethanie. I'm both excited and a little trepidatious. I want to help. I truly do. But my extended cousin has a cockeyed vision of what I can manage for her.

My knock on the doorjamb of Bethanie's office distracts her from her computer, but her harried expression turns delighted. "How was your workout?"

By the time I get from the door to my seat, I come up with an easy demur. "It was interesting. The Grannies are all lovely, of course."

"They can be a handful. I hope Logan went easy on you, first time and all."

"He was…fine."

Bethanie squints an eye. "Fine, as in fine-looking? Because that's a resounding yes. Or fine, as in his class wasn't fine at all? When that word comes out of my mouth, it's usually more of an epithet."

My poor cuticles are the unfortunate victims of my discomfort. "It's nothing."

"I'll take 'Understatement for $200, Alex.'"

She waits and waits until I finally cave. "If you must know, he asked me to dinner."

Bethanie gasps and flops back in her chair. "That cad! Let me give the Grannies a callback. We can have tar and pitchforks ready by dusk."

"Very funny, ye daftie."

"Then tell your new friend," she teases, pointing to herself, "who's clearly missing something, what the problem is."

"Bunny seems to share your opinion. I'm not prone to overreacting, I promise. It's just I can't explain why this has me flummoxed."

Well, I can, but I'm not repeating the confession I made to Bunny. I don't have self-confidence issues. I'm a standard medium on the attractiveness scale, and I accepted that a long, long time ago. What I'm not okay with is a man who's clearly out of my league thinking I need his charity.

Bethanie shrugs. "I'm willing to blame jet lag for all anomalies, but seriously, you've barely had your feet on good, Texas soil for twenty-four hours."

"Which is why I'm feeling like a royal cow. From Bunny's reaction and now yours, it's clear I've lost my marbles, and I've shown my hind end to Logan, and he didn't deserve it."

He didn't deserve my wrath, but we're not going to dinner, and that's that.

A smile with no pretentions of being anything less than wicked crosses Bethanie's beautiful face. "He might have liked that. Word is, he's a legs-and-butt guy."

Heat scorches my face, and once again, I'm certain I'm a right eejit. For the love of the Loch Ness monster, I'm hardly ancient, but Bethanie suddenly seems eons younger and light-years more hip.

Is *hip* even a thing nowadays?

"Look, I've known him for about ten years now, although I was drinking back then and didn't have too kind a view on most humans.

Still, he's always been kind to me, and all evidence supports the theory that while he's sexily mysterious, he's a genuinely good guy."

"How can someone be mysterious after a decade?"

"He doesn't date locals and has an astonishing aversion to gossip. Word is he had a girlfriend in Atlanta for a while, but no one could confirm."

I can't stop an eye roll. "Oh, bollocks. Isn't it beyond passé now to play the I-don't-do-commitment card?"

"At the risk of sounding like head cheerleader on Team Logan, I don't think that's it. His best friend is Wyatt Jenkins, who also happens to be a good friend of mine."

"Wyatt, as in Emmett Everson's partner?"

"You really do have an eidetic memory for names. Yes, that Wyatt. Anyway, once, when I was still drinking and Wyatt was making sure I didn't kill myself, he said that Logan really does believe in love. Like the real deal, forever thing. Wyatt and Logan played college ball together, and Wyatt was an extra in a movie shot at the castle that brought Logan to town. He used to be a stunt double for his brother, who's a B-list actor, or a low A-lister now, but Logan never talks about him. Like, *ever* ever."

I stretch my memory for a famous American actor named Jameson but come up blank.

As if she's read my mind, Bethanie fills in the void. "His brother is Brock Michaels. Uses his first and middle name professionally."

"Ah! The rugged, square-jawed, I-don't-smile-and-take-no-prisoners action guy."

"That's him. Wyatt says something happened between the two of them back in the day, and Logan became Brock's opposite. Brock plows through women like a harvester at bailing time, but Logan won't. He could but doesn't."

"Come on, he sounds like some kind of god."

"He does kinda sound too good to be true, doesn't he? Thing is, he doesn't like drama. Basically has an anaphylactic reaction to it."

Oddly enough, I nearly had the same reaction to him. I laugh at the truth before me. First, the officer on the plane. And now Logan.

Apparently, I'm allergic to sexy men.

"Now that we've done a thorough information dive on Logan, let's move on to what I'm here for."

Bethanie gives me the I'm-on-to-you chuckle. "Okay, let's get started."

With the efficiency she displayed at the airport, Bethanie blocks out how I can be Kiki's stand-in. Most of the contracts are negotiated, which makes sense as the event is barely a month away. My main purpose will be to meet with vendors, finalize timetables, and escort people around the castle and grounds as needed. All in all, it's what I've done for thirty years for Douglas and his brothers, with the difference being I'll be talking about setting up a party, not drafting out parts and service techs, subcontractors and calendars to plumb an office building, and the million things I can rattle off with my eyes closed.

There's a reason project managers are worth their weight in gold. They're the unsung heroes of any event, but the last thing I need is to cause the gala to implode like an old building set with C-4.

I wring my hands in my lap, hoping I'm hiding my near panic attack. "It's a really bad idea to have me mucking about when I know faucets and toilets, not foie gras and tiaras."

"You won't be doing anything alone. I'm literally ten yards from the turret where you'll be working. Kiki's going to cover the budget and contracts."

I look at the spreadsheet she handed me when I walked in, and once I focus, I can see I'm overreacting…a little. "What if we give it a trial run? I'll see what I can get done this week, and if the castle's still standing instead of in a pile like a badly pulled Jenga tile, we'll take it from there."

I swear a tear of relief forms in Bethanie's eye. "Oh, thank God. Kiki's a bit of a one-woman dynamo, and I'm happy here in my little office, in my little niche. She and I've become a good team, but there's no doubt she's the ringmaster, and I'm the third-act juggler. You've wrangled contractors before. We just need to get you used to some different lingo."

These barmy hens don't know what they've done. Going round

with a PVC supplier's one thing. I don't have the experience to wrangle dance floor installations and champagne fountains. But I'm tired of repeating myself, so I decide to give it a go. My performance on day one will be more than enough for them to come to their senses.

"I'm going to hold you to that. Show me where to set up, and I'll get to work."

"Kiki insists you take her office. It's where all the files and information are."

"I can't be taking the chatelaine's office. It doesn't feel right."

"Don't argue. It's logical and time-saving. Besides, Harville believes if her office is occupied, she'll feel too guilty about displacing you to try to sneak in. Which she's already done."

Any pressure I previously felt triples. I'm to pull off a gala when I've never so much as attended one and do a good enough job to keep a pregnant woman from being put on bed rest? Why on earth did I decide to take this trip?

"I assume Pastor Harville's no-cursing vow was seriously threatened by such shenanigans." I'm a laugh a minute now, only to keep from tearing out the front door. If Penny the Dragon were real, I'd jump on her back and ask her to fly me far, far away.

"I've honestly never seen that man mad before, but the old saw about beware the quiet ones? Yeah, that."

"I can't say I'm surprised. Even over the phone, Kiki's extremely determined, but to aid and abet this plan to keep her resting, I'm happy to get started right away."

Och, the lies I'm telling. God's sharpening up a lightning bolt with my name on it.

"Far be it from me to stop you, but don't work too long, okay? I don't want to wear you out and have the entire MacInnes clan and the castle ghosts mad at me."

"Aye, right, and I want to make sure I donnae let you down."

Bethanie flaps a hand at me and grins. "To quote the inimitable Eunice Greene, pishposh. You're the one doing us a favor."

Shooed off, I head down the hallway and am in sight of the iconic doorway to the even more iconic office. Images of the women who built and managed this estate float through my mind, and I can almost see a movie of the proud, intelligent, and fierce MacInneses who have weathered the highest of highs and lowest of lows while seated behind an heirloom desk a few meters beyond this entrance.

I can see Evajean in her long skirts and crisp white blouses, Gavina in her Levi's blue jeans and chambray shirts, Violet in her mod prints, and Kiki in her no-nonsense polyblends. Not that the legacies are about fashion, but it's an easy film reel in my mind, seeing them coming and going, stacks of papers in their hands, pencils pushed haphazardly into coiffures or behind ears. I'm here only temporarily, but as certain as I am that I can't do the job to their standards, I can admit that I'd like to be a brief success story in the saga of Castle MacInnes.

I reach for the handle as my imagination runs wild, and I half see Evajean, Gavina, and Violet in a semicircle behind me, urging me on.

The image pops like a soap bubble when my phone rings, and I nearly jump out of my skin. A quick glance at the screen has a smile back on my face and the surge of happiness I need. Sadie, named after Douglas's mum, tends to text me once a week or so. Short bursts of what she's doing or what the baby's up to. I miss Frederica, named after her other gran, but Sadie and Nicholas moved to his native Spain not long after they married. I held Ricci, as they call her, a few times, but it's not like my life has made it easy to jaunt to the other side of Europe on a whim.

"Hallo, Sadie. This is a nice surprise."

"Hi, Mum. Listen, not much time. We've got a huge trip planned to Greece, and I need you to come—"

Shock zips through me like the time the boys left a wire exposed on a remodel, and I found it in the dark. To my regret, Sadie and I have never been especially close. We're not estranged or anything so dramatic, but ever since her high school years, our lives intersect only when she needs me for something. I can't believe my girl wants me to join them on a posh vacay. Could it be my girl is growing—

"—and keep Ricci for us. You and Dad never went anywhere, so I bet you have tons of points on your rewards card to use for a flight, even if it is at the last minute."

Wait. She wants me to come to Spain. On a moment's notice. On my points. To babysit.

The electric shock turns to a dull throb.

"You want me to come to Spain. Because you need a babysitter."

"Aye, right away."

Deep breath, Lexi. Deep breath.

"Hang on. I need to step outside."

I move across the short distance to the balcony I so enjoyed this morning. I take the same rocker I used earlier, but the metal's decidedly warmer now. It takes less than a minute, but I need the time to get a hold of my temper.

"Okay, I'm back." I trace my fingernail over the filigreed table to my right. "I'm confused why you're calling me. Surely it's easier to have your mother-in-law keep the baby."

"Augustina and Joseph are going with us. Augustina's sister was going to stay with Ricci, but she fell and broke her ankle, and there's no way she can keep up with a toddler. It'd really be best if you could be here by Thursday."

So, in two days. Literally forty-eight hours.

The ache turns to a stab. Right in my gut.

"Let me see if I can recap. You're calling me, with barely a how-do-you-do, to demand I fly to Spain in the blink of an eye so you can go on a dream vacation with your in-laws."

"I wouldn't ask if it wasn't an emergency, Mum. I need you."

Clearly, my girl got hit with the oblivious stick, because I don't think my voice could be any more incredulous if I went to acting school.

"Well, there's a few wrenches in your plan, mostly that I'm in America, which you would know if you'd read any of my texts for the last, oh, month. I even sent you my itinerary in case of emergency."

"Oh, yeah, you did. I'm sorry to mess up your trip."

And there it is. The certainty in her voice that I'll drop whatever I'm doing to come to her rescue. Maybe that's my fault. I taught the kids to be independent, but they've always known I'm here for them, am in their corner. Maybe I'm the only one who understood I meant I'd be there for them *in emergencies.*

"I cannae, Sadie. Sorry."

"That's grand, Mum. The closest airport to us is—"

"If you'd listen, you'd have heard me say I *can't.*"

"Of course you can. It's a bit longer flight and all, but—"

"Sadie, stop talking. Since you're nae hearing me, I'll make it clear. Even if I could manage to get myself on another international flight before I've had two decent cups of coffee, I *won't.*"

"But I need you, Mum."

"Nay, you need a babysitter, and I wasnae even your first choice. If you'd stopped and thought for one second about where I am or what my plans are, this conversation would be moot. I don't exist to be your personal 999, to be used only at the last minute. My days of jumping-to simply because you're in a panic are over."

Sadie sucks in a breath, and if this call were on video, I'd see her mouth go pinched. "I can't believe you're doing this because you're jealous of my mother- and father-in-law."

That line of attack doesn't surprise me. Her husband's family is significantly wealthier than Douglas and I could ever dream of being, and my little material girl had stars in her eyes from the moment her dark, sexy Spaniard started calling on her.

"I admit, I had a flash of envy that you're going to Greece, where I've always wanted to go, but I never even entered your mind until something gummed up your plans. Honestly, though, Augustina and Joseph aren't factors here. They're delightful people who've been nothing but lovely to me the few times we've met."

I can tell she's winding up for a dissertation on why I need to change my mind. I concede I would have done exactly as she asked a few years ago, been at her immediate beck and call, but something has shifted. I suppose sudden widowhood does that, but regardless, I put myself out of her misery.

"Listen, Sadie, I've a thousand things to do today, and I'm already behind. I hope you get this all worked out. Have a nice holiday. Send me pictures."

Before she can get in another word, I disconnect the call.

Strange thing is, although Sadie probably wouldn't believe me, I mean it. Despite the searing hurt tearing through me like a heated chef's knife, I want her to go and have a marvelous time, regardless of how blindly, ragingly insensitive she's been, because Sadie has her husband. She's young and vibrant and alive, and she needs to make memories with him as fast and furiously as she can, and yes, even with her in-laws.

From thousands of kilometers away, I silently implore Sadie to do it now. Don't wait. Don't postpone. Don't cancel amazing trips at the last minute because of one business emergency or another. Don't let your husband say, *We'll get to it, love. I promise.*

Douglas and I were always getting to something. And now we can't.

My steps to the turret this time are more determined. Firm. Intentional. I push open the door and flip on the lights, instantly delighted at the room awaiting me. It's out of a movie, really. The stone walls and floors are softened by an enormous area rug, and two inviting chairs face a wooden desk piled high with neat stacks of files spaced with mathematical precision over the surface. A few feet behind the chairs, a comfortable couch waits, ready for cozier conversations.

What I wouldn't give to pop back in time and listen in on some of the talks that have happened here.

It's perfect. I couldn't have designed the room better myself.

With a deep breath, I cross the threshold and head for the ornate but cushioned chair. I can't claim it forever, but I'm going to dive in and enjoy my temporary trade.

There's an envelope on the desk with my name on it, held down by a small box. Inside is a gorgeous cairngorm necklace, a stone I know well, and the piece of home makes me smile.

The note is short and sweet.

Lexi,

I can't thank you enough for coming over and helping me during this crazy time. This cairngorm has been worn by the chatelaine of Castle MacInnes for coming up on two centuries. I'll have to ask for it back when I can return to my duties, but until then, I want you to wear this and know you've got generations of MacInnes women beside you and behind you.

I look forward to meeting you soon!

Love, Kiki

I touch the pendant, then pull back when the stone heats underneath my fingertip. Not burning, instead radiating welcome. Warmth. Invitation.

I'd usually be unable to accept such an unexpected gesture. It's not in my nature. But I can't stop myself from fastening the clasp behind my neck. Of course I'll give it back to Kiki when she returns, but I'm delighted to be temporary keeper of the cairngorm as much as the turret office.

I set the fanciful moment aside and get to work. Besides, nothing keeps grief and sorrow at bay like keeping busy.

CHAPTER TEN

BUNNY

I ALMOST RACE AFTER LEXI, but manage to maintain my dignity, and now, as they say, the moment has come. I can almost hear Emmett scolding me to *quit waffling.*

"So, uh, thanks for coming, Gene. Have a seat. I apologize, but I need to run to the back for half a sec."

My voice isn't the one I normally use, the steady tone I work to maintain with the man I'm enamored with even more than my brewery. How ridiculous can I be? I'm the one who set up this meeting. Yet here I stand, a woman of well over forty, tongue-tied like the star quarter-back has asked me to prom, except Gene hasn't asked me to anything. In fact, I'm supposed to be pulling a Sadie Hawkins and asking him.

"No worries. Take your time."

I walk at a normal pace toward the back, but as soon as I'm sure he can't see me, I put my faux leather wedges into high gear until I'm between the brew kettles, punching the top name on my favorites list to video call my best girlfriend.

Almost immediately, Dani's face pops up on the screen, thank all the celestial beings. I don't pick one in particular, as I'm not sure which divine body she's into right now. Last I knew, it was the Kabbalah and all things related to her Jewish ancestry. I am fairly certain my BFF's quest to find herself by studying the world's religions isn't how the Broder family imagines Danica Broder coming back into the fold.

It's not my business to tell my friend her *Eat, Pray, Love* journey won't get her the inner peace she's seeking. She'll eventually figure out what everyone else has known. She's been enough all along, just how she is. Besides, I, a Grade A lapsed Protestant, have no room to tell anyone how to soul-search.

"Hey, girl." She takes a tenth of a nanosecond to go from smiling to concerned. "What's up? Your energy's spiking off the charts."

I don't credit special powers with her observation. I'm sure my eyes are wild, and I can hear my own accelerated breathing. Winnie-the-Pooh in a honey coma could tell I'm off-center.

"No time for an aura adjustment. Gene's here. For the meeting."

Dani stops French braiding the section of hair she's partitioned with pins, hair that's long and lush and dark. Basically every descriptor my hair is not.

"*The* meeting? Should I cue the *Mission: Impossible* theme music?"

"You're a laugh riot, you know that? What is it with me and smartass friends?" I look around to ensure my whispering hasn't attracted a certain someone's attention. "I only have a second to talk. I don't want to keep him waiting."

In the blink of an eye, she stops teasing and turns into the woman who kept me grounded when I entered the rarefied air of Dallas high society and who kept me sane during my two-year divorce from hell and expulsion from those heights. She had plenty of sage advice, seeing as how she's one of the oldest Broder grandchildren and was born into and gave up a social stratum I only briefly visited.

"What do you need?" She gives an unconscious adjustment to a tangle of necklaces, each with a sun, moon, or star pendant, while reaching for her favorite tarot deck never far from her hands. "Do you want me to do a super-quick yes-no?"

"No, no readings. A panic attack was trying to bowl me over, so I wanted to take one minute to call and get my head on straight. I don't want to be rude, though, so I'm gonna get back out there."

"Then consider yourself straightened. I'll send you some energy streams to keep you even, but promise you'll call me as soon as you can."

"Always. Love you."

"Love you, too." She leans closer to her phone's camera. "You got this. You've waited too long as it is. And the answer's always no until you ask."

"I know, I know." I widen and blink my eyes to get them lubricated. "Talk to you in a few."

I end the call, and by the time I'm within Gene's sight line again, I'm calm. Or, more truthfully, I appear composed, bearing three bottles of my new creations and ready to hopefully impress my fellow member of the Magnolia Bloom Merchants Association.

I keep my face pleasantly neutral and contain the smile that wants to break free from my steely determination to play it cool. Besides Emmett, Dani's the only one I've confessed the full extent of my crush on the teetotaling bartender who revitalized the Magnolia Moon. Unfortunately, Gene's never given me the slightest hint he has similar thoughts about me. Fear has kept me somewhere between casual friend and fellow member of the MBMA.

Twenty-going-on-thirty years ago, I thought I was a manslayer. I thought I could get any guy I wanted with the snap of my perfectly manicured nails and a come-hither smile highlighted by my crimson La Prairie lipstick, or whatever overpriced and overhyped makeup I was wearing back then. I can admit now I was more than a bit of a stereotype. Young, upper-middle-slash-lower-rich-class brat who didn't work a day in her life but somehow felt my daddy's money made me special. Tall and lithe by the good grace of the genes I've been gifted with, smart because I loved to read and excelled in school, but didn't do a damn thing with degrees carrying an eye-popping price tag.

That master's degree in medieval women's studies wasn't coming in handy in the beer business.

Now I'm standing behind a bar in a tiny microbrewery in a little town where few people know my embarrassment-worthy past, scared to death to find out if the owner of my pretend rival dance hall might want to go to dinner with me. I've been afraid to find out for a year now. Truthfully, longer, but I'd rather not dwell on that right now.

I lament how far I've fallen—from my glory days as a maneater to less illustrious chickenshit.

A car wreck and a broken face that would make Frankenstein turn away were the near-fatal catalysts forcing me to take a long, hard look at myself. It makes sense an actual mirror was the first place to start, but it was my marriage to the plastic surgeon who restored my outer beauty that made me realize how self-involved inner-me had become.

And good Lord, why did I show poor Lexi those pictures?

I line up some highball glasses in front of the man who makes the moniker "silver fox" too tame. Six-two. Muscles for days without being muscle-bound. Black hair liberally dosed with ghostly gray in a short, spiky mess that says *touch me!*

Oh, I'd love to.

But Gutless Wonder replaced Bulldozer Barbie a long time ago.

I clear my throat even though Gene has been patiently watching me for the last however many painful seconds I've been dithering. "Thanks for coming over."

"You've said that. Happy to help. Your idea sounds great, and shrubs are the hot new thing."

I pick up the soda gun and shoot some seltzer into a glass. With an attempt at a flourish, I twist the top off the bottle. "Old thing made new again, you mean. There's nothing novel about simple syrups, but regardless, this masterpiece is a hot process. I've got two cold-processed ones, too."

I add a splash of the ginger mix I've chosen to begin with, bruise a twist of orange—enough to release the scent and add the faintest hint of oils to the concoction—and give it a quick whirl with a bar spoon. After floating a napkin in front of him, I place my offering with a soft *thunk*. I'm no cocktail-meister, but it's not a horrible showing, if I do say so myself.

He swirls the glass, breathes in the spicy ginger and unmistakable orange, and takes a sip.

I had no idea how anxious I am until I realize I'm holding my breath. Dang it, this recipe's good. "My part-time help and wannabe mixologist Isaiah said it's his favorite. He's been pushing me to get a liquor license so he can play, but Bethanie's advised me not to dilute the brewery brand, that if I want to add hard spirits, I'd be better served to create a more upscale venue dedicated to them, maybe next door. The space has been available for a year, and I've been mulling putting an option on it for months."

He nods and taps his glass. "This is really good. Refreshing. It would be great as is or as a mixer with a neutral alcohol like vodka or gin like you told Lexi."

Thrilled far out of proportion to his kind critique, I hide my school-girl giddiness behind my second offering—a cold process this time, with watermelon, honey, and lime.

I push a fresh tumbler across the wood with a hand not quite as steady as I'd like and give myself a sharp command to get it together. I make one for myself and take a sip to moisten my suddenly dry mouth. "This one would be great with champagne or sparkling wine."

He sips, pauses, swallows. "I completely agree."

He's equally kind for the entire flight I've prepared and sits back after the last sample.

"So, Bunny, these are all great. What has me confused is why you're wanting me to showcase these at the gala. You can promote the heck out of them at your station."

I scrub at a nonexistent spot on the bar. "I'm not going."

I guess I spoke more softly than I intended, because Gene leans forward, turning his left ear toward me. "Excuse me, what?"

"I'm not going, okay?"

"Oookay. And why?"

"Doesn't really matter. I love Kiki for her determination to priori-tize local merchants, and I'll hang out in the office to handle any issues, or in the kitchen with Eunice. I can be her sous-chef. I have no desire to be in the middle of the hullabaloo."

He doesn't answer for so long, I'm forced to stop polishing the random pilsner I've picked up. If I don't, I might rub the etched logo off the darned thing.

He's doing his sit-quietly-until-they-break thing. I've seen him put his Jedi mind trick into action before, but it's always been on one of the other members of the association, or a fellow chamber of commerce attendee. There's a problem with being infatuated with a bartender who's also a twelve-step sponsor, as he has a double dose of the talk-to-me gene.

Ha-ha. My turn for unintentional puns.

Problem is, he also has the professionalism wall built high and tight. He's happy to talk about you. Not so much about himself.

I've tried. I've hinted. I've flat-out asked. The most I've gleaned is he was in the military for twenty years, spent a lot of time angry and in a bottle, chased his wife away, and has a child of unknown age—well, unknown to me—who hasn't spoken to him in a decade.

Instead of turning the enigmatic vibe back on him and trying to be mysterious, I stand there like the dorkiest kid at the high school dance whose main job is to hold up the back wall.

Gene raps "Shave and a Haircut" on the rail and then tosses his thumb toward the best table in the place, the one in front of the huge window that lets us spy on the folks strolling the square. "Come on. Let's people-watch for a minute. I'll take one of those homemade root beers Isaiah came up with."

He starts moving as if my acceptance is a foregone conclusion. I feel a ripple of irritation because, well, my compliance isn't in question, but I'm a teensy bit frustrated that he knows it.

I draw us both a fresh glass and follow behind, telling myself it's not such a bad thing to get to watch his long legs and tight butt as we traverse the quietude of my pride and joy.

"I had no idea how easy it is to make root beer. Isaiah's the best employee I've ever had, and I fully intend to bottle it, along with the shrubs."

"Coke and Dr Pepper better watch out."

I snort, a sound hardly the ladylike quality I'd like to present, but

Gene's that kind of guy. The one who sets you at ease even as your stomach is simultaneously seizing when he nails you with those green eyes with the gold flecks, his mouth in an inviting half smile, and he's leaning toward you with his forearms on the table, his body all tall and lean and comfortable, and—

Jeez Louise, Bunny. Get it together already.

"I hope you're right, but I'm not trying to get send-myself-into-space rich. My goal is no debt and the ability to help my employees."

"Which is all fascinating but avoids the question of why you're going into witness protection over a fundraiser."

"That may be a little more dramatic than I intend, but really, Kiki doesn't need two people handling the alcohol portion of the evening. Let's face it. You've got a lot more experience with big crowds than I do."

He gives me the signature left-side tilt to his beautiful lips. "The Due West Saloon's doing pretty well."

"True, but I hardly pull Magnolia Moon crowds." I take a fortifying sip of root beer and meet his patient gaze. "But to get us back on course, I'll answer your question if you agree to answer one of mine."

"That's not how this works."

I raise both eyebrows. "Says who?"

"Says me, since you're the one who thinks she has a problem and is asking for my help."

"I'll withdraw the request, then. If you're going to dig into my psyche, I get to dig into yours. We're..."

Drat the man. He lets the silence extend until it's slightly painful. "Friends?"

"Yeah, friends.

"All right, I'll concede. I'm okay with twenty questions."

My mouth opens before I can get it in line. "Not truth or dare?"

I feel the heat scorching up my neck but try to maintain my who-am-I-kidding façade of coolness. I mean, what if he dared me to kiss him? That's incredibly far-fetched and would be out of character for Gene, but I can't take the chance while I deride myself to acknowledge it's more of a wish than a fear and straight out of a badly written rom-com.

"That sounds intriguing." His smile is delightful and sexy and teasing. And friendly.

I shake my head, stopping this before it can go any further. "I can't believe I said that. I'm not so good on the daring part." Unfortunately for my attempt at casual nonchalance, my voice wobbles as I confess the truth.

Gene's innate kindness makes the teasing fade from his voice. "We'll back the bus up and start over. Let's start with you and me getting to know more about each other beyond our bios on the city website."

Which is exactly what I wanted to do for the past year, since he bought the Magnolia Moon and turned the already-important set piece in this town into an even better dance hall and music venue. I loved Tidy, the former owner, for the four years I knew her, but she was more than ready to retire to her little ranch outside of town and tend to her cows, horses, and sheep.

I lift my glass and tilt the rim toward him in an obvious invitation to toast. "Since I called this meeting, I'll start. Tune out the parts you've already heard."

"Deal."

"So, I came to Magnolia Bloom five years ago during an excruciating divorce. The short version of the embarrassingly long story is my ex bought this brewery as a joke. Sort of like his version of *Schitt's Creek*, except he hasn't lost a dime. He has some extended family in Atlanta, and we used to come to Magnolia Bloom, in the good days, for weekends away. We were even married in the castle."

Gene's brow furrows. "Really? No rainbows and butterflies for you?"

My smile is wry, but I've had a long time to come to terms with all the signs I missed, giant flags waving right in front of my face. "We didn't marry in the chapel. You must know the MacInnes magic only applies there. We had a huge affair under white silk banners on the east lawn, Lake Maggie suitably calm and beautiful in the background."

"I vaguely remember the mystical marital guarantee only applying to the chapel. I've been there for a christening or two, but no weddings yet, so I haven't put much thought into the woo-woo workings of the estate."

"Typical dude. Anyway, suffice to say, I haven't damaged the MacInnes reputation for successful marriages. In hindsight, my ex's derision should've been a huge clue we were never going to work. I loved everything about chapel. It's small, sure. I mean, 'chapel' is kind of a clue, but when I'd be at the castle for prewedding meetings and such, I'd go in there and sit, relax. I don't think I've ever felt more peaceful."

"That's quite a testimonial. Be sure to tell Bethanie so she can use it in her marketing."

"I'll do that. Anything to support yet another of Magnolia Bloom's success stories."

"Between her, Traycee, and Kiki, we've got a good-sized recovery group going here. It's great to see, but tell me more about how a wrecked marriage brought you to town."

"To cut straight to the chase, the only thing I asked for in the divorce is the saloon, my clothes, and my jewelry. You'd be stunned at how much money you can make selling designer stuff online these days, so that gave me enough cash to get the tavern up and running."

Gene looks around the public room with an approving eye. "You've done a beautiful job."

"I'm proud of it. It's been a lot of hard work, but I wouldn't change a thing. Which leads me to ask what brought you here."

"Short answer is Kiki. I was lucky enough to be part of her journey to her happy ending, or happy beginning, as castle chatelaine, wife to the town's favorite pastor, and soon-to-be mom. I had a small bar about halfway to Atlanta, which is where we met, and she called me when Tidy decided it was time to retire. I was ready for a change, and I guess it was meant to be."

"Tidy's a firecracker, for sure. I'm glad her moving on to her next chapter brought you to town. She couldn't have handed off the Moon to a nicer person."

Subtle, Bunny. Very subtle.

"I appreciate the vote of confidence."

I try to steer my thoughts and the conversation back into the safe lane. "You've also brought some real wisdom and sanity to the merchant meetings. The old guard has needed a shakeup for a long time."

He gives me a mock frown. "You're a relative newcomer, too. Why didn't you take up the mantle?"

"Not my style. I'm happy to be a cheerleader or team member, but not the leader."

"Is this connected to why you won't go to the gala?"

Instead of a frown, I give him the slow blink. "That was sneaky."

"Sounded pretty on the nose to me."

"The truth is, I've seen the guest list, and I don't want to see a bunch of people from a painful time in my life. This fundraiser's for an important cause, and while I'd hardly be the in the spotlight, I don't want to field snarky comments and barbed asides. It may have been five years, but the gossip hounds would probably love some fresh meat to toss around."

"So you're hiding."

"Damn right, I am."

Gene doesn't need to know my own family chose my ex in the divorce, climbing onto the bandwagon he created by painting me as a bitter gold digger. You'd think my own kin wouldn't believe something so crazy, but apparently hitching their comfortably wealthy wagon to my ex's super-rich train was more important than defending me. And truthfully? I was a bit of an arrogant airhead back in the day, but that was a long time ago. I changed long before the divorce, but damnation comes quickly and forgiveness rarely in that world.

I get nauseated thinking about the person I used to be.

Which all rounds back nicely to the discussion at hand.

"I have no desire to be around the glitz and the glamour. I want this endeavor to raise an armored carload of money for the new hospital, but I intend to assist from way back in the shadows."

"Sounds like someone hasn't faced her past."

Even though that was offered in the nicest of voices, anger surges and takes over what was my nerves. "Don't twelve-step me."

I don't want to be his project or his sponsee, which I can't be because I'm not an alcoholic or an addict, and I don't need his brand of amazing help. I want to be his love interest, his obsession of the good kind, the woman he thinks about when he's alone. I want him to count the minutes before he's with me and smile when I'm the only thing on his mind when some song comes on the jukebox.

"Okay, I won't. But I'll make a deal with you. I'll do all the stations for the Moon and Due West and get my manager to oversee the rest. That way, you can come to the gala with me." He lets the dramatic pause hang. "As my date."

CHAPTER ELEVEN

LEXI

By the time four o'clock's about to chime, I've got a solid handle on Kiki's filing system, have briefed myself on most of the gala plans on a cursory level, and think I'm reasonably prepared for a meeting with the man from the company that'll provide temporary flooring and the large tent. My job today is simple enough. Walk him around the east lawn and get basic measurements so he can do an estimate. After that, it's a meeting with the table-and-chairs guy, including the minutiae needed for five hundred people—tablecloths, plates, stemware, silverware, napkins, serving stations. And then I'll meet with the music guy, after which I get to call it a day.

My mind's boggled as I try to calculate an eighty-by-one-hundred-fifty-foot tent, then add in the space needed for dancing. It's not the size so much. I can estimate piping, fittings, valves, joints, toilets, sinks, drains, and all the rest for a ten-story office building in my sleep, so *big* isn't the issue. It's the metric-to-imperial conversion that has me groaning.

My cell phone chirps at me, jerking me from the spreadsheet where I'm adding a column for my metric measurements. After the way my conversation ended with Sadie, I half expect to see her picture on my display, then feel sad I'd even hoped she'd check back in and apologize for being insensitive. Still, I'm surprised to see my sister calling.

I swipe the screen, and Zelda's beautiful face goes from frozen to live, and I feel the momentary envy that hits me every single time I see her. "This is a surprise. How're you?"

"I'm brilliant, thanks. I'm coming to Glasgow to sign a contract with a new client and thought we'd do lunch."

The twinge of envy turns to irritation. "Whilst that sounds wonderful, it would be difficult. I'm in Texas, so it would be a long trip."

"Texas? What in the world are you doing there?"

I stuff the urge to go into full snark mode and manage to keep my voice civil. "I sent you my itinerary in case Mum and Dad need you while I'm gone."

"Sorry. I must've skimmed over it. So you're checking out the American cousins?"

"That, but it's really an excuse to get away. The people here have been lovely. I'm sure you've seen pictures of the castle Maggie's collected. You do recall our great-grandmother, aye? I'm a little concerned with your memory."

"Very funny."

"Just checking. She sent out links to the diaries and other data she has on this branch."

"I recall that. Anyway, I need to dash. Ring me up when you get home, and we'll reschedule."

Before I can agree or argue, Zelda ends the call, and I'm left staring at my phone and wrestling with my emotions.

"Did your phone do something wrong?"

The voice coming from the hall takes me aback for two reasons. One, I didn't think my meeting was for another ten minutes, and two, I can't think of a reason why Logan Jameson is taking up almost every square centimeter of my doorway.

It's not merely our disastrous first encounter. I've rerun the scene through my mind almost enough times to find it funny. Not quite, but I'm getting there. Mostly, I came to the conclusion that even if he is every bit as wonderful as Bunny and Bethanie claim, I can't get past the fact he's one of those rare people who is that striking, that commanding, that perfect.

Yeah, yeah, there are no perfect people. Perhaps it makes me the shallow one that I can't get past his looks. I've never been around anyone superstar pretty.

Realizing Logan is waiting for my response, I answer truthfully. "As a matter of fact, aye.

My phone seems to be allowing only annoying callers. I'm convinced throwing the blasted thing against the wall is a sound solution."

"You believe violence is the answer?"

His grin's gone cheeky, so it's clear he's bammin' me. "Absolutely. One good knock against schist stone will set near anything to rights."

"All right, then, hand it over. I've got a pretty good fast pitch."

I raise both eyebrows at him. "You think the little lass needs the big strong man to help her? I'll have you know I was queen of center field my entire time in high school. We always made the playoffs, thanks ever so much."

While that's true, and I was good enough to be a starter, my skills weren't enough to get a scholarship to uni. My unhealed memories of there being no money for me to go flare anew. Zelda burned through most of our parents' savings with rescues from her endless escapades and her extended years in Edenborough before she got a degree she's never used. My sister has grown out of her seeming unending adolescence, but that didn't change the choices I had to make.

"I'm impressed. Now I need to get you back into the gym, and we'll see who can throw the biggest medicine ball."

Instead of taking the gauntlet he's thrown, I set my phone aside and fold my hands on top of Kiki's leather desk blotter. "My sporting skills aside, is there something I can do for you?"

"Sorry if I'm too early, but I'm your four o'clock."

A glance at my spreadsheet has me double-checking the initials in the vendor column. "You're JLJ?"

"In the flesh. Joseph Logan Jameson, but I never wanted to be a Joe, so I've always gone by Logan."

"Ah, well, mystery solved. Will you be needing anything before we go walkabout?" I'd like to rail at the heavens, demand an explanation for what I've done to deserve this torture, but instead I simply beg I don't make a complete numpty out of myself.

"I've been here many times and have done a few weddings about the size of this shindig, but it never hurts to get reacquainted with the venue area. Besides, a stroll around the grounds is always a treat."

A stroll. It sounds so...datelike. I didn't give my clothing choice much thought when I got back from Bunny's, but now I'm glad I have on crisp white culottes and a navy top in a jaunty nautical theme. After my fashion wakeup call at the airport, these are the most stylish things I have with me, and I'm glad I didn't save them for another day.

I immediately castigate myself for stressing over this whole situation.

Why am I worried? Joseph Logan Jameson is simply a contractor, one of many I'm going to have to check with. I'm being a certified eejit, and I have to stop this instant.

"Right, then. Let's go."

If there's anything I'm good at, it's herding suppliers and tradesmen. Why am I not relying on my years of experience with a very similar process? I've got this handled. This quick meeting will be seamless, and then—

"You look lovely, by the way."

Then? *Then* he goes and says something like that.

"Thank you. You're too kind." That I manage to *not* say, *You look great, too,* has me nearly faint with relief. After the "nice muscles" debacle, I don't think I could survive a second malfunction of the filter between my brain and mouth.

I lead the way down the stairs from my turret to the east grounds. It's amazing I already consider it mine after a grand sum of six hours working in the magical space.

The afternoon heat is broiling, but we stick to the shadows of the massive pecans and oaks and, of course, the magnolias. With the shade and breeze, it's tolerable, but I'm glad for the distraction of confirming seating plans, tenting, and flooring. Most of this was already decided, and Logan promises to send me all the confirmations from his suppliers by day's end. He speaks with easy assurance and gives off waves of the "nice guy" vibes Bunny and Bethanie both allege so passionately.

I check my list again. "So, you're gym man, flooring man, tent man, table-and-chairs man, and stage man. How many times am I going to see JLJ in column Q?"

"I'm sound man, too. I'll be setting up the mixer and speakers. I play bass, keyboard, and acoustic guitar when the local troupe needs me to sub in, but I'm not part of the band this time. I've even sat in with Ally a time or two when she's here on local gigs. Mostly, I like to keep busy."

I stop under a trio of magnolias guarding the entry to a dense copse I've been told to visit. This grove is special to the MacInneses, and I wish I had the signature scent on top of the comforting shade. Unfortunately, I'll have to come back in late spring to see the breathtaking white blossoms. Or maybe it's fortunate, as I'll have no choice but to return to see the magnificent blooms in person.

"You're quite the renaissance man, it appears. Kiki says we sold, as she put it, a metric crapton of tickets once we announced Ally's doing a set, so your services will be in high demand. And speaking of high demand, you better plan extra room near Buddy's bar to accommodate the line for Bunny's shrubs, although I'll follow her protocol and call him Gene."

Logan's smile is something I could see a hundred times a day, and it would never get old. His face is expressive, his eyes dark and liquid, but his mouth is insanely magnetic. At the moment, one side is tipped up in a half grin, and he lifts a brow, too.

It's my turn to do the tilty-lip-lifted-brow move. "I kinda think 'Bunny and Buddy' is funny, but she's sensitive about it." I fan myself with my papers and add a shrug. "I can't be the only person who sees she's crazy about him, and I saw it after being in the room for five whole seconds."

He takes a few steps left and leans a shoulder against the trunk of an oak that's seen more Texas summers than our combined years. "Everyone but Buddy—I mean, Gene—knows it."

I sigh on my new friend's behalf. "I won't talk about her behind her back. Suffice it to say, I'm the last person who can cast stones at anyone else's relationships."

We listen to the soothing sound of the water of Lake Maggie lapping at the shore. I make a mental note to come back out after my day is done, fully doused in DEET, as not only is my Scottish skin prone to sunburn, midges think I have the sweetest blood in the Northern Hemisphere.

"It's kind of a universal truth that you don't get to decide how someone else feels, even if we wish we could."

I cut him a glance, wondering if this not-so-subtle jab is for my utter gaff at the Iron Core, but his expression's serene and innocent of guile. It feels like honesty. Bald, bold truth in words I'm not ready to hear.

As a parent, I know how true his statement is. I've seen friends disastrously try to affect who their children date or marry, and I swore when my weans were still in nappies that I'd never be that kind of mum. I guess I didn't extrapolate my wisdom to handsome gym owners halfway across the world.

That doesn't mean I believe his easy compliments. Those I can naturally chalk up to the Southern manners I was introduced to on an overseas flight and see on display everywhere I go. On one hand, it's comforting that that's the way things are done around here, but on the other, I have to confess it would have been nice to believe DeWayne, and now Logan, really did find me attractive.

I've been brutally honest with myself for too long, though, to believe such nonsense.

We finish the last few meters to the castle on a lighter note, mostly about the star-studded lineup for entertainment. Those are items on Bethanie's list, but I'm aware there's an A-list comedian and Ally all set to be the main acts. A big-time actor is doing the auction, and then a band will play for the crowd to dance the night away. It's genius, in my humble opinion, for a fundraiser for a regional hospital, but if I've learned anything about the MacInnes women, they don't do anything by halves, and Kiki's carrying on the legacy with flying colors.

We're about to part ways, and Logan pulls out a business card. "Call me so we can set up that private training we talked about."

"Private training?" The unexpected turn to the conversation leaves me stunned. Witty repartee does not come as quickly to me as, say, where the new order of silicone tape has been placed or when the toilets will be in for the new house we're finishing.

"Don't you remember? You said you were dying to join my beginner's weight-training class, and I said I'd see if I could squeeze you in, and then you said, 'Oh, please, Logan, that'd be ruddy brilliant.'"

I bite my lip, trying to give at least the appearance of being stern, especially with his utterly horrid imitation of a woman's voice. "I said that, did I? The woman who's Scottish, not English, and doesn't say ruddy?"

"I remember it clearly. Scout's honor." He holds up three fingers, but it's his smile that makes my heart hit a speedbump. "I hope you'll let me start over and make a new first impression."

Since it's I who needs the redo, I find myself reluctant to say no. Logan's earnest warmth, genuine kindness, and devastatingly handsome mien are quite a combination to resist.

But I must.

It seems the libido I thought died with Douglas has decided to reincarnate itself with a man I've been acquainted with for less than a day, and to say I have no idea what to do with this new information understates the case.

"Your girl here has six weeks to pull off a ball without destroying the entire MacInnes reputation, so we'll both be too busy to do more than wave at each other in passing now and then. But you're kind to ask."

"I like to think I am, but kind has nothing to do with it. The last thing I need, as a major contractor for the event of the year, is for the coordinator to be so stressed she ends up ruining my reputation, too.

It's all about me, you see, and making sure you stay relaxed and on top of your game."

He's impossible, this man who is far too handsome to be this nice, despite what Bunny and Bethanie say. Then Bunny's name popping into my head brings another thought I've been avoiding. I go back to the moment when Gene walked into Bunny's tavern, and I witnessed the light, the joy, the desire that consumed her like a flash fire. I can't recall experiencing any of that in my near thirty years married, and it's painful to do it standing in front of a man who has my pulse rising and my guilt bubbling.

"I'll give it a think and let you know." The *think* will be how much I'd like to have his hands on my muscles and just about anywhere else, but the *let you know* will be a definite *not a chance*.

Logan raises his hands in surrender, and we part ways, leaving me to do what I always do. I head to my new office and dive into work so I don't have time to give in to an imagination gone wild.

CHAPTER TWELVE

BETHANIE

I'VE NEVER DENIED I'm not much of a cook. I *can* cook, but I don't like to.

Which is why, instead of bringing some fancy breakfast casserole to the meeting, I'm at the Magnolia Market at seven thirty in the morning. Normally, I pop in early to say hi to Dad and Mina before they start their day, but my goal right now is entirely self-centered. I'm here so I can nab a batch of doughnuts before Ivy Sinclair can put them out. Since I'm the daughter of the owner and a former staffer, I feel only marginally guilty when I sail into the employees-only section where Ivy is working her flour-and-sugar magic.

"Hey, Ivy. Good morning."

"Bethanie! You nearly gave me a heart attack."

I didn't mean to startle her, but in her defense, it's pretty early, and my dad doesn't come in to steal his morning treat until about nine.

"Sorry. Didn't mean to, but more importantly, you can't have a heart attack. At least, not until after you give me a dozen of your crullers for a meeting I have to go to in about an hour."

"But you're having coffee with your daddy, right?"

My grin's overly big and goofy, but I don't care. "Absolutely. Mina's joining us because she missed out on the weekly confab last time. She's back from Copenhagen and visiting Fina and Anders."

A timer sounds, and Ivy heads for the large commercial ovens.

"Both of them are still so happy they have to have anchors tied to their ankles so they don't float away."

"It's great, isn't it?"

Ivy goes to a cooling rack and fills a precious box full of twisted dough and sugar. "It sure is. Here you go. Now get outta here so I can do my work and not get fired."

She puts the box on the counter between us and restarts her kitchen hustle. My dad would board the doors and windows if Ivy tried to quit, so her getting terminated is about as likely as my dad rooting for Oklahoma in the Red River Rivalry.

Icebergs. Hell. That sort of thing.

"You can let go of your job security worries, but I'll get out of the way." And try not to eat half the box.

She heads for the pantry, waving a goodbye hand over her head. I take my prize, vowing to resist the warm sugar smell, which has led more than one person down the temptation highway, and pass the coffee bar and café seating I convinced Dad to put in not long after I got my head on straight. I've always liked marketing, and I'm proud of the creativity my brain has come up with now that it's not pickled.

I get giddy out of proportion to reality when I see smiling customers leaving the store, holding their lattes and cappuccinos, obviously pleased with their drinks. I had to do the hard sell on Dad, convincing him I could help promote his business like an actual adult. He was reluctant, but so eager to support me as I began my new life sans the bottle that he signed check after check for the rest of my ideas once he saw the bistro's success.

I find them waiting for me, Mina with her iced mocha and Dad with his straight black, and a vanilla latte will be on the table before my butt hits the chair.

Mina's smile is box-of-lightbulbs bright. "Hello, beautiful. How's your morning?"

I lean over and kiss her cheek, then lean toward Dad so he can kiss mine. "I'm fabulous. Picking up doughnuts for the committee meeting for the gala over at Bunny's in a little while."

Dad nods approvingly, as much because he's proud of me as he's excited about the town's growth. "How's everything going? Lexi settling in?"

It's no surprise Dad's been read in on everything going on with the castle, what with his mother-in-law being a Grannie and the chief source of information as well as food.

"She's getting there. She was petrified when she got here, as she had a misunderstanding about what Kiki wanted, but she's a trouper and dug right in. Enough about that. How was Copenhagen?"

Mina clutches her hands to her chest. "It was amazing. And Fina and Anders are building this house that looks like it's about eight million square feet."

CT gives her an indulgent smile. "That might be a tiny exaggeration, but it's going to be a palace. They're almost as happy as we are, I'm proud to say."

"That's wonder—"

"Miss Bethanie!" A high-pitched voice belonging to Roy's daughter, Chloe, precedes her into the café.

I shift around, smiling at the little pixie who was a bright spot in my dark past. She always picked my line if I was working the register during her daily visit to the market. Roy always hovered by the front door as she made her selection and came to me to pay. I'm not sure why, but it became a game for me to teach her how to count change, and she took great delight when the day came she could tell me how much she'd get back from her carefully hoarded allowance.

"Well, hello, Chloe. You're here a bit early for candy."

"We have a late-start day at school, so Daddy said I could get candy, but I can't eat it until after school because he has to pick me up for a doctor's appointment, and we can't stop by then, so I promised I'd wait." She sucks in several dramatic breaths, grinning. "I pinkie swore and everything."

"Good for you."

"I like your line the best. Are you going to be the cashier again?"

For the millionth time, I want to pick her up and squish her in a hug. I've never done so, of course, but she's such a cute little ray of sunshine, the opposite of her grump-a-lump father I see scowling out of the corner of my eye.

"Not anymore, but I do miss it. Especially you."

She drops her backpack and begins to rummage inside it. "I have to show you. Wait one minute."

The adults exchange delighted smiles.

"Here it is!" She hands me a rumpled test sheet to smooth out. It's a math quiz, and at the top is a B+ with a big smiley face beside it.

"It's the best math grade I've ever gotten, and I told Mrs. Matthews that I was glad it was a B because B is for Bethanie, and you're my tutor, and you're the best."

"That's amazing." I set the paper on the table and bend down so we're eye to eye. "You are so, so smart, and I'm super proud of you."

"I told Mrs. Matthews to make you a teacher at my school because you help everybody."

I swear I'm going to melt right here and I work overtime to blink back hot tears. Chloe's making great strides, but her developmental delays are a direct result of time spent with her usually blacked-out mother. Roy didn't even know of Chloe's existence until two years ago, and he fought furiously to get full custody. Mina said she heard the counselor believes Chloe will be at grade level by next year, but it's Roy's unflagging dedication making that happen.

And we can all assume his ex cemented Roy's views about people who're consumed by alcohol far more than his experiences as a law officer. No telling how many drunk Magnolia Bloomians he's cuffed and put in the back of his squad car. Oh, wait. I know of only one.

Me.

Chloe knows none of that, thank the stars. She's barely in second grade, so her memories of her time spending ten and twelve hours a day in front of a television with a box of dry cereal are fading.

If chugging Lucky Charms would work that well for me, I'd buy stock in General Mills. Unfortunately, that's not how it goes. My recall's painfully vivid, and I have zero doubt Roy's memory is long and crystal clear. I force myself not to look in his direction, for while I believe he doesn't mind Chloe talking to me, Mr. Impatient's ready to be on about their day.

"Thank you for showing me your test, Chloe." I can't resist tucking a wayward curl under her pink headband, which matches her pink backpack, which coordinates with her pink sandals. "Have a wonderful day in school."

"Thank you very much. I gotta go, though. Daddy's giving me the hairy eyeball."

Dad, Mina, and I all sputter in laughter. "Where did you hear that expression?"

"Uncle Nathanial said it, and Daddy told him to shut up, and I told Daddy that we're not supposed to say that, and Uncle Nathanial laughed. He does that a lot."

Yes, her uncle Nathanial is quite the jokester, and I have no doubt he pokes at Roy through Chloe every chance he gets.

"Well, bye, Mr. CT. Bye, Mrs. Mina. Bye, Bethanie."

Without waiting for our responses, she's off, backpack swinging, skipping to Roy and launching herself at her tall, stoic father without a moment's hesitation.

He catches her and gives a brief nod in our general direction, but is out the side gate and headed toward his patrol car, his jaw grinding visible even across the small patio.

Mina shakes her head. "That boy is gonna have a stroke if he doesn't learn to relax."

Dad gives me a look. "Fathers are often discounted when it comes to worrying about their children. Roy's going to be on guard for a long time."

The tears are still in my throat, but I manage a shrug and swipe at the tear that's escaped. "I'm glad Chloe has an amazing father. Like I did."

Mina sniffles, and Dad pulls me sideways into a hug that nearly topples me. We all grab napkins and get ourselves together, then I sit to enjoy our coffee before going our separate ways.

Dad and Mina hold hands as they walk toward the new Escalade Dad got her as a just-because surprise, and joy briefly breaks through the clouds camped out over my heart. An unexpected happily-ever-after isn't in my future, but I can appreciate my father's happiness from afar. He's a good man. The best man.

And he deserves nothing but good days after what I put him through.

I clean up the table and pick up my treat box, taking a deep breath and reminding myself I have too much to worry about to bother with my misty-eyed daydreams.

So why does my gaze pull left and down the road where Roy's tail-lights disappeared?

CHAPTER THIRTEEN

LEXI

I ARRIVE at Due West a good twenty minutes ahead of schedule, but I abhor being late. We're having a committee meeting, and Bunny volunteered the saloon for this morning's get-together.

She opens the door for me, and I can hear both of her commercial coffeemakers gurgling away as I hand my new compatriot two boxes of confections from The Sweetery. Bunny said it's already thriving, and the newest member of the Magnolia Bloom Merchants Association is as colorful as her creations. She was certainly polite as I paid for the order, but Bunny says while she thinks Felicity's going to fit in fine, she keeps a wall up all the time. She's not rude. It's more a signal that she's a card-carrying member of the wounded-hearts club.

I've discovered something in my first week here. Bunny West is a gem, sweet as her iced tea, and whip-smart. We've become something of a dynamic duo, building to a terrific trio when Bethanie joins us. We're a bit of a barmy mix, but I haven't laughed this much or felt as included in more years than I'd like to admit.

Bunny lifts a mug in my direction. "Two sugars, one cream?"

"And this is why you're a business maven. I bet you remember everyone's favorite pint and will soon memorize which person likes which of your new shrubs that are going to take the world by storm."

Her chuckle is as delighted as the gratitude in her eyes. "Isaiah is ten times better than I am, but I keep a few special people at the top of my remember-this list. At least you don't drink it black. I don't understand how anyone can do that."

"Takes all kinds, as my gram would say."

"Indeed. Pastry?"

"No, but thank you. I'd say Eunice is trying to put another stone on me I don't need, but I guess that's not fair. She's on this health kick, and she might convert me to the joys of riced cauliflower and fresh spinach eventually, but she still wants to feed me. All. The. Time."

"She's a tornado, that one."

Before we can form a Eunice Greene admiration society, the door opens again, and Kiki comes in, shadowed by her tall, handsome, and hovering husband.

"Kiki. Harville. Good morning."

He nods and gives us both a warm smile.

Kiki moves to the bar with far too much grace for someone clearly in her third trimester of pregnancy. She looks more like a soldier on a mission, her face set, her steps determined. "Mornin' to you both. Any chance one of those pots is decaf?"

Bunny nods. "Absolutely."

Kiki casts an eye at her husband, who hasn't yet said a word. "My jailer allows me a single, minuscule cup, and I've been saving my precious allotment all morning."

She grumbles, but it's clear she's still smitten with her sexy pastor, a man who she told me was the last person on the face of the earth she believed she'd end up with. An agnostic preacher's wife? Who'd've imagined? But lightning struck, and they work things out. As a MacInnes and the castle chatelaine, Kiki is universally loved, but these two together could put us all in need of an insulin shot.

Bunny hands over the eight-ounce portion of our mutually favorite elixir, pretending to shudder that it's unadorned. Kiki laughs before she takes a grateful sip. She told me all her years in the military taught her not to waste time on sweetener or cream.

I'm sure Bunny doesn't mean for anyone to see, but I catch her giving our fearless leader's burgeoning belly a glance, and a second of longing flashes behind her eyes. She told me motherhood is a ship that sailed for her a long time ago, and my heart goes out to her. As I'm well aware, life isn't fair. Bunny should have five or six kids to chase around, and I should have half a century more with Douglas, but it appears the universe hasn't asked us our opinion.

I give a mental Scottish kiss to fate and cover the moment by turning to Kiki. "I'm glad you could make it. We were prepared to set up a laptop to do a remote feed, if need be."

Her frown is not only fierce but formidable. "I'm not an invalid, but I have to be careful. Which is why I'm so dang grateful to you. I'm pretty sure Ally's staying in Australia because I try to corner her and hug the stuffing out of her every time I see her talking you into coming over and making this all happen."

I laugh at the image. Ally has come a long way since I first met her, but she's still not overly touchy-feely. "I'm happy to do anything that takes something off your plate."

Everyone heads for the table, and Harville, who's taken the seat to his wife's right while I've taken the left, looks over her head in my direction. It amuses me but earns him a frown from her.

"I can't tell you how much I appreciate you diving right in." His voice is deep, resonant, comforting. I'm not a regular churchgoer, but I'm looking forward to attending his services soon.

"It's a joy, but you can show your appreciation by naming the baby Lexi."

They laugh at my lame joke, but Kiki gives Harville a playful punch on the arm. "I'll name her anything you want if you take this bear off my hands. Could you throw him in one of the turrets until she comes?"

She softens her pretend threat with a kiss, and I have to look away as a spear of jealousy cuts through me. They have such an easy and precious affection with each other, and I decide envy is a better word for what I'm feeling. Jealousy is ugly and mean, and those words are nowhere in the wistful ache squeezing my heart.

Any comeback from Harville on being banished to the tower is stalled by the bell ringing, and the largest table available in the saloon fills with the Magnolia Bloom Regional Hospital committee heads. My gratitude for my superpower surges as I make a mental tally of the new attendees.

Bethanie leads the way, followed by Emmett and Wyatt, then Cammie and Trey, and Bailey and Jake, then Doc, and finally, Logan.

I do another tabulation of putting faces to all the names to keep from thinking about my thundering pulse. I've seen Logan a few times over the week and have even gone back to the gym with the Grannies for another workout session, but I managed to concentrate on kettle bells instead of quads that deserve their own postal code.

At least he's had mercy on me by wearing jeans and a polo, although the sunshine-yellow color is marvelous on him.

Like I don't have enough trouble concentrating.

According to the files I've memorized like my life depends on it, Emmett and Wyatt are handling the contributions to the auction from major art donors. Cammie and Trey, the soon-to-be newlyweds, are the attorneys of record for this endeavor. Bailey has taken over most of Doc Carter's practice, except he's congenitally unable to stop working completely and is apparently invaluable in defining the needs of our future patient base. Jake Broder is the general contractor and a gallant gentleman, pulling out Bailey's chair and kissing the top of her head before he takes a seat beside her.

Memories of the many hours I spent with Douglas and his brothers flood me. Though filled with laughter, they used incessant references to ball sacks and bodily functions to hide their genuine affection for one another. There's never been soft looks or gentle gestures. Still, for all they might be right glaikit sometimes, I loved them, one and all. If I'm being honest, though, these intimate connections make me painfully aware of how I've never had such easy camaraderie in my life, though I never knew what I was missing.

And now that I do, I'm not sure what to do with it.

I'm glad no thought bubbles are appearing over my head, revealing my inner wrangling. It's not like I had a barren desert of a marriage. Far from it. Douglas and I were good friends, good parents, good partners, and good lovers, but these moments of downright mushiness make me feel even more the foreigner.

Blessedly, the door opens one last time, and in walks Gene and Roy. Bunny's in poorly concealed love with the former, and Bethanie's got a hidden hot zone for the latter.

Kiki taps her coffee cup with a spoon. "All right, gang, here's the newest monkey wrench in the works. Y'all know Poppy and Digby Kingsley are our biggest donors."

I look at my laptop and click the donor tab. Wowzers. I'd say Kiki has a gift for understatement.

There's a collective groan, and I feel my forehead wrinkle in confusion. Kiki helps me out. "You'll no doubt get to meet Poppy soon, as she likes to think she's on this committee, and when you do, she'll be wearing at least a collective hundred carats between wedding rings, tennis bracelets, a single pear-shaped pendant that has its own dedicated insurance agency, and earrings that need scaffolding. After she's made sure you've cataloged her personal depletion of the De Beers inventory, she'll say—"

Four people from the table jump in. "I don't like to call attention to myself, but…"

The drawl on the *but* takes at least three full seconds.

I snort a laugh and cover my mouth. "I'm getting a vague sense Poppy's a tad disingenuous."

Bethanie's sigh is a dissertation all by itself. "That would be an understatement, but the fact remains that Poppy and Dear Old Digby are giving a whole lotta shekels to this venture."

Bailey's grip tightens on her pen. "To ensure that the heart center is called the Digby Kingsley Wing, but if that woman tries to put her nose into the design, I'll—"

Cammie pats her sister's hand. "I'll get a restraining order for you, Sis, if I have to. I got you."

Kiki lifts her hand from the table. "I'm as guilty as anyone for wanting to take a swipe or two at Poppy, and no doubt she earns it, but we all know this is how the game's played. And to get us back on track before we go completely out to left field, what does Poppy want, Bethanie?"

"Remember how Logan's studio over in Dallas had that *Dancing with the Stars* charity showcase a few months ago?"

I cast a cocked brow at Logan. "What a surprise. Another business Logan owns."

A united chorus comes from around the table. "Half owns."

Logan flushes charmingly. "Cut it out, all of you."

"This makes at least ten, but who's counting?" I can't help teasing. It's so much fun to watch the giant man squirm.

Kiki gives the table a soft rap. "Anyway, Poppy, being the chair for that event, had her dance highlighted."

"Of course." Bailey's disdain is spoken softly, but it's crystal clear.

Despite his embarrassment, Logan chimes in. "She had the winners from Blackpool a few years ago come over to teach her and Digby. Svetlana and Viktor are still here for another few weeks. They've been making a killing doing private lessons."

"Blackpool?" I admit my shock reveals a tiny preconception about my newly found American connection.

"Blackpool is—"

"Och, aye, I know. I'm the one from the UK at this gathering, aye?" I gain a collective laugh for my cheek, but feel I need to explain before I sound like a snob. "A few years ago, Douglas gave me dance lessons as an anniversary present, and we went to Blackpool. Had a marvelous time at the beach and then watched the competition at the Empress Ballroom, so if you have the winners here, I'm impressed." I realize I'm babbling and snap my mouth shut.

"What's your favorite?" Bless Harville for breaking the suddenly awkward moment.

"Dance? Foxtrot and cha-cha for rhythm and bolero for smooth."

"No tango?"

"Gads, no. Everyone picks tango. I like it well enough, but it's not top o' my list."

Buddy—or rather, Gene since Bunny's in the room—catches my eye. "I can't say I play much bolero or foxtrot at the Moon, but I'll bet a good portion of the till you'll slide right into two-step and nightclub."

Kiki, being an excellent meeting manager, brings us back to order. "This discussion is perfect, because the punch line of the story about Poppy and Digby is she's informed me that she'd like to reprise the *DWTS* event at our gala."

Bunny's eye roll nearly makes her topple backward. "But rest assured, she doesn't want to bring attention to herself."

The laugh escaping Kiki isn't amused. "Problem is, it puts me in a quandary. I can't alienate her, but I'm not about to let her overrun this event with only five weeks until go time. But more at issue than timing is, while Poppy thinks she's the modern-day Ginger Rogers, I went to that party—Ginger and Fred have no threat to their reputations with Poppy and Digby."

Logan lifts a hand. "Since the gala is as much about showcasing the Magnolia Bloom merchants as it is a kickoff for the hospital, why not combine it with Poppy's megalomania? Let's do a mini—stress on mini—showcase. We could do four dances. Open with Poppy and her ego—I mean, Digby—followed by a routine with some of the MB merchants as a group, then two numbers with our Blackpool stars."

To my surprise, it's Jake who pipes in. "MB merchants? What part of five weeks did you not understand?"

"I sponsor a table at all of my partners' showcases, so I've seen plenty of these things, and trust me, people put routines together in a month, and no one would be expecting anything spectacular from us. It's more about the hometown aw-shucks and then a jaw-dropping performance."

Even from across the table, I can see ideas spinning in Kiki's eyes. "If we did this Magnolia Bloom's mini *DWTS* as the opening act, then go to the comedian, then Ally as the finale, the evening's guaranteed to be a huge hit. Perfect timing to have everyone in their seats and primed for the auction."

"And their checkbooks loosened up by plenty of beer and wine." Emmett is ever the pragmatist, apparently.

"Or mocktails with Bunny's shrubs." Roy's opinion on his preference is clear.

Bunny's cheeks pinken, but she's clearly delighted. "Do you think four numbers is enough?"

My stomach gives a lurch when she shoots an obvious glance at Logan and me. "Logan and Lexi could do a routine so we could put a shine on our new committee member."

I choke and shake my head like a squirrel trying to count a bag of spilled nuts. "No, no, no. Besides, I'm not a member of the Merchants Association."

Bunny dismisses my objection with a flip of her hand. "That's only for the group number. You and Logan could be a palate cleanser after Poppy and Digby."

"I'm game," Logan declares, his eyes only for me, "but I want Lexi to be my partner on the team, too."

What? What is he doing? He can't—

"There's no 'too' here." My voice goes a bit wild, and I'm sure my expression's wilder.

The crosstalk around the table completely dismisses my objections. In the end, they—and I point out my vote has not been tallied—decide that another individual number might string the act out too long, but everyone agrees I have to dance with Logan for the team number.

I'm also not given any time to reaffirm my definite no on this issue, because Kiki moves the meeting along to individual reports. That means I'm too lost in making notes on the spreadsheet as each person takes their turn to do anything but sputter inside my own head.

My chance is truly gone when Kiki closes her tablet and smiles broadly. "Dang, y'all, we've got us a right fine shindig goin' on here."

We all laugh at her drawl. While she might be a native Texan, she doesn't have the accent people expect, much like the rest of the people around the table. Doc is probably the only exception. Sure, I can hear it in them all, but it's nothing like Hollywood tries to depict. I understand, seeing how Scots are always badly done, but I have no doubt anyone could find me in a dark room in a Celtic version of Marco Polo.

I decide to wait and inform Logan Jameson that while I may tend to stay quiet, I'm not a pushover, and I'm not going to be forced into dancing with him.

No matter how damned sexy he might be...

CHAPTER FOURTEEN

BUNNY

I'M PACING SO HARD WAITING for Lexi, I'm afraid I'm going to drill a hole in my office floor. I suspect she's genetically hardwired to be early, so this is all on me.

I'm staring at the security camera, and as soon as I see her on the boardwalk, I thread my way through the crowd in the taproom and head for the front door, practically pulling the knob out of the frame as I yank it open.

She jumps back, putting a hand to her chest. "Hell mend ye, Bunny! You nearly scared me white-haired."

"Sorry. Come in, and I'll apologize with a glass of the best beer in Magnolia Bloom and the three surrounding counties."

"If I didnae need one before, I do now, but I'll forgive you."

I lead the way to the far door and out back to the small patio I put in right after I signed the papers making the tavern officially mine. The afternoon sun's shining at the perfect angle to make this little space feel like a country Eden.

"Oh my, this is pure barry."

I don't need a search engine to translate. Her slow pan of the area, taking in all the details I've added over time, confirms she thinks it's as beautiful as I do.

"Thanks. This was my therapy for almost two years. I watched endless hours of tutorials, learning how to set a foundation under my paving bricks, which plants to use on the borders, how to use a pickax, mix Quikrete. Lots of stuff."

"It's brilliant is what it is."

I give her a quick tour around the space, telling her about shopping trips that yielded the yard art I painted and refurbished for the final touches. With chef-kiss timing, the pints I told Isaiah to draw when Lexi arrived are brought out, and I gesture for her to sit down at the table I reserved. Best seat in the house, unless it's raining.

"Lexi, this is my favorite server, Ravi, but he's forbidden from lording it over the other servers' heads."

She takes in Ravi's shy blush with a sweet and understanding smile. "It's nice to meet you."

"You, too, ma'am."

I chuckle as he hurries away. I'm determined to pull him out of his shell, but it's not going to be easy.

Lexi lifts her beer for me to clink rims. "Sláinte mhath."

"Cheers back at ya."

"Your wee Ravi seems a lovely lad."

"Indeed. He's one of the younger in the Broder clan. Just graduated from high school and is off to college in a week or so. I'm truly going to miss him."

"I've met Jake, but I don't think I've met any of the other Broders yet besides Sarah."

"Jake's the reason I have my bestie, next to my new Scottish BFF, of course. His cousin, Danica, had the gall to move to Albuquerque to take art training and abandon me here all alone."

Lexi snorts at my attempt at being pathetic. "Och, aye, all alone, are ye? Poor lassie, someone give her a pet on the head."

"I'd appreciate a little more sympathy from our new friendship."

"You've come to the wrong lass, then. I've been surrounded by nothing but plumbers and carpenters the better part of my life, most of 'em Scot, a few Irish, and the rest a mishmash. I've nae had much experience with the needy sort. If, on the other hand, you need a good kick in the bahoochie to get you off your pity pot, I'm here for you."

"I'll bear that in mind." I wait until she takes a healthy sip of my choice for the afternoon. "So, what do you think?"

"It's magic, that's what I say."

"That was the first recipe I ever got right. I had a few wowzer bad ones in the beginning, I'm telling you. This one's become a crowd favorite, though, and keep your fingers crossed for me. I've got a buyer from one of the biggest grocery chains in Texas coming to see about stocking it."

"Congratulations, that's braw. I'm happy for you."

Like someone flipped a light switch, my mood goes sad. Dark, even. "Yeah, it's just, after I got off the phone, it hit me that all the reasons I tell myself I have to stay in Magnolia Bloom are a lie I want to hear, not the truth."

Lexi blinks, then her eyes squint in confusion. "I still have half this pint, so there's nae chance of me bein' steamin' yet, but I can't figure out what's happened."

I sit back, rubbing my temples so I can get my act together. "That came out of left field. Sorry."

"It's all right, love. Tell me what made you go dour."

It takes some effort, but I force a smile. "I'm being…what's that expression you used? I'm being crabbit? Well, that's the perfect word, and I don't want to spoil our evening."

"Nonsense. You asked me over for a pint and a blether, and I'm all for it. We can tear the tartan all night if you want to get something off your mind. Don't pretend to be all taps aff for me."

I burst out laughing, thankful for her pulling out her Scottish slang to yank me out of my sudden doldrum. "What in the world does 'taps aff' mean?"

She takes a solid draw on her beer, and I have to say I'm impressed. My Scot friend is no tiny sipper, like some women feel they have to be. "It means 'tops off.' In Scotland, pure sunshine can be rare, so if there's the littlest bit of sun and heat, men will strip off their tops to soak it in like it's the best party of the year. There's nips everywhere, I'm tellin' you."

My gut laugh earns us a few head turns, but I don't care. "Oh, Lexi, please say you'll stay here forever. You're a riot."

That earns me a slanted brow. "I thought you said you were leaving Magnolia Bloom. How could I bear it here without you?"

As if it's the most natural thing in the world, I reach over and take her hand, squeezing her fingers to somehow convey how precious she's become to me in an impossibly short time. "Don't listen to me. I change my mind as often as I used to change shoes."

"Even so, tell me what's got you all emotionally peely-wally."

I release my death grip and take my own appreciative slug of my favorite brew. "I told you about the shrub-testing and Gene asking me to go to the gala as his date. I've been a wreck ever since."

"Didn't you give me shite about getting all up in arms when Logan asked me out? At least I'd just met the man. You've been tail over teakettle for Gene for a year, or so you said."

"I'm not sure that's exactly right, but the basic gist is, as I've worked with Gene on the business association and other town meetings, I've grown more and more attracted to him. It wasn't love at first sight, or any of that stuff."

"So is it any less real for it?"

"Of course not. I just mean I'm unsure when I tipped over into being...."

"In love?"

I bury my face in my hands. "Yes, and it's so pathetic."

Lexi pulls my wrists down, leaning in, meaning she's about to get serious. "Bunny West, your bum's out the windae. You're gun-shy is all. He's asked you out. Go!"

"Says the woman who won't accept a dinner invitation from Logan, and what the hell did that mean?"

"It's talking shite and nonsense on steroids, meaning you're talking with your bahoochie. Being an utter fool—"

"All right, already! Don't pull any punches there, my friend."

"I donnae know how after all my years being surrounded by men and their nonsense until I wanted to scream, but listen, I'll go out with Logan if you'll go out with Gene."

Well that escalated quickly. I expected her to challenge me, but now she's padding the bait with what I want for her. How am I supposed to say no now? She's got me, and she knows it.

"You're devious, Lexi Stewart."

"Aye and nae. Growing up, all I had was my sister, but she was the center of her own world. Then when I met Douglas and married at the tender age of eighteen, my world became all men, all the time, until a few years ago when we hired some lady plumbers. Some of the best workers we have, but that's another story. Point being, I learned early to speak my mind, or they'd run over me like an out of control lorry."

I've seen enough episodes of *Call the Midwife* to understand her reference, but I feel like I'm staring down a steamroller. "I can see that, but I have the feeling, despite your claims, you're only a little bossy."

She wrinkles her nose at me. "Caelan and Bram, Douglas's eejit brothers, tried to turn my hair silver on a daily basis, but the thing is, for all their nonsense, they're good lads. I watched them botch chances with several good women before they grew up and were worth more than a tarnished ten pence. So I was thinking that maybe Gene believes he's not worthy of you. Or, more likely, thinks his past makes him undesirable."

Everyone in Magnolia Bloom knows Gene as the teetotaling bartender. He was a raging alcoholic and takes full blame for destroying his marriage and his relationship with his son. It's not that Gene talks about it a lot, but there's no hiding a secret in a small town. More to the point, he uses his past as a cautionary tale when the moment is right.

"I honestly believe Gene tells his story to help people, but I also think he uses it to mortar a brick wall around himself."

"Right, then, it's time for you to use those pickax skills you mentioned a moment ago, aye?"

"Hmmm…maybe. But you're not getting off the hook. If I agree to your crazy plan, when are you going to ask Logan to dinner? He made the first move. Isn't it your turn?"

"We're supposed to grab a bite at the new pizza place before dance practice tonight. The group is going, and you have to come because we're going to form the couples and get started on the choreography."

"Wait, what? Tonight?" So much for the peace brought about from the beer. "You didn't tell me I had to be involved."

"What? I think you're mistaken. I told you." She puts a finger to her mouth, her expression far too innocent.

"No. You. Didn't."

"Och, well, my head's been mince this whole week, being so busy. But you're a major business holder. Your attendance is required. Sorry about that."

"Sorry, my great-aunt Fanny. You knew this whole conversation you were going to have dinner with Logan, and you roped me into going with Gene on false pretenses."

"I did nothing of the sort. I merely helped you decide to do what you've wanted to do all along. If anything, I enabled you. Or even better, I empowered you."

I give her my wickedest glare. "No so fast, my Scottish lass. If there's a group, this does not count as going out with Logan."

Her blush can't hide the truth. "It certainly does."

She makes a buzzer sound. "Wrong answer, but thank you for playing." She leans forward, her face stern. "You're not winning this one, missy. It's not a date if there's a table full of people. If you're going to hold my feet to the fire with Gene, then I'm holding yours. You have to ask Logan out on a proper date, or the deal's off."

"Now, wait—"

"Not a chance, sister. That's the deal. Take it or leave it."

I can almost hear the cogs turning in her brain, but in the end, it appears her desire to play yenta overcomes her reticence to change roles and become Logan's pursuer instead of his pursued.

"Okay, right, then, you daft hen. I'll do it."

I offer up my hand for a high five, which she returns reluctantly, but I'm thrilled. There will be five hundred people at the gala, so it'll hardly be intimate, but I've cornered Lexi into an evening alone with Logan. Total win for me.

"While you sit here being so pleased with yourself, I've got to go to the loo. I'll take another pint of this magic, though."

"I'll be right here waiting."

Deciding I can be every bit as devious as my new friend, as soon as Lexi is out of earshot, I grab my phone and speed-dial Emmett. I'm probably interrupting dinner, but Wyatt will forgive me, and this is important.

"This had better not be another shrub emergency." Emmett's cranky, but I can hear Wyatt laughing.

"Not shrubs. Remember that conversation we had about Lexi a couple days ago? Well, it's time to initiate Operation Fairy Godmother."

CHAPTER FIFTEEN

LEXI

I WANT to be angry with Bunny for tricking me into having to ask Logan on a real date, but I'd tricked her back into having to go out with Gene, so it's a win. Besides, I'm only going to be here for a couple of months, while, if things go according to my hope, she'll stay here in this town she loves and build a future with the man she loves even more.

So who's the smarter hen, now, eh?

Still, I've had to put on my big-girl knickers and find a dose of false courage as I head down to the Iron Core. I've surmised that asking him at work will be less intimidating.

For me.

My nerves, apparently, didn't get my message about behaving. The second Logan spies me, he heads my way, ending the call on his cell phone as he walks.

"I have to tell you, you're not dressed appropriately for my dead-lift class."

I glance down at myself, then feel foolish. Like I have to check to know I'm still in my black trousers and the plain white blouse that goes with everything.

I need to hurry up and be done with it. If I dither, I'll not do what I've come for, so I blurt it out.

"Would you like to go for a piece?"

His eyes go wide and his posture stock-still. "I'm...I'm sorry, what?"

I rewind my question in my head, but it seems pretty straight forward to me. It might not have been the most elegant invitation I've ever issued, but he sure looks flustered over being asked to tea.

"Um, I was wondering if you'd like to grab a bite, maybe a piece... I mean, you say sandwich, and I don't know, some soup. Or whatever."

Great, Lexi. Keep dithering like a total rocket. He'll be calling the sanitarium and not the restaurant to make you a reservation.

He covers a laugh. I really wish I knew what I said that's so funny, but he doesn't enlighten me.

"I'd love to. My last appointment rescheduled, so the universe must be smiling on me. I'm totally at your disposal."

Hell and damnation. That's not the way this is supposed to happen. My plan was to ask him out for a quick nip into a local pub, maybe, or one of the shops. His response, according to my script, was to say he's too busy. Then I'd act disappointed and leave, having fulfilled the spirit of the law in my agreement with Bunny. I could honestly say I asked him out. That he couldn't go wouldn't have been my fault, and with one fell swoop, I'd be off the hook.

The key word, of course, is how this was *supposed* to happen.

"This is right in the middle of your workday, so if another time is better—"

"Not at all. Give me five minutes. I'll go change, and we can leave."

He gives me a piercing look, as if he's well aware I'm searching fast for a way to hedge.

Damn and blast. Now I'm good and stuffed, so I guess I'd best make the best of it. "Right, then. I'll wait here."

I gesture vaguely toward the couch and chairs comprising a seating area. In turn, he sweeps a hand toward the man who just came up behind him and has taken a stance at the front counter.

"Quinton, have you met Lexi?"

The man who has a more mature version of Logan's amazing physique breaks into a smile. "No, I haven't. Ranelle, that's my wife, said Emma, who's her mama, said you're from Scotland. Welcome to Texas."

Logan interrupts to say he'll be right back, and I add another set of names to my memory. "I love it here already, and Emma's my second-favorite Grannie, but don't tell her that. I have them all thinking they have the number one position."

Quinton's laugh is as easy as his grin. "Your secret's safe with me. So how do you find our little town?"

"It's a slice of heaven. A wee bit on the warm side for a Celtic girl, but I'm happy to adjust."

"Ranelle says Emma says you're fitting in like vanilla wafers in banana pudding."

"I take it that's a good thing?"

"Young lady, you can't get a better compliment in the South."

"Right, then. Good to know."

By the time Quinton offers me something from the cooler, and I politely decline, Logan's back, sporting those thigh-caressing jeans and a sky-blue polo. As fast as my heart is racing, the last thing I need is a spike of caffeine.

He takes my elbow in the Southern way I'm still not quite used to and gives Quinton a wave. "See you tomorrow. I'm off on a date with a sexy lady."

"You kids have fun."

A group of teens coming in makes me feel like I'm walking through a gaggle of geese, and it deflects me from his sexy lady comment. So much so that by the time we're alone on the sidewalk, I let it go.

"Did you have anywhere specific in mind for our first date, or should I pick?"

"This isn't a date."

"It's not? You came in, asked me out, we're going to do the food-and-drink thing. Feels like a date."

"It's a pre-date."

He nods slowly. "A pre-date."

"Aye, so we can get familiar each other a wee bit. Just talk. So no place posh and not here in downtown."

"For this not being a date, you're sure being picky, which I should note you said you weren't."

I give him a side-eye. "And you're about to make me rescind the invitation."

"No, no, not necessary. I'll behave."

"I'm sure you're being untruthful."

"All right, no more teasing. Do you have a spot in mind?"

"Something easy, since we've got to go dancing. It's hard to be light on your feet with a heavy stomach."

"How about a burger? We could go to Cooter's. He's got the best in town."

"You're bammin' me. Cooter's?"

"Teasing you? Not even a little. Cooter Gilroy's family has run the Burger Barn for half as long as Magnolia Bloom's been around. That and the towing service, but the two aren't connected. The restaurant's not much to look at, but surely it'll satisfy your condition."

"Cooter's Burger Barn it is, then." I give in, wanting us to get this over with.

"You won't be disappointed." He gestures toward an enormous white pickup truck in the reserved spot just ahead of us. "Your chariot awaits."

Trying to find my humor again, I nod toward the diesel monster. "That's quite a beast for a personal trainer."

"A personal trainer who's usually hauling equipment. Not to mention tools and flooring and tables—"

"And chairs and speakers. How could I forget, Mr. Half Owner In Ten Companies?"

"As long as you don't think I'm compensating, that's all that matters."

I chuckle, letting him help me into the passenger side. Even with a running board, it's a jump to get in. We have big lorries at home, but they're big by Scot standards, not American.

The drive out into the more rural area's lovely. This week's been solely comprised of time in the castle, the grounds, or around town, so this is my first trip away from the city center.

Logan did preface his restaurant choice by saying the Gilroy family has had their business for nigh onto seventy-five years, but I'm not quite prepared for the weather-beaten wooden building that lists to the right. I'm also not entirely certain the place wouldn't fall down in a stiff wind.

Logan chuckles at my expression. "Don't worry. I wouldn't risk your health or your safety. And I promise, you'll be a Burger Barn fan for life by the time we complete our *pre*-date."

I slip out of my side of the truck. "You're not going to let that go, are you?"

"Not a chance."

He's his ever-gallant self and holds the door, ushering me in ahead of him. If I wasn't sure from the building's outside, the inside transports me to somewhere around 1950. Still, the seating area and ordering counter appear reasonably clean. With no apparent health hazards, if I'm in for a penny, I might as well be in for a pound. I take a tray and move under the handwritten *Start Here* sign and slide the tray along the rails reminding me of my primary school lunchroom.

The menu, also in rough printing, is tacked to a corkboard that has soaked up decades of ambient grease. The prices have been crossed through and changed so many times, I'm not exactly sure what they say.

Logan waits patiently as I try to decide, thinking if the people of Magnolia Bloom actually eat three-quarter pound burgers on a regular basis, I understand why Bailey's putting a cardiac care wing in the new hospital.

Swinging doors with fogged-over portholes fly open, and a man who could be anywhere from fifty to ninety barrels over to the cash register and looks at me with a distinct hurry-up expression.

I order a cheeseburger, chips, er, French fries, and a glass of water. Logan tells the man to make it two, but makes his drink a Dr Pepper. I almost cave and change mine to match, but decide there's no need to start an addiction to a fizzy juice it would cost a fortune to get shipped to Scotland.

I have no illusion he'll allow me to pay, but I do offer my thanks. "So we're clear, the next one is on me, aye?"

"There's going to be a next one?" He tilts his head at me, and I shake mine.

"If you're lucky." Goodness, where did that cheek come from?

When we finally sit down with trays laden with greasy, deep-fried, and delicious-smelling options, I open our conversation with what's been eating at me for the last thirty minutes. "When I popped in and asked you to tea, you got flummoxed. I said something wrong, but I cannae figure out what."

The flush I saw before under his rugged, dark skin returns, and now I'm even more confused. What does *he* have to be embarrassed about?

"You didn't say anything wrong."

I narrow my gaze, knowing good and well he's fibbing. "You're blushing, and that's saying something."

He takes a desperate sip of his soda. "You said, 'Would I like to go for a piece?'"

I frown. "Aye, I realize I should have said sandwich, but that's what we say where I'm from. Like tatties are potatoes, and a biscuit is a cookie, and tea is dinner, unless you say cup of tea specifically. I'm trying to remember the American terms, but sometimes mine slip out."

"Come on, you have to watch some of our movies or television. When you said 'piece,' I thought...."

Oh. My. God.

This is ten thousand times worse than *nice muscles*. He thought I meant piece of...

Ass.

As God is my witness, I didn't even think such a thing.

I scramble wildly for my purse. "I have to go."

"Lexi, don't. It took me two seconds to figure out you meant nothing like what my immature, boy-brain thought, which immediately shorted out. Please don't be embarrassed."

"Embarrassed? I'm about to go up in smoke right here in Cooter Gilroy's Burger Barn, which probably isn't insured, and I'll put the man out of business. But since I'll be dead and gone, it won't matter. Please tell my weans I died from something exotic, not utter and abject humiliation."

"Listen, if you want to play who's more embarrassed, I try to be a decent guy, but where my thoughts went in that nanosecond isn't gentlemanly, not even remotely."

"You're nae helping!"

He reaches across the table and pulls my hands away. "Lexi, please, look at me."

It's all I can do to comply, but when I do, I fall into the liquid warmth of his eyes and the true chagrin on his face.

"If you don't mind, I'd rather fall into a hole in the floor. I bet there's one around here."

"I do mind. I mind a lot. I'm finally getting to spend time with you, no matter what we call it, and I wish you'd decide this was wicked funny more than anything else."

Funny? The fact my brain has gone to places it has no business going and is coming up with a whole film's worth of images from his version of my invitation? Like how hot all those muscles would be under my fingertips, or how amazing those lips would feel on mine, or my neck, or my—

I snatch my hand away and drain my water in three gulps. I'm amazed it didn't start boiling as soon as I touched the glass. I suck in a piece of ice and chomp it down, too, but it doesn't help calm the lava flow in my veins.

"Lex, eat your burger before it gets cold. Trust me, this is a meal you want warm."

Lex. Douglas always called me Lex when he was having a go at me, or when he was in a particularly jovial mood, usually brought on by several pints down at our local pub.

I'm stopped short because I like the sound of the diminutive of my name coming from Logan. It should feel like a betrayal, right?

So why doesn't it?

"Hey, where'd you go?"

"Took a tiny trip down a memory." I blink to clear my blurry vision and find a smile for my handsome not-a-date. Picking up a chip, I hold it out like it's a tumbler of the finest Glenfiddich. In his usual good humor, Logan uses the one of he's just dunked in red sauce to "clink" with me. We dig in, and it's clear from bite one he's right. It's a fine burger, grease and all.

I try to let go of the fact that until that last moment, I didn't give Douglas a thought this entire day.

It seems I'm starting to move on after all.

CHAPTER SIXTEEN

BETHANIE

"HELL, yeah, I want to be in Operation Fairy Godmother! This is an awesome idea."

Bunny's grin is as big as mine. "Fantastic. I'll tell Emmett we're a go, and he'll text you what we want you to do to get this party started."

"I'll be waiting with baited breath." I give a mock frown. "That's such a disgusting saying. Why do we use it?"

"Mostly because it's b-a-t-e-d, as in restrained, not b-a-i-t-e-d like fish, but it's gotten muddy over the years. If you want to check for yourself, open your twentieth internet tab and do a dive on it."

I look at my crowded menu bar and wince. "I'm not as mysterious as I'd like to believe, huh?"

"S'okay. We all love you just as you are."

She clicks off, and I determinedly scroll through my open searches, closing down at least ten. In my defense, most are related to my job, researching marketing sites and digging into their metrics to see if the shiny "place your ad here" graphics are merely pretty pictures and not valuable spaces for my limited investment budgets. I'm lucky enough to have a healthy one for the castle and Dad's market, but I've picked up a couple of smaller clients who are working on a shoestring.

That's what I find challenging. It's an advertising puzzle with ever-changing pieces, but I do a darn good job helping people reach for their dreams. In the process, I'm getting to reach for mine. I have no need to go to New York or LA or any other place where marketing staff are either piranha in a tank, or treated like the bugs I have to constantly wash off the front grille of my car. No, thank you. I'll stay right where I am and be a little bitty fish, but a happy one.

A mostly happy one. As soon as I get over my juvenile crush on the most unobtainable man in town, I'll be super peachy.

My phone dings, and I read the text from Emmett giving me my marching orders. I'm to head over to the new upscale boutique on the square. Marissa is a fallen-from-grace wedding and gown designer who has come to Magnolia Bloom to make her creations without bitchy runway critics and magazine writers from San Diego to San Francisco to LA tearing her up nine ways to Sunday. She's the kind of Bloomian we love. Here to remake herself and be part of a giant, if sometimes flawed, small-town family.

I'm to give Marissa the names of all of us who've waited too long to get their dresses for the gala, and I note with a chuckle that he chose me to go first. I'm to use his very specific list of colors and patterns for each of us so that when we herd Lexi into the shop, she won't have time to get nervous. I'm not quite certain why he couldn't have texted Marissa himself, but I have a feeling it's a not-so-subtle move to make sure I show up, too.

It appears our resident art expert knows people a little too well.

In that I've become a pretty good rule-follower in this new life of mine, I'm at Marissa's of Magnolia Bloom in no time. She's waiting for me, the picture of poise with a greeting both cheerful and welcoming.

After the requisite hellos, I ask for her number to forward the all-important text, and in moments, she's a whirlwind, pulling dresses and setting them in some formula exclusive to her on three rolling racks.

"Okay." She finally stops and takes a deep breath. "You're

supposed to be dressed and on the stage when they get here, and we're T-minus twenty to show time, so here's the plan. I'm going to take five minutes and put your hair up in a simple twist, then get you dressed." She gives a second look at her selections. "Thank God my stock arrived from my old store in time, or Emmett might have run me out of town."

I'm in awe of what she's pulled together like she's a speed skater with a stopwatch moving in fast-forward. "You're as organized and on top of things as he is. He'd never chase off a kindred spirit."

She points to a garment bag with *MARISSA'S* embroidered in green letters on a creamy magnolia blossom, and motions toward the dressing room. "Let's see the first belle of the ball."

Even though I want to, it would be useless to argue. Emmett would bust in here and give me the holy what-for, so I take the bag and head through the velvet draperies without grumbling. This is all for Lexi and Bunny anyway. Even if I wanted a designer gown, I can't afford one. I've got a healthy savings account and can pay my bills, but I don't have Marissa's of Magnolia Bloom-level funds yet.

I slip into the gown of raw silk, the fabric and soft rose color the definition of not-a-bridesmaid-or-prom dress. I've managed to lose my booze weight over this last year, but I'm not exactly Bunny West lithe. I'm more curvy-girl-likes-to-eat-but-is-doing-her-best, but I nearly tear up at the delicate cowl-neck front and keyhole back. The empire waist is the perfect amount of formfitting until the skirt flares at my ankles, and the color against the slight tan of my skin is the most beautiful thing I've ever seen.

I look good. I feel good. And it's been a long time since I could say those things at the same time.

With my dark hair pulled back in a soft swoop from my face, and even without jewelry and makeup, I feel like there should be a director's chair behind me and she's about to shout *Action*.

I step out, pausing so Marissa can pull the zipper the final few inches. Taking the skirt in hand, I climb onto the pedestal set in front of five huge mirrors arranged in a semicircle for optimum viewing.

She gives me a quite-sure-of-herself nod. "That's perfection. I knew I was wasting my time pulling those other two."

If I could form words, which I can't, they're interrupted by the door bursting open and my favorite candy imp racing into the room.

"Miss Bethanie! I saw you through the windows on the way to the market. You're so beautiful!"

"Thanks. Isn't this dress wonderful? Miss Marissa is the best designer in the whole world. What do you think?"

I smile at Chloe, pretending not to notice Marissa has inched closer in case little hands reach for the insanely expensive fabric.

She nods vigorously. "Oh, yes, she's the bestest. Wait right there."

And then she's out the door in a flash.

I return my focus to Marissa. "This is the most fantastic dress I've ever seen, and if it's only the beginning, I'll be in sensory overload by the time we go through Bunny's and Lexi's options."

"Thank you. This design is one of my favorites. It's simple but elegant. However, you don't look good. You look *amazing*."

The door reopens, and I turn, expecting to see the gang, but I find myself nailed by the widened eyes of a certain sticky-fingered girl's father.

"See, Daddy? I told you. She's a princess!"

Roy's looking at me with an expression that's the definition of gobsmacked. I can't say I blame him. This is the spectrum opposite of city jail scrubs, my hair matted and scraggly, my fingers black from booking ink. And when he sees me around town these days, my uniform is basically jeans and snarky-printed T's.

"Right, Daddy? Right?"

"Yes, sweet girl, she does look like a princess."

I'm glad I'm in bare feet. If I'd already put on the waiting dyed-to-match heels, I'd have fallen and broken an ankle.

"You *have* to take her to the ball."

When I think I can't be any more shocked, he looks me right in the eye and gives me an apologetic smile. Then he kneels to talk to Chloe, tapping the end of her nose.

"I can't do that. I have to work the gala as a policeman. I'm not going as a guest."

"But you're a prince, Daddy, and she's a princess. You have to."

"You, little troublemaker, are the sweetest five-year-old in the world."

Her little face turns lava red. "Daddy, I'm *seven*. Well, not until tomorrow."

Roy's hand presses over his heart. "My apologies. Can I make up for my horrible mistake by taking you for some early birthday ice cream? Miss Felicity has double chocolate in today."

Just like that, the frown turns upside down and Mount Vesuvius settles back into rest mode. "I'll get over it...if you get me two scoops."

"Deal. Let's go now so we don't spoil your supper."

She takes his hand and is practically racing him out the door. He looks back at me and winks, and it's all I can do not to clap and call out, *Well played, Chief.*

The interior of the shop seems achingly quiet when Marissa and I are alone again. Her smile is bemused, while mine, which I've pasted on in the way I've perfected, covers the crevasse in my chest that widens with every sighting of the too-sexy star of my fevered dreams.

Marissa's gaze cuts between me and the door. "That was interesting."

I shake a nonexistent wrinkle from my gown so I can avoid her. I have a feeling tears would stain the silk, and I don't want to have to pay to dry-clean a dress I'll never get to wear.

The entry bell rings, saving me from an explanation, and the shop becomes a sea of faces and a river of *oohs*, *ahhs*, and *ohmygods*.

I'm thankful, because fielding a barrage of compliments and instructions to *face this way, no, that way, now turn around* keep me from thinking about the dark brown eyes locking with mine, the smile sending tremors up my spine, and the wink nearly taking me out at the knees.

I expect Emmett to be his usual jokester self, but instead, he moves close and takes my shaking hands. "I saw your badge-wearin' cowboy coming out of here. Want to tell me why you look like you're your rubber ducky get swept out to sea?"

"Not really. I need to keep it together. If I start baring my soul to you, I'll be a mess." I look in the mirror and touch the drape of my dream dress's cowl. "Does it make me a certifiable lunatic to admit I'm glad he got to see me in this before I have to put it back?"

"No, honey, it doesn't, but don't count me out yet."

"What does that mean?"

"All right, everyone." Emmett has ignored me and is corralling the crowd. "It's obvious we don't need Bethanie to try on anything else, because this one's perfect, so she can go get dressed while we wrangle Bunny into that aubergine fantasy she's drooling over."

"I'm not drooling."

"Honey, I'm going to have to put a bib on you." He flaps a hand at me. "You, go. Bunny, dressing room."

Bunny takes the hanger he hands her and follows me down the hallway. "That man should've been a general."

"He had to be in a past life." I'm grateful Emmett has let me save face and restore my dignity before I make a basket case out of myself.

I beat Bunny back to the main salon, my humor restored as I gush over the dresses waiting for Lexi to try on. My heart clenches when she touches one of her choices, and her voice breaks.

"There's nae way she'll have dresses to fit me. These posh shops don't carry my size."

Marissa glides in, placing a comforting hand on Lexi's arm. "I give you my word. I've prided myself on being able to fit almost any customer, and you aren't remotely close to stressing my size selection. Enjoy a glass of wine, and we'll get you back there after I pull your hair back. It won't take but a second."

Our conversation screeches to a halt when Bunny steps into the light from the hallway, moving with a grace that turns me green with friendly envy as she steps onto the platform.

"Marissa, you're missing out on the perfect spokesman for your brand." I whisper the words, not wanting to embarrass Bunny, but I'm delighted when Marissa agrees.

"I think you're right, but she might not have room in her busy schedule, sadly for me."

I've known Bunny for so long, I'm no longer starstruck by our resident beer-meister's beauty, still, my breath whooshes out of me as I look at her. Unlike Lexi and me, Marissa has pulled Bunny's hair to one side with a comb and let the long length flow over her shoulder in a cascade of sunshine-infused honey. The deep purple dress is worthy of an Oscar party, and we stand behind her in silent, rapt attention.

Bunny's gaze shifts from the back of the fitted sheath with a high thigh split, and she startles when she catches us all staring. She flushes and lifts a self-conscious hand to her ear, stroking the scar that's so faint it's impossible to see except in bright light, and only then if her hair's up in a ponytail.

"Y'all, stop."

Emmett moves, stepping forward to do the honors of the final zip and hook-and-eye closure on a dress that, by every standard, is modest. Her toned arms are exposed by the deep cut angling to a high, mock halter, but all the requisite bits are hidden from view. That's why it's a thousand times sexier than something cut from hither to yon, because the exquisitely embroidered mesh bodice fuels the imagination.

Although tall, Emmett's dwarfed by Bunny on the pedestal, but he tilts his head back and gives her his trademark smile. "One and done. This one's the winner."

We lock eyes in the mirror, and I nod, swiping at a threatening tear. I'm back in my T-shirt and jeans, so it doesn't matter anymore, but still, I don't want to be a snotty mess before Lexi gets her chance.

Which is exactly what happens in the Great Gown Try-On. Marissa has left wisps of Lexi's auburn hair loose around her face, and she gets the requite sigh-and-smile reaction as she takes center stage. As promised, the dress is indeed plenty big for Lexi. In fact, it's going to have to be taken in, as it's currently being held together in the back by giant clips.

Marissa gestures to the mirrors, directing our attention. "Everyone concentrate on the front. By event day, I'll have this altered and perfectly fitted like Flora, Fauna, and Merryweather conjured it with their magic wands."

Emmett's breaks his trance. "The mistake women with a few extra pounds make is wearing things too loose. Makes you look like you went shopping in the tent department at the outdoor supercenter. The key, as we see so beautifully modeled before us, is letting your curves have their moment to shine."

Lexi looks like she's been bathed in moonlight in the pewter baronet satin. The bateau neck shows off her amazing collarbones, and the fit, even if created with clips, lifts her bust into va-va-va-voom territory. The fabric skims her hips and thighs, then flares into a classic mermaid skirt that couldn't be more perfect.

I inch forward, still holding her deer-in-the-headlights stare. "If the evening ends up overcast, it won't matter. We'll put you on the dais because, Lex, you look positively glorious and would light up the whole room."

Her flush returns color to cheeks that had gone white. "I've never put anything this amazing on my body in my entire life."

"How sad for Scotland, but how wonderful for us," Emmett teases, knowing that getting her to laugh will ease the shock from her system.

Bunny returns from her quick change and joins in the chorus of voices rejecting Lexi's arguments that it's too tight, and she should wear a darker color. "Listen up, missy. You're wearing that dress if we have to collectively wrestle you into it. In fact, if you'll agree, Bethanie and I will come to the castle early to get ready. Emmett has already said his cousin Tara is ready and willing to do hair and makeup for us, so we won't be the belles of the ball. We'll be the queens."

Marissa takes over as chief wrangler, tells Lexi to get dressed, and directs Bunny and me to claim our garment bags.

A pang hits me, but I shake my head. "I can't. I'd love to, but while this has been tremendous fun, this isn't in my budget."

"There will be no arguing. My agreement with Kiki is I get billing in the program for your dresses, and that's precious advertising space. Bethanie, you of all people know I'm getting the better end of this bargain, considering the roster coming to this shindig."

Between her, Emmett, Bunny, and Lexi, I'm far outnumbered, so with an embarrassed but grateful heart, I take my new treasure. My heart's incongruously light, compared to how sad the afternoon started, as I take the tail end of the stream of bodies headed out of what is sure to be one of Magnolia Bloom's most successful shops in no time flat.

It doesn't matter that I can't be Chloe's princess.

Or Roy's.

I'll have to be content as a grateful fairy godmother for Lex and Bunny for our evening extravaganza. Besides, Emmett and Wyatt and the rest of the committee guys will dance with me until I'm exhausted enough to put away my foolish Disney dreams.

CHAPTER SEVENTEEN

LEXI

IT'S no surprise I put off visiting the famous grove behind the castle, considering how much I've had to do. I'm sure it's a forgivable offense, and I'm not complaining. I've been more involved and had more fun these last weeks than I have in ages. It's equally unsurprising that the grove is every bit as beautiful as Kiki said it was. In truth, far more, because in moments like this, I understand how even the best-intentioned words can fail.

The cairngorm necklace I've grown fond of wearing warms in the hollow of my breasts as I move farther into the welcoming embrace of the towering magnolias. I pull up short when a woman emerges from the back edge, a bit surprised to find someone else here.

"Sarah! So sorry to intrude."

Sarah Broder is the most no-nonsense of the Grannies, and I've enjoyed her style from the get-go. I love Eunice and her steel-hand-in-a-warm-glove approach, but Sarah doesn't bother with the mittens. Since I've been around mostly men since I was a lass of eighteen, Sarah's inability to pull her punches feels like home.

"You're not intruding. At least I got all my clothes on before you got here."

I pretend to be shocked, but biting my lip gives me away. "You promised you'd text me if there was going to be naked coven dancing."

She nods approvingly and adds a wink. "Sorry. Must have forgotten to hit send. Next time, I promise."

"I'll hold you to it, but I'll slip off now."

"Nonsense." She gestures toward an iron bench. "Come sit for a minute."

It's amazing how easy it is to be with the Grannies. Each one's a bit different, but all of them entice you to bask in their wisdom and humor. I hate it when I get pedantic, but these moments remind me why it's dangerous to be youth-obsessed. We miss out on so much because we won't take five minutes to talk to those who've seen so much more, done so much more.

And why I'm going to be inconsolable when I lose Gram.

"Have you been in the grove before?" Sarah relaxes on the bench as I take a seat, turning toward me and resting her arm along the back.

"I meant to come earlier, but things got busy so quickly. It's like everyone says, though. I swear this is an enchanted forest. It feels... different in here."

"Oh, it is. Always has been. Story goes that Evajean and Alisdair planted the very seedlings you see in their towering glory. One for each of their children and then spouses and grandchildren. That's why there's so many clustered in one place."

"That's a sweet legend, and I need a calculator to log them all."

"It's lovely to believe, but enough about trees. Tell me what's on your mind."

I catch the tip of my tongue between my teeth, a habit I formed years ago when I needed a second to stop the words I wanted to say to Douglas and the boys. Usually, some form of telling them they're being shite-filled eejit bags. I'd refine my words to get them to listen and do the right thing, instead of going hell-bent with their harebrained ideas that would cost us ten times the labor and parts and money.

"I needed a quick break. Things are heating up to the countdown, and my nerves are a bit peely-wally."

"Sickly?"

"Aye, exactly. These past few weeks have been wonderful, and I'm so grateful everyone has taken me into the fold like I've been here my whole life."

"That's the real magic of Magnolia Bloom."

"I cannae agree more, though the lore about the lace is interesting. My great-gram, Maggie, and her progeny still make it with reverence."

"Which is part of the mystique, I assure you. It drives visitors crazy they can't buy it. It has to be given to you by one of the MacInneses."

"Where do you keep yours?"

I meant the comment to be teasing, but Sarah goes so still my heart hurts.

"I'm afraid my swatch didn't work. I lost the man I loved a long time ago, but I don't want to speak badly of the legend."

"I'm so sorry. I didn't know your husband had passed."

Her smile is sweet and sad and a tiny bit vixen-ish. "I didn't lose my husband. He's over at the country club playing golf as we speak. I said I lost the love of my life."

"Ah, forgive me."

"Nothing to be sorry for. You haven't been here quite long enough to hear all the super-top-secret stories that everyone in MB knows."

"You have me intrigued now, if that was your intent."

"Maybe a little. I was more hoping to nudge you into a confession or twelve."

"I'm afraid my life isn't nearly so interesting and certainly not at the super-secret level."

"I'd bet that's not true. For me, the really juicy stuff was the bits I kept under a mountain of denial and regret, but holy moly, when it all bubbled up?" She gives me a lucky-you-weren't-there shrug. "Not pretty."

I struggle between I-know-what-you-mean and abject terror. She's hit the bull's-eye of my soft candy center that I try to hide with a hard outer shell.

"I've always said I have nae regrets about my life. I'd be a right whingey brat to complain, considering the lifestyle I've enjoyed. Oh, sure, the early years were hard, but that's part and parcel of most people's marriages when you get together young, full of dreams and steamin' on passion."

"But do you really? Have no regrets? Or is that the story you've told yourself so many times you almost believe it?"

I sit back hard against the warm iron, stunned into silence. Of all the Grannies, Sarah's the one I've been around the least, and I realize now why the others call her the Sphinx.

Scrubbing at a freckle at the base of my thumb, I find the guts to be honest. "I'm not comfortable digging into this. I've never found much value in navel-gazing and reimagining the past."

"I believed that for a long time, too. I never found the nerve to put on my boxing gloves and punch back until I watched my grand-daughter Danica struggle for years now. I kept all my crap buried and cocooned myself in that ridiculous mantra of suck it up, stiff upper lip. I finally figured out I didn't want to keep calm and carry on anymore. I wanted to get mad and rage against the machine and walk in protests and the kinds of pot-stirring I denied myself my whole life." She stops and gives a self-deprecating laugh. "One of the advantages of reaching a certain age."

I have to agree. Although Sarah and I are a generation apart, and I'm still in my forties, time alone, on top of becoming a widow, has changed me.

"I understand, to a degree. I'm hardly self-actualized at the top of Maslow's pyramid, but I believed myself close until the universe decided I needed a few teeth kicked in."

"She can be a real bitch, that one. I truly am sorry for your loss."

"You're kind. It's been long enough now that the initial shock has worn off, but I'm stuck in this no-man's-land."

"Are you still mad at him?"

I look at her with new respect. "You're the first person, in the whole time I've been processing—more than a year now—to ask me that. Everyone else says, 'Oh, you just miss him,' and 'You need to fill the empty space with your new grand or your weans.'"

"I'd throw the bullshit card on that, for sure."

"Aye, I've wanted to, but it felt so disrespectful to Douglas to say I wish I had five minutes with the man so I could pound him."

"Now there's an honest statement if I ever heard one. When I lost the one who held my heart, I felt the same way. I felt *he* betrayed *me*, not the other way around."

For the first time in fourteen months, some tension leaves my shoulders. I feel...seen. Validated. By a woman I've known for a few weeks.

She looks down, then back at me with some chagrin on her face. "I need you to know I love my husband. He's a good man, and we've had a good life. We're good to each other, and we've accepted that comfortable has to be enough."

It's my turn to toss her line back. "Is it, though? Enough?"

"Yes, it is. I can look at my life now and see I've done most of the things I've wanted, some late in the game, but the boxes are checked off. I've got plenty of golden years left, but I'm at peace with my choices. You, young lady, are not me, and you have decades more than I remaining. So what do you want to do with another fifty-plus years? You're literally in midlife now, with age expectancies rising all the time."

I blink, trying to process the magnitude of what she said. Fifty-plus years? But she's right. If I follow in Gram's footsteps, late nineties to a hundred isn't unlikely at all.

"I believe that's why I'm so mad. We were preparing to travel and do all the things we put off while raising children and building a business."

"You and almost everyone else in the world."

"Aye, you're right, but..."

A thought's come to me I simply don't want to explore or admit so I concentrate even harder on my thumb. Of course, Sarah sets her teeth into my hesitation right away.

"But?"

"So, in my head, in the way back, the deal I believed we had was my giving up going to uni and marrying him, at eighteen no less, meant..."

"Meant you got payback later."

"That sounds so harsh, so transactional, and that's not it. I loved Douglas, and we had a good life."

"I'm sure you did, and I'm sure it was. Most importantly, you're not a bad person for realizing there was a touch of quid pro quo back in the day. Good gracious, I'd bet most women can say that, and a few men, too, but we go about our lives pretending we don't have those unspoken agreements or expectations as young people."

While I'm on this truth train, I have to admit I took the easy route. Yes, there were real financial issues at home when I was a girl dreaming of her future, but when reality was thrust upon me, I could've taken the hard road. Worked and gotten student loans, figured something out or, after we married, gone to classes part time, even if it would have taken years to finish. I gave up my dream. He never asked me to, but then again, he never asked me about anything I wanted, deeper than surface-level needs. His part in the puzzle was his comfort in my being the mother to his kids and partner in his business. That was what *he* wanted, so in his world, why would I have wanted anything else?

In the end, though, it was my responsibility to claim the life I wanted, even back then, and I didn't. It isn't fair to accuse the dead of reneging on the deal, blaming him for his failure to make my choices worth it. I chose his affection as good enough, real though it was. Kind of hard to throw stones at him when he didn't even know I was keeping a score sheet.

Hell and blast, *I* didn't know I was keeping this tally stick. Until now.

Considering how red my hand is, the freckle should be gone by now, but all I've done is nearly give myself a blister. "I feel like a horrid person right now."

"Nonsense. You're perfectly normal, and I'd place a healthy bet with a Vegas bookie that most people would be nodding along, if they were honest with themselves." She gives a what're-you-gonna-do waggle of the hand resting in her lap. "Here's my confession so you'll feel better. I turned down the man I loved. I did my 'duty.' I married the 'right' man. I raised my children the 'right' way. Then, when I had a second chance to be with him, even though it's pretty obvious it would have meant exiting my marriage, I said no again."

Sarah rubbed her forehead as though she could wipe away the pain the memories were bringing up. "I was a fool. I had two chances, and I threw them both away, and now I'll never get a third, not that I deserve one. I never broke my vows, and I would have left legally and as kindly as I could if I'd had the guts to. But I didn't. And now I'm watching my granddaughter struggle to be the person she needs to be in a family determined to put outer image over inner peace. I'm going to stop them, if I can. I'm going to help Danica, if she'll let me. Thank goodness she's twice as stubborn and three times as smart as I am, but she's doing this the backwards way, all jutted chin and clenched fists. I want her to be joyous."

Words are useless, but I have to whisper, "I'm sorry, Sarah."

With a deep breath and shoulders squared, she puts her armor on again and reaches over to touch my cheek with gentle fingers. "I may not be yours, but let me be a stand-in granny and bop you with my get-over-it wand. I don't mean that harshly, and I'd never tell anyone how long they have to mourn, but my heart says you're ready to say your piece to Douglas. So do it and grab on to a second life with both hands."

She rises, but motions me to stay in my seat. "Take some time in the quiet. Go down to one of the docks and dangle your feet in the water. If you want to talk some more, give me a call."

With the grace I've come to associate with her, she leaves the grove, the picture of confidence. I never would have guessed she harbors such hurt had I not been privy to her secrets in this special place.

As beautiful as the shade is, I take her advice and take the short hike down to the lake and one of the smaller docks the MacInneses use for their watersports. While I can't say I'm used to the heat, I've never lived where splashing around in a lake is a common thing. Hiking up the hems of my jeans, I toss my shoes behind me and kick back at the tiny waves rolling toward the shore. In the distance, a motor hums, but whoever is grabbing some late-summer playtime is outside this cove, and I'm selfishly grateful I don't have to share this moment with anyone.

Well, anyone but Douglas.

The cairngorm warms again, letting me know it's waiting. I slip the chain over my head and nestle the stone in my hands. I've been to the Cairngorm Mountains. They're stunning. Breathtaking, actually. The water's so crystal clear you can see the jagged peaks and thick foliage reflected in a perfect mirror, but that water's probably thirteen Celsius at its warmest. My toes are no thermometers, but Lake Maggie's quite a bit warmer than fifty-five degrees local. And the foliage around this inlet is beautiful, for certain, but I'll keep to myself that it doesn't begin to compare to the mountains and lochs of home and the birth-place of the stone I'm clutching like a lifeline.

I came to America to get away, to take a break. I didn't intend for my trip to be life-altering.

I didn't intend for Magnolia Bloom to be the place where I tell my husband goodbye.

Bolstered by the piece of home nestled in my palm and the magic of the pure beauty all around me, I do what I haven't done in all these months. I stare into the water and start talking to him.

"I need you to know, you big lout, that I love you. I always loved you. We were good for each other, you and I. So what, we didn't burn hot like the stars and all the poetic stuff? We made two beautiful weans, and it breaks my heart you won't get to see Ricci grow up. Won't get to act like a right eejit around her and be the best grandda in the world. But we'll all be all right. And I want you to be all right, driving Saint Peter crazy with ideas on how to make the loos in heaven more efficient."

The tear that plops into my palm and onto the cairngorm is hot, but not bitter.

"Just promise me you'll be ready, someday, when you get a tap on the shoulder, and you hear my voice behind you asking, 'Hey, love. Can I have five minutes more?'"

CHAPTER EIGHTEEN

BUNNY

THE DAY'S FINALLY HERE. Thank goodness my jam-packed schedule with getting everything ready has kept my brain whirling around sanitizing bottles, preparing labels, and ten thousand other details keeping me from being a Vitamix set on high over Gene.

To his credit, he's been a gentleman, as always, even when I totally chickened out and reneged on our date to the gala. My excuse wasn't a complete lie. The last-minute delays on the bottles I ordered nearly gave me an ulcer, and filling them with beer, root beer, or shrubs took me and Isaiah until midnight last night. Gene offered to come over and help, which I so badly wanted to accept, but my spine liquefied, and I assured him that "my staff" and I had it all in order.

After being mowed down by an avalanche of guilt, I caved and promised I'd sit with him at dinner. It's a small redemption, but this way, we'll be surrounded by people from the get-go. Well, we'll be surrounded by people if I can resolidify my backbone and stop hiding in Eunice's kitchen. I know he's already here. I saw him doing a final sweep of the Due West and Magnolia Moon stations as I peeked around the corner of the castle like a really bad spy skulking in the shadows.

I stuff down a too-pretty-to-eat treat and rearrange the remaining ones to hide my theft.

"What're you doing in here?" Bethanie asks, her unexpected appearance making me scream and twist around like I've been shot.

"Don't do that!"

"Do what? I have to run to my office for a list I forgot, and here you are, hiding like Cinderella with the pots and pans." She gives me an arch look. "No, wait, that's not how it happened. Cinderella got her beautiful butt out into the crowd, made everyone drop their dentures because she's too beautiful to be real, and made a prince fall in love."

"I've set my sights lower, like not throwing up all over the dance floor."

"Quit kipping the pâté, and you might avoid that."

"It was just one."

"Um-hm."

A rustle at the door makes us both turn. Bethanie appears as surprised as me to see Lorraine Pepperdine, wearing an apron emblazoned with "Grannie in the streets, dragon in the sheets" covering most of her evening dress.

"What are you girls doing here? The party's started."

This is true. The band has fired up. Early arrivers are mingling or dancing to the strains of an upbeat two-step that filters across the lawn, and I don't know how anyone could stay off the dance floor.

Anyone besides chickens like me, I suppose.

Bethanie breezes past her, obviously with no time left to waste. "I'm a woman on a mission. Lists to grab, people to pester. Coming through."

Lorraine shakes her head, casting a glance at Bethanie's not exactly ladylike race toward her office. "I understand the bee in her bonnet. What's yours?"

"Nothing at all. I'm about to head out."

My attempt at nonchalance fails. Mostly because the Grannies have a collective bullshit-ometer that no one escapes.

Lorraine crosses her arms over her chest, leaving the head of her sultry, smoking dragon peeking out at me, which was decidedly disconcerting.

"Which doesn't explain why you're here. All the beer and booze have been ready for hours now. If you're looking for an ice-cold Lone Star, this ain't where you'll get it."

I know she wants me to either laugh, or get on my way, but I do neither. "Did you know Adolphus Busch built the first large mechanized brewery in Texas in 1884, and that was the birth of Lone Star Beer? I suppose he deserves some credit for me having my very own saloon, and interesting factoid, they brewed it in a building that looks like a castle, which would have pleased Evajean, I think."

The quietest of the Grannies, which is by no means indicative that she's the shyest of the lot, glares down her nose as my babbling trails off. "Fascinating."

The polyester in the mesh of my dress had better be heat resistant, because my blush might test its melting point.

"That man's been lookin' high and low for you."

I don't pretend not to know who *that man* is. I nod, since I can't speak around the frog that's brought an oversized lily pad with him to reside in my throat.

"Get out there, then. Time's a-wastin'."

"I will. I just need another minute."

Lorraine unclasps the apron's neck strap so she can remove it without messing up the beautiful updo one of Tara's crew tamed her bright red locks into for the evening. "Girl, I'm not normally one to speak my mind too much, but I'm going to tell you something. If I'd waited for Walter Pepperdine to ask me to the Sunday Social fifty years ago, I'd still be sittin' on a shelf. Or worse, married to someone who didn't make me laugh every damn day. Quit hiding. Take your shot. It's better to know now than waste a lifetime wondering."

With usual Grannie efficiency, she hangs her apron on a hook and sails out of the room, one hand making sure her curls haven't been disturbed and the other pushing open the outer screen with fingernails painted a deep crimson that matches her dress.

Whoever said redheads can't wear red has never seen Lorraine Pepperdine dressed to the nines and about to wear out her husband's new boots before the night's over.

I don't waste a second pretending to be surprised Lorraine knows why I'm dithering. I'd bet this month's profits that most of Magnolia Bloom knows.

Such is the truth of living in a small town.

I'm in the middle of stuffing another cracker with cream cheese and a sliver of salmon into my mouth when the door opens, the music going loud again, and I turn, ready to endure Lorraine's *and another thing.*

Only it isn't Lorraine, or any of the other Grannies.

It's the man of my daydreams, and night dreams, too. Looking utterly, impossibly handsome in a Texas tuxedo. His crisp white shirt, bolo tie cinched with an etched silver slide, and a black cutaway jacket are exquisite against the deep midnight of his Wranglers and his shined-to-perfection Luccheses. He's holding his perfectly steamed Stetson in one hand, which is a good thing. If he'd had it on, I'd probably faint right here like some Victorian heroine with a fit of the vapors.

He stops inside the threshold, the music muting as the door closes. He looks as though he's as transfixed by me as I am by him. It's gratifying to see his Adam's apple move several times, as if his mouth has gone bone-dry.

That's only fair, since mine's a desert. And I have a mouthful of cracker I can neither swallow nor spit out.

"You look…. Good God, I can't find the right word. 'Stunning' is inefficient. 'Breathtaking' fits, but is hardly good enough. 'Glorious' might come close, but then again, not really." He turns his hat in his hands like he's nervous. "If you've got a thesaurus around here somewhere, I might be able to find it."

The man I've never seen remotely on edge appears a thousand times as off-center as I am. Buddy Gene Autry is standing in Eunice Greene's kitchen, blushing like a high school boy at his first prom.

Over me.

With Herculean effort, I swallow hard, and the canape drags the frog down with it. "Thank you. I could use a hand from Merriam-Webster or an old copy of Roget's myself, sir, as you are one handsome cowboy tonight."

Gene recovers, grinning and pointing to the empty spot on the tray beside me. "You know they have food outside, right? Drinks, too, I'm led to believe."

I grab a napkin and dust my hands off before I do something unbelievably gauche, like wipe my suddenly sweaty palms on my dress.

"I've heard that rumor."

"So would you care to join me in sampling some appetizers? Dinner won't be for another hour, at least."

Lorraine's voice echoes in my head. *Take your shot.*

"In a minute. Would you like to nab some of this brie with me first?"

Good God. If the fate of human civilization depends on my flirtation skills, we're doomed.

"I could be talked into that."

Hoping I don't look deranged, I take two plates from the stack staged on the counter, create the quickest canape sampler on record, and hurry to the space barely clear enough for the both of us to sit at the end of the big table.

I nudge one of my two baby carrots around with my short but perfectly painted index finger.

"Gene—"

"Bunny—"

We both laugh, but he nods. "Ladies first."

"I appreciate the chivalry because if I don't get this out, I may not be able to." I rest my hands in my lap, but crush my napkin so my fingers stop trembling.

That's the theory, anyway. Now, I have a shaking napkin.

"So, I...I wanted to say I'm sorry for being glaikit. That's one of Lexi's words, and it's now my favorite."

"And it means?"

"Foolish, thoughtless. One of about a thousand terms the Scots have for stupidity."

"I don't agree. You're none of the above."

"Oh, but I have been thoughtless. But that's because I'm nothing short of panic-stricken." I look down, abject terror about to mow me over, but I dodge it and draw my gaze up again. If I'm going to shoot my shot, I'm taking dead aim. "I go back and forth, needing to tell you I really like you and suffering from the dreadful hope I won't make a fool out of myself."

"Dreadful hope, huh?"

"Yes, abysmal. Wretched. Ghastly."

"I see." He reaches over and takes my hand, slowly bringing it to his lips and kissing my knuckles in the sweetest of gestures. Thank heaven I'm sitting, because I'm certain my knees wouldn't work. "That is the nicest thing anyone's said to me in a long time."

Not the response I was looking for, but hey, he didn't laugh.

Gene lets my hand go and reaches up to tug his earlobe. "I confess I've been a little confused sometimes. I've been afraid to get my hopes up, because for the life of me, I can't see what interests you in this used-up, old drunk."

The uncertainty in his voice drains all the wobbles out of me. With my newfound bravery, I sit up and raise my chin. "Buddy Gene Autry, that's the most foolish thing I've ever heard come out of your mouth, and you're not a man known for foolishness."

It's his turn to push around a cracker and not eat it. "I don't know how much you know about my past, but it's not pretty. I spend my days trying to do what's right, help folks where I can, be a good person, because I did a lot of things wrong. Very, very wrong. I'm not a man who deserves to have a goddess like you on his arm. Honestly? It was easier to convince myself you were being nice and pretend I was seeing things, hearing things. Things I wish I could believe, but know better than to take in."

I sit back, my gaze locked on this incredibly handsome, sexy man with so much pain behind his emerald-green eyes. Eyes usually laughing, or rolling with pretend mockery, or quietly holding the ones of whoever's talking to him.

Normally, I'd have to look away. I'm not comfortable getting this close, this real, with anyone, much less a man I'm wickedly attracted to.

"We're a pair, aren't we?" My question comes out softly, like the hand I'm holding out across the table. "Emmett teases me mercilessly about being a bottle-blond Dallas socialite, but that's galaxies away from who I am now. I was so sure you'd be like the people outside on that lawn who think they know me."

"Sounds like they knew an old you, kind of like the *me* I try to forget."

"I think we shouldn't forget who we used to be, but we shouldn't beat ourselves up anymore." I school my disbelief as he takes my hand, and I wrap my fingers around his bigger, stronger ones. I pull the warmth from him into my cold skin like precious, soothing oil. "I'd like to go out with you. Spend the evening with you. Maybe...." I swallow. Hard. "Maybe the morning? Or just see what happens?"

I'm caught in a prism of emerald and gold flecks, captured in a web of delicious crinkles at the corners of eyes that have seen too much, hurt too much.

"I'd like that very much."

He reaches between us, moving with infinite slowness, sliding his palm around my chin and cupping the back of my head as if I were the most fragile porcelain, and he's using the utmost care not to damage me. But I'm not fragile, and I'm not porcelain, so when his lips touch mine, I reach out and pull him to me to let him know how much I want this.

Him.

With a strength I knew he had, but never saw in action, he lifts me from my seat and settles me in his lap. I have zero objections, snuggling in and shifting my arms to pull him even closer.

Minutes pass. Hours? Days? Not sure. Don't care. My lipstick's far beyond repair, but who cares? Apparently not Gene.

The music's suddenly louder. Knowing we're busted, we stop our tongue swapping, but neither of us moves.

"Don't mind me." Eunice breezes into the room. "I need to check on the extra champagne for the dais stored in the pantry."

I press my forehead to his, and we both giggle like high schoolers.

"Well, this is awkward." Gene's voice is deep and husky, and I have plenty of proof he's as...moved as I am. I slip from his lap and tug at the seams of my dress, shifting them back to their proper alignment. He stands as well and holds out his palm. "Dance with me?"

I realize Eunice didn't close the main door, just the screen to keep the bugs out, and the notes of a slow rumba float into the kitchen.

I accept his invitation, and he pulls me in tight, trapping our clasped hands between our bodies as he slides a warm arm around my back. I nestle my cheek on his collar and from the first step, our bodies are in perfect sync, moving as if we've been dance partners for years.

As his cheek settles against my forehead, I feel something inside me thaw and a tiny bud of hope unfurl.

CHAPTER NINETEEN

BETHANIE

I'M a little breathless by the time I make it back to the tent. I came to a screeching halt as I was about to barrel back through the kitchen, because I heard Gene's voice, then Bunny's, and I'd be a monkey's uncle before I'd interrupt whatever's starting in there.

I hope it's good, and not merely because I'm Bunny's head cheerleader. I'm Gene's, too. He's a good man, and even though he's decades ahead of me on the recovery highway, there are some wounds that take ages to heal, if they ever do. I want him to be happy just as much as Bunny, but I'm the last human on earth who can give advice on matters of the heart.

As the hours roll by, my shoulders relax more and more from their climb to my ears. The mini *DWTS* is a complete success, with everyone laughing in a good way over the merchants' number. The oohs and gasps awarded the finale numbers with Svetlana and Viktor turn into thunderous applause.

Mr. A-List Comedian keeps his language tame enough to earn us a soft-R rating, but he's not so crass as to spoil the evening.

Then, ah, then, Ally takes the stage, and while I don't want to be avaricious, I feel wallets open wide by the time she finishes her set.

I'm in the back, one of Bunny's amazing shrubs in an ice-cold glass in my hand, when a tall shadow blocks the light. I didn't know there was such a thing as a dress police uniform, but apparently there is, and damn if I don't need a bib as I take in that much studmuffinness in one glance. And my next thought is how, by all that's holy, is the man not sweating like a steamer at the dry cleaners while he's wearing black wool head to toe, white gloves, and patent leather shoes so shiny I could fix my lipstick in my reflection? I know darn well those suckers are uncomfortable and not exactly known for breathability.

He doesn't say a word, content to help me hold up the back tent pole while the auctioneer rattles off his hundred-mile-an-hour shtick. He turns to me, his eyebrows nearly touching his hairline when the painting of Gavina's that Juliette restored to breathtaking beauty goes for damn near half a million dollars. It's a grand finale by all accounts.

"Wow." That's the sum total of what I can say as the crowd starts to exit their seats, and the band takes the stage again. From here on, it's all music all night, and we got through without a single bobble.

I rap my own forehead with my knuckle.

"What was that for?" Roy's trademark growly voice sounds confused.

"I jinxed myself. Quick, let's go get something to drink, so I can escape the curse."

I hear a muttered, "Ooookay," but he doesn't argue, instead offering his elbow and escorting me across the huge floor quickly becoming one giant dance space as the catering crew whisks away tables and chairs with nearly silent precision.

We both take ginger shrubs, and our new vantage point gives us a clear view of Kiki and Harville. They're hugging each other like they won the lottery. Lexi and Logan are doing their own high five. Wyatt leans over to plant a giant kiss on Emmett's ecstatic face as the auctioneer directs the art crew to take the painting that's stolen the show inside for packing.

"You did it, Bethanie."

Gratitude surges through me, but I shake my head. "You know as well as I do that this took a village. I'm superduper happy I got to be a part of it, is all."

"No false modesty. Not tonight."

He takes a step toward the open floor, and I frown in confusion as he takes off his gloves, stowing them under the belt holding his jacket against his sigh-inducing body. Then he holds out his hand.

"I want to dance. With you. Just once."

Every nerve I have shorts out in one spectacular supernova. I have no idea how long it is before my mouth finally moves, my brain automatically defaulting to humor. "Have you been bingeing George Strait again?" Or nipping the Dripping Springs Vodka while I wasn't looking?

"Maybe, but he isn't the first man to whisper those words to a beautiful woman, and I don't want to waste my chance. I know I shouldn't. I know we shouldn't, but indulge me."

My fingers could whip cream into butter right then and there if I were holding a whisk, but he doesn't tease me. He takes me into a proper dance frame, and with a synchronicity I can't believe is possible, we waltz like we've got skates on and the floor is polished ice.

I've danced a lot this past year. Fridays at the Moon are an institution around here, and it's crazy how much fun this is when you're not falling over your feet like a buffoon, or passed out in your car in the parking lot. Turns out I'm pretty good at it, too. So much so that I only sit out a song if I want to.

But this.

Wow. This.

Our bodies brush as we turn, and I miss the momentary contact with an ache when he spins me so effortlessly I feel like Svetlana has inhabited my body for a moment. Thing is, I don't care how sexy our Russian dancer is, small-town police chief Roy Hilton makes my brain go, *Viktor who?*

The song is coming to an end, making my heart break, but he sends me out, then spins me back, taking my back and my waist and bending me over his balanced knee in a dip that I don't have time to fight.

And nothing can stop me from feeling like I've lassoed the moon I can see outside the open tent wall and pulled it into my heart.

He brings me up with as much ease as he let me down, and I'm wondering if the ambulance is still staged out of sight, because I need a tank of oxygen, two probably better.

"Roy—"

My prophecy chooses that instant to come true. Maybe I need to thank the car alarm that starts blaring from the parking lot, because at least this way I don't say something I can never take back.

"Stay here." His growl is back at full strength.

Ah, well, fairy tales always end. Mine just a little sooner than I wished.

But as to staying here, not a chance. I changed from my heels into my much lower, but still pretty, sandals hours ago, so at least I'm not in danger of breaking my neck as I run after him hell-bent for leather.

The good news is, the situation is easily resolved.

Roy yanks the keys from Digby Kingsley's sloppy-drunk hand and silences the Bentley's insanely loud siren that Dear Old Digby obviously set off when he fell against the door before sliding to the ground. Roy helps the stupid-rich realtor from Dallas to his feet, leaning away from the breath assaulting him as Digby pats the gold shield right at eye level.

"Right ho, my good man. I'll take those now."

Why the hell Digby puts on a pretend English accent when he's eight sheets to the wind, none of us has ever figured out. Roy waves away the two of his men who come to a skidding stop a few feet away. As they leave, he holds the keys out of Digby's reach and pushes him back against the car, but I'm impressed it's with far less force than our illustrious police chief wants to use, based on the look in his eyes.

"Digby, you idiot. You can't drive."

"What, what? 'Course I can."

"Listen up. You tell me who to go get from inside, or what cab service you want to use, but unless you want to sleep this off in my jail, you'd better not touch the door to this car. Right now, the only thing I can cite you for is public intoxication, but we'll let it slide if you get your ass home without touching a steering wheel. Otherwise, we add driving under the influence and endangering a public servant."

"Now listen here, old chap—"

"Cut the shit, Digby. You've got one chance. I suggest you take it."

With surprising swiftness, Digby regains his balance and nods, wobbling only the slightest bit as he heads back to the festivities to find, I assume, Poppy. Why they weren't leaving together is neither my business nor my concern.

Quiet falls around us except for the crunch of gravel under the wheels of other cars leaving the estate. I pray none of those drivers is impaired, but I'm reminded, brutally, that I have no control over any of that. Our bartenders have a crew of bouncers in the wings to confiscate keys and escort anyone who goes too far out of the area.

When it's clear Digby isn't going to try to do an end run and retrieve the spare key we both know is hidden somewhere on this showroom machine, Roy rounds on me.

"I told you to stay at the tent."

"Yes, you did. And I didn't."

"You could have been hurt. What if this was some crazy robbery gone wrong? There's enough money in here tonight to tempt who knows what element."

"Which is why I have public security, a la you standing right in front of me, several of your off-duty officers, and a host of private contractors who are in full ninja stealth mode around the castle and the grounds."

His growl precedes, "I'm aware. I signed off on the plan."

"That's right, you did." I put a full golly-gee-shucks tone in my voice.

"Bethanie, you are the most stubborn, pigheaded—"

"Nothing new there, Roy. You've known this about me for ten years."

"I guess for a minute I thought—"

"Well, you thought wrong."

I about-face and start walking, desperate to put space between my heart and the almost-perfect moment that almost happened.

CHAPTER TWENTY

LEXI

KIKI'S HUG, followed by Bethanie's, practically cracks a rib. And I couldn't care less. I'm still flying too high to even acknowledge how sore my feet will be tomorrow.

It's been a long night. A long, wonderful night, and exhaustion aside, it's sad to see all the people working with impressive precision to take down the event site. It took days to get it all put up, and now it's almost gone.

A shadow falls over me before a bottle appears in front of me, and the very essence of a tall, dark, handsome man takes a seat beside me.

"These are the last two of Bunny's best label."

"Well, bless you for being quick, then."

I clink rims with Logan and take a grateful sip of the ice-cold elixir, testament that it was at the bottom of the bin all night.

We're almost alone under the huge tent he'll have hauled away in a day or so. For tonight, for now, it's us, the sparkly lights, and the quiet of the night broken only by the remaining cleanup crew doing their work. We're agog that Kiki left an hour ago, and I even convinced

Bethanie that I truly wanted a few more minutes out here before heading to a hot shower and a soft bed.

And, if I have to confess, I also wanted a few minutes with Logan without five hundred people milling about.

"I'm beside myself how well the night went." Beside. Behind. In front of.

"Pretty telling you went from sure you couldn't do this to a modern major general, wrangling this whole thing into fine form."

"No shinin' me up, Logan. I was part of an amazing team. I'm still gobsmacked, feeling I was in a walking, talking jewelry store."

He gives me his irresistible one-sided smile. "Don't be impressed. Half the people in here were more in love with their tiaras or tie clips than each other." He shakes his head and slugs back a healthy mouthful of lager. "Don't mind me. I have to be careful I don't become the bitter brother I'm told I am."

"By your brother the actor, I take it."

"Yeah. My mom's birthday is coming up, and he texted to tell me he has Somewhere Very Important to be and can't be there, and would I pick something up for him on my way and throw his name on the card."

"He's a right bawbag, then."

Logan coughs a laugh, his eyes twinkling at me.

"What?" I open mine as wide as I can. "I said I was around the posh all night, not that I am one. I'm more comfortable talking to folks about their loos being backed up than their new Maserati sports car."

"Which is one of many reasons I enjoyed spending most of the evening with you."

Joy courses through my veins on the heels of the alcohol bubbles. "It was rather perfect. I even enjoyed our silly dance."

"Silly? I beg your pardon. I was the quintessential cowboy coming home to my lady love after a long cattle drive."

"Absolutely! I had no problem imagining you on a horse in a ten-gallon hat."

"That's better."

Maybe it's the quiet. Maybe it's the darkness. Maybe it's the beer. Who knows? But I lean toward him and wrap my arms around him.

It's a stereotype, but no one expects a man so muscular to be graceful, but once again, Logan has proven everyone wrong. I should be grateful he took me out on the floor the five times he did, but in his defense, my dance card was delightfully full, too.

"I'm sorry we didn't get in that cha-cha you wanted."

"It's all right. I got a waltz, and that's better."

He shifts so my head is on the pillow of his chest and slides his arm down my back to tug me closer. I sigh, wondering if this feeling is what heaven is like.

"Would you like to dance again?"

His voice is a deep rumble under my ear, and I nuzzle my cheek against him to absorb every last note. "I'd love to, but we'd have to move, and more importantly, the musicians have left."

"Oh, ye of little faith."

Slipping away from me, he nabs his phone from the tabletop and heads toward the sound stage, fiddling with something, and a moment later, the strains of *I Don't Want To Miss a Thing* fill the night. I smile, knowing darn well he's picked a song that can be danced almost in place, if someone was so inclined. I volunteer to be such a someone.

A while a thousand people might find his choice corny. I'm not one.

I find it deeply touching, and I need to send a thank you note to Aerosmith for giving me the perfect song where we can be so close together water couldn't come between us. Any judgy people can go find the bartender and ask for a lemon to suck on.

Feeling like I'm in a dream, I walk toward him, and he spins me in with an expert twist of his wrist.

"That was very fancy, sir." My voice is a little muffled, as I've rested my forehead on his collarbone and buried my nose in the placket of his shirt. He should smell like sweat and a long night. Instead, I inhale bliss.

"I always save my best moves for last."

Now that sounds promising.

Of course, his leads are easy to follow, but then again, it's hard to mess up when we're doing basic boxes so our bodies can stay snuggled together. I shift back to that yummy place high on his chest, as if that shoulder was carved out just for me. When he tilts his head so his cheek rests on my hair, I declare the night perfect.

When the song ends, as they all have to, I reluctantly pull away.

He looks down at me, those eyes so deep and dark I nearly drown in them, and his face turns serious. "I'm so sorry to do this, but there's been an emergency."

I look around, my pulse going from languid to heart attack, and I'm sure my expression is wild. "Emergency? What? Where?"

"Right here. The emergency is I can't wait any longer to kiss you."

My breath comes in a pant of both relief and an entirely different sort of panic. These last weeks have been filled tip to top with unending tasks, and yet, we found minutes to carve out together. The lessons for our routine were loads of fun, filled with laughter and teasing that kept the evenings from being intimate.

This, though, is everything those were not. This is quiet. Alone. Soft.

He's clearly waiting for me to respond, so I lean back, meeting his eyes. "I'd like that, but I'm terrified."

His brow furrows. "That I'll hurt you?"

"Nae, silly man. I'm terrified because, for all intents and purposes, I've been kissed by one man in my entire life. I'm not afraid of *you*. I'm afraid of *me*. That I'll be terrible."

His low rumble, that signature laugh, hits me in my belly because we're still stitched together in the middle of an empty floor. "You say the funniest things, Lexi."

"I'm nae trying to be funny."

"I know, but it never fails to amaze me that you have no idea how incredible you are, how beautiful, how sexy."

"I'm—"

"Don't even think about arguing with me. When you came down the steps to the lawn a few hours ago, I would have sworn the moon had risen early. You're a vision in that dress, like you've been bathed in moonlight. And all night, I've watched you reflect your glow onto everyone around you."

I feel like the sun is scorching my neck, not its evening counterpart. "Who knew, on top of all your other skills, that you're a poet?"

He shakes his head at my attempt to deflect. "One look at you made me want to be one. I've spent weeks waiting, and finally I feel I have the chance to do what I've wanted to do since the moment you walked into the gym."

I push a hand between us so I can brush my fingertips over his jaw, trace them down his neck, rest my palm over his heart.

"I'd like that."

He doesn't wait, or let me waffle. His head bends down, mine bends back, and when our lips meet, I gasp.

I expected our first kiss to be like everything about him. Quiet. A little shy. Reserved.

Oh, no.

This is heat and demand and need.

He uses one of those strong hands to shift my head so he can explore more, his tongue diving against mine, inviting—no, demanding —that I meet him back.

Every muscle, every nerve ending, every synapse is on fire. For him.

I'm breathless and consumed.

I've never been more alive in my life.

When he pulls away, both our hearts are beating so wildly I'm afraid we'll rock the tent poles.

"Lexi, I want you."

Now is not the time to dither. No more. "I want you, too."

"Would you come home with me?"

"I could, but I have a lovely suite right there." I tip my head toward the castle, which seems both so close and a thousand kilometers away.

He rests his forehead against mine and chuffs a laugh. "That sounds wonderful, but I don't have any protection with me."

Well, now, that's not something I was thinking of. I haven't thought about it for about twenty years.

"I had a hysterectomy, so I haven't had to think about birth control in two decades."

"It's not that, per se. I don't want you to worry about anything. I haven't been with anyone in a long time, but we can't pretend these days that it doesn't matter."

"This isn't something I thought I'd be talking about in my wildest dreams, but Douglas is the only man I've ever been with, but if you think it'd be best, we can wait—"

"No…I mean, I've been tested so I'm safe. I just don't want you to have any doubts."

"I don't."

He lets me go, moving far enough away to look at me again. "Have I spoiled everything?"

"What? You really are daft."

"I tried to tell you I'm no alley cat Lothario. I'm more awkward Austin Powers than suave James Bond."

"Thank the stars. I'm grateful for a little equal footing, then."

He reaches over, using both palms to frame my face and pull me in for another kiss. "I really do want you."

I nod toward the turrets. "Then why are we dallying?"

Every dream I've had of being swept off my feet comes true as he breaks away and swipes my legs out from underneath me, lifting me into his arms and twirling me around—as if I wasn't already dizzy enough—and marching across the east lawn. No amount of protest makes him put me down, and it isn't until we're standing outside the door to my little apartment and he lets my body slide down the length of his that I'm standing once more.

"Are you sure?"

Ah, bless him, this man. "Aye, Logan, I'm sure."

I unlock the door, and despite my yelp, he picks me up again and kicks the door shut behind us as he heads for my bedroom.

With fingers that shouldn't be quite so nimble, he plucks the pins from my hair and threads his fingers through the released length as his mouth roams between my lips, my neck, my throat. My ears. My nose. My forehead.

Those fingers are equally adept with my zipper, and with the moonlight streaming through the window as if Mother Nature has decided I need a spotlight, my dress pools to my feet.

I'm not nearly so smooth as I unbutton the shirt that's been in the way of my imagination all evening. He takes pity on me and shucks it and his pants so I can move into the arms of the man who looks as though he'd like to devour me.

I pull his head to mine and let him know I'm entirely on board with that decision.

CHAPTER TWENTY-ONE

BUNNY

Is it possible to actually walk on air? I'm beginning to think so as my repaired Jimmy Choos don't feel like they're touching the floor when I glide over to let Emmett in for our morning coffee.

"Well, looks like somebody got laid last night."

I squinch my nose at my confidant as we take seats at the front table, and I slide his mocha frap to him. Dani gave me almost as much grief on our catch-up call when she chewed me out for waiting so long to tell her all the details.

I didn't give her all of them, and neither will I spill my entire bag of beans to my nosy friend.

"And the night before. And the night before that."

The week since the gala has been a bit exhausting…in the best way possible. I didn't think Gene and I would move so quickly, but once we broke the seal, all bets were off. I was nervous, beyond petrified, and Gene was…Gene. Wonderful. Warm. Understanding.

And damn, the guy has moves. At the gala, his term was *used-up,* but I can testify the term doesn't remotely apply to the Richard Gere of

Magnolia Bloom. I'd say he was *saving up*, and I'm the lucky lotto winner.

The bell over the door tinkles, stopping the remarks I know are coming, and I smile at the delivery man who's bringing me an envelope marked Express. I'm not expecting anything, so I'm even more intrigued than Emmett as I sign for the package.

When the door shuts, Emmett stabs at the table. "Hurry up already."

"Listen, Mr. Bossypants, this might not be something I want to share with you."

He sniffs. "As if."

I don't bother retorting and rip the mystery missive open. I pull out a small stack of documents and read the top letter, then rifle through the attachments.

"For the love of...." Emmett is practically growling. "What is it?"

"It's an offer to buy Due West." I fall against the back of my chair. To say I'm stunned is an understatement.

With a complete lack of his usual grace, Emmett dives for the papers and starts reading.

"Damn, girl. That's some offer."

"Seems a little high, don't you think? For a little craft bar in a tiny town?"

Emmett takes my question seriously and considers it for a long minute, shelving his usual shenanigans and becoming all business. "Possibly, but there were a lot of investors at the gala. That's what the event was for, right? Not only to bring backing to the hospital, but to grow the town as a whole."

"True, but I wasn't expecting this."

"You've been making noises about leaving MB."

"Yeah, but not loud ones. And how would Ms. Investor from Denver have heard?"

Emmett purses his lips, rereading the summation. "Who cares? You know how fast gossip travels in this town. Someone may have told someone who told their second cousin who told their—"

"I get it. It's still shocking such blabbering garnered this much interest."

Reaching into his jacket pocket, Emmett pulls out his phone and spends a minute madly typing. Then he gives a little whistle and pushes the screen toward me.

"Maybe this explains it."

I skim the story about a trust-fund baby who prides herself on investing in the Next Big Thing before anyone gets wind of the opportunity.

"I'm not sure I want to sell to someone who wants to commercialize everything about Magnolia Bloom."

He nods, but adds, "I don't, either, but we can't have it both ways. We can't want the town to grow and then rebuff the people who want to invest. I have a reasonable expectation that between the city council and the business association, we'll keep a mix and maintain our hometown feel."

"I hope you're right."

"Of course I'm right."

I snort. "Thank you, Baron Smartass."

"Please, if you're going to give me a royal title, I'm at least a duke."

"Well, Your Royal Dukeness, what should I do?"

"Say no, obviously."

"Obviously?"

"Saying yes would mean you have more money than half the state, and then you'll leave. So toss these puppies in the trash."

I hear the fear behind his glib nonsense. We've become close over this half decade, and the realization of what taking this offer would mean isn't lost on me.

But isn't it what I've wanted for years? To prove my brain isn't peroxide-pickled? Haven't I wanted success in business to sort of be my Princess Diana's revenge dress, wanting to casually flaunt it in front of the Dallas glitterati with my version of, *What? This old thing?*

The bell tinkles again, and I'm afraid to look. What is it this time? An armored car with pallets of gold bullion?

Emmett solves my dilemma by saying, "Hey, BG. Nice to see you."

My friend, of course, has taken the Buddy/Gene thing to another level, combining his initials, which no one in the entire town does. Ever.

"Emmett, looking dapper as usual." Gene advances to the table and offers his hand, which Emmett takes, adding a wink with his handshake. Gene's return grin doesn't pretend to misunderstand.

What is it with dudes?

My second-best bestie and my first-best lover are entirely too cocky. "All right, you two, cut it out."

They both give me entirely too innocent *what?* expressions.

Emmett, damn him, stands and announces, "Time to go. Besides, y'all have a lot to talk about."

He abandons me and Gene looks at me with open curiosity.

Grabbing at any way to get my thoughts in order, I snatch Emmett's cup and head for the kitchen. "Coffee?" I toss over my shoulder.

"Sure."

I know he takes it black, so I don't buy much time, but at least the two minutes it takes to return to the front room let me get enough air in my lungs to stop gasping like a beached fish.

I didn't intentionally leave the paperwork on the table, but the damage is done when I put the cup of hot Texas pecan in front of him.

He looks up slowly, no hint of what he's thinking revealed on his handsome face. "I apologize if I wasn't supposed to read this. I sat down, and it was kind of hard to ignore."

I sit, fidgeting with my mug. "It's all right. I would have talked with you about it eventually. It arrived not twenty minutes ago, so I'm still in stunned mode." I scoot the pile closer to him. "Go ahead and read it, or I can give you the gist."

"Do that."

The basics, including numbers and time line, are covered quickly, and Gene's face goes from interested to grave to worried. "I guess the obvious question is, what do you want?"

Before I can stop it, as I have a thousand times before, my mouth blurts, "A baby."

His entire body goes still, and he blinks a good four times before he speaks. "Wait, what? I don't recall that being in the letter."

My "ha-ha, very funny" comes out strained and not at all amused. "My head's going in a thousand directions, all because of the what-ifs this has brought up, and you're right. The question is obvious, and I went from having enough money to grind my ex's face into the dirt to having a baby to, hell, I don't know, building orphanages in Uzbekistan."

"Crazy money would let you do all of the above." He takes a sip of coffee, wincing at the temperature. I forgot to warn him. "So, you want children?"

"I haven't thought past one, but if not children plural, a child singular would be amazing."

"With that offer, you could have a whole basketball team and have plenty left over for nose-grinding."

I wobble my head left, then right. "I suppose. I guess my revenge fantasies mean I'm not quite as mature as I pretend to be."

"I'm not sure any of us are when given the chance to actually do the things we've imagined. Most of the time, we're stuck with surreal scenarios we know can never play out."

"Which is probably a good thing."

"Definitely a good thing."

"So…what do you think?"

Of all the things I'm not expecting, it's him standing up, his energy an unmistakable tangle of agitation and uncertainty. Gene is known for his calm demeanor and placid nature, not looking like he'd choose a trip to Saturn without a space suit if given the option.

"Bunny, you've got a wonderful offer in your hands that could make several long-held dreams come true. But I'm not the person who can come with you on any of those journeys. I don't want to enter the rarefied world of big money, and I failed miserably at the one chance I had at parenthood." He runs an agitated hand through his hair. "More than anything, I want you to be happy, but I'm not the right person to help you, if this is what you want."

I sit, speechless, when he leans down and kisses the top of my head.

And leaves me...

Shattered.

CHAPTER TWENTY-TWO

LEXI

I SNUGGLE into the perfect hollow where his massive arm attaches to the pillow of his chest. I've claimed this space every night since the gala. The fact it's morning, and we're at his place, takes a minute to process. The small apartment I'm using felt comfortable from the moment I'd opened the door, and I easily settled in. Spending time at Logan's is a different animal, and I still look around his beautiful home and wonder if this all isn't a dream.

Instead of one of the renovated Victorians so popular in Magnolia Bloom, his midcentury modern design fits him perfectly. The living room has a wall of pristine windows that make me jealous at how light and airy the room feels, and his furniture was clearly selected for comfort, yet is still impressive. I appreciated the luxury of the surrounding well-tended acreage, teasing him when he showed me around that my home in Bearsden would fit in one corner of this space, and by local standards, I have a roomy setup. At home, though, only the posh set can afford this much land.

He took my roasting in stride when I asked if he was half-owner in a landscaping company, too, as I waved my hand toward the lush foliage and the deep green of his lawn. I shook my head at his to-be-expected, "Yes, but I do most of this myself. It may be cliché, but it helps me decompress to come out here and dig around in the dirt."

He proceeded to tease me back, saying it's my fault things are getting a little weedy outside, because he's been too busy attending to the beautiful things inside.

I'm getting a little more comfortable with his easy flattery, but I can't say it's natural yet.

A warm kiss to the top of my head and the accelerated heart rate under my ear alerts me he's awake, and the whole scene is as yummy as warm scones and jam in bed.

"Do you want to talk about him?"

Of all the questions I thought Logan might ask, this one's definitely last. Then again, Logan has defied my expectations at every turn. I still can't believe I'm shagging a man almost too handsome to be real, yet I find him to be the kindest soul I've ever met.

"Douglas?"

"Are there any other *hims* you'd like to discuss?"

I search for a centimeter of fat to pinch and fail, settling for tickling a man with abs that could be used to bend copper piping. "I'm nae sure I said I wanted to cover this subject at all."

He shifts so we're on our sides, face to face in the insanely comfortable bed he ordered to fit his tall frame. Bunching a soft pillow under my head, I settle in. The old me would have run away, probably to the kitchen to start coffee or breakfast, or to the laundry room to tackle the ever-present loads of wash. Avoiding emotional turmoil is something I excel at, having practiced my entire life, but a week of spending every spare minute with him has changed me. To his credit, he didn't bring up Douglas before now.

Rolling toward me, he plants a long, slow kiss on my happily waiting lips, then settles back. "I don't want to be pushy, but I figured maybe we'd tackle it sooner rather than later."

Later is the elephant in the room we haven't touched—me going home. I haven't broached the subject because I don't know what any of this means, or what I want, or what my options even are.

In my continued crusade of no dithering, I decide to dive right in. The proposition's like going for a swim in a loch too late in the summer. You risk hypothermia, but it's better to get it over with, as tiptoeing in is worse torture.

"I'm not sure what you'd like to know. I met him when I was sixteen. He was a mate of my sister's boyfriend at the time, and we married a few months after I graduated high school. We have our two weans, with Travis coming along a little sooner than we planned, but we had no regrets, and after we had Sadie, we decided two was enough. As to the rest of our lives, it was all entirely normal. Raising kids, building a business, staying busy."

"But you said the other night you were fighting being angry."

I didn't mean to tell him that, but we stopped by Bunny's for a pint, and the little nugget of unintended sharing slipped out.

I trace the mound of his bicep, accentuated by the fact he has his arm curled, and he's resting his unfairly gorgeous head on his hand. He brings my fingers to his mouth and gives my thumb a gentle bite that makes me shiver, but he doesn't say another word, or do any of the things bursting in my head.

"I'm struggling with a lot of things." I stop. Do I really want to go there? Confide these things I can't yet accept myself? I meet his eyes, and there's nothing but kindness staring back at me. Well, shite. Might as well go on with it. "I didnae know I was supposed to have a midlife crisis. Before he died, and before I met you, I was content with my life. Now I'm trying to sort through all these feelings. Were things perfect? As Eunice says, *Pish*. They never are, but damn it, I was happy. Now I'm doubting everything, from being too scared to go to uni on my own, to wondering if I've taken the easy way and coasted for nearly thirty years."

"What did you want to study?"

His question makes me realize I talked with Bunny about my sister and the choices I made, but I haven't covered this topic with him.

"I wanted to be a chemist. My family life was a bit wobbly, but science appealed to me because it makes sense. When you put X with Y, the result is going to be Z whether you want it to be something else or not. To change the outcome, you have to change the input. But what point would it serve now? It's a little late."

"Is it? Modern thinking about second-life careers has turned on its head. You could do whatever you want. What about becoming a pharmacist? MB's going to need more than Palmer's Drugs when the hospital's finished."

"Your question implies I'm staying in Magnolia Bloom. I have a home to go back to."

"I'm saying you have options, things to consider you might not have considered before."

Before now.

Before you.

My phone buzzes, and I roll to reach for it. I don't have set office hours or anything, but I do tend to let Bethanie know when she can expect me. Because the event ended doesn't mean the work's done.

To my surprise, the text isn't from anyone associated with the castle. It's from DeWayne Tomlinson. He's coming back to Texas for a visit that coincides with Halloween and wants to take me out. These past few weeks have changed me more than I realized, because instead of immediately dismissing the sweet invitation, I'm touched. And flattered, to be honest. DeWayne isn't movie-star handsome like the man patiently waiting for me, but he's definitely good-looking and has all the other attributes I like. Kindness. Humor. Manners.

"Bad news?" Logan's question makes me look away from the screen.

"Nothing like that."

"But you're frowning and smiling at the same time."

Do I tell the man I'm in bed with that another man has asked me out on a date? That seems wrong, but the devil that sits on my shoulder some days scoffs, asking me why I'm censoring my answer. The angel on the other tells me to keep quiet.

I opt for a lane down the middle. "It's from the nice gentleman I shared a row with on the flight over. He's from Dallas, although he's stationed in England in your Air Force. He's coming back and will be here at Halloween."

"So invite him to the shindig at the castle. It's a great event."

I look away, despite my determination to be honest. "That's the thing. He'd like to take me out."

He goes still. Not cold, just...anticipatory. It seems obvious something of the kind would be coming from the turn in our conversation, so it requires a lot of my newfound confidence to remain silent. More important, to stay here in his bed, breathing in the citrusy remainders of his aftershave, waiting for...what? His approval? His disapproval? Why do I care either way?

To say I've never been in this situation is patently understated.

"Do you want to go out with him?"

The question makes it impossible to hide from the fact I dove right into Logan's arms the second I accepted he was attracted to me. Moreover, I'm lying here with him, talking about the future. Even if all of this is hypothetical, I'm doing exactly what I did with Douglas. Started planning things around a man.

All my newfound self-assurance dies between one breath and the next. I've enjoyed endless days of seeing things in a different light, seeing myself in a different light, and now I'm one raw, live wire, and the anger I felt toward Douglas becomes a haze of frustration at the whole world. It's not Logan in particular, I know that, but it doesn't stop me from rolling out of bed and throwing on my clothes.

He watches me, his confusion clear, but he neither follows me out of the room nor tries to stop me. He leaves me alone with my uncertainty, letting me whirl in my thoughts on the back porch with a cup of coffee barely touched on the crackle-finished plexiglass top of his outdoor table.

"Can I join you?"

How a man that big can be so quiet's unnerving.

"Of course. I'm sorry about that."

"Don't apologize. I opened the subject, so I can't be upset about how the conversation turns."

"Honestly? I had no idea any of that was going to bubble up."

"I'm glad you were honest with me, even if it's not the answer I wanted."

I mentally retraced our conversation. "I gave you an answer?"

"Absolutely. You might not have said the words, but it seems pretty clear you aren't ready for anything serious yet." He sits down, his cup so warm there's a hint of steam above the rim of the stoneware. "To be clear, I'm not asking for the rest of your life. I'm asking for the rest of your time here. If, though, you need to sow some wild oats, I heartily volunteer to be your International Harvester, but if you need to visit some other fields, I'll admit it won't thrill me, but I'll understand."

Despite myself, a burst of laughter escapes. "That's the funniest thing I've ever heard."

"Isn't sowing wild oats the quintessential bad analogy for—"

"Shagging around? Indeed, it is, but my funny bone's tickled at your offer to be my, um, personal tractor."

"The offer stands, but I'll warn you, sleeping around—hell, even casual dating—isn't like Hollywood portrays it. For me, anyway."

"What is it like for you, then?"

"Lonely."

He's got that long, glazed look, his focus far at the end of his property. My heart squeezes, confounded at his answer. It isn't what I expected and confirms that, once again, I've stereotyped someone based on looks. Knowing Bunny should have broken me of that embarrassing habit.

I reach over, taking his hand and pulling it into my lap, my fingers threaded through his.

"Logan?" He blinks himself to rights and turns his head to me. As usual, I get lost in those deep, warm, melty brown depths and almost can't ask what I need to know. I push through, realizing I've had more heartfelt, emotionally laden words with him in a few hours than I've had in my entire life. "Why would you wait? Why would you want to?"

"Because I always said I'd know when I'd met the right person. And now I do. I don't want to chase you away, but I also don't want any shadows interfering, if this ends up the way I hope it will."

"You're disgustingly perfect, you know."

His head moves in a slow side to side that makes my eyes widen.

"Wrong. I'm deeply, horribly selfish. Until you're sure, you need to understand I won't be anyone's second choice. I won't be anyone's convenience. I won't be anyone's coin flip. And I won't be anyone's regret."

Using both hands, he slides his fingers into my hair and pulls me to him so he can kiss me with promise, longing.

And hope.

CHAPTER TWENTY-THREE

BETHANIE

I FEEL horrible even acknowledging the thought, but I'm jealous of Bunny and Lexi. I wish I wasn't. I want them both to be deliriously happy, but I didn't get the Disney ending at the gala. They did. Hands down, they both deserve it, but it doesn't stop the pulse of wistfulness from sneaking in.

A two-pop knock on my office door precedes Nathanial sauntering in and throwing himself into one of my guest chairs.

I arch a brow. "By all means, come in and make yourself at home." I pretend to read something on my computer. "Oh, no, you're not inter-rupting. I don't have a thing to do, so your unplanned, unannounced, and uninvited intrusion into my space is delightful."

"I need help."

That's the thing with Nathanial. In his world, he's the sun, and everyone orbits around him. Since he's handsome, affable, and usually a laugh riot, he generally gets away with it. Unfortunately for him, today is not the day to yank on my last nerve.

"Sorry, I don't have a psychology degree. Oh, wait, is this about getting your balls back from Eunice?"

"Got 'em last week, but don't make me remind you that jokes are my arena."

My lifted brow descends into a full frown. When I got sober, the universe seemed determined to throw me into Nathanial's path. We'd find ourselves at the lunch counter at Peaches and Pie at the same time, in line at the post office, at JJ's gassing up our respective vehicles, even at the tax office when I had to go down in person because I waited too long to register my car by mail. In the beginning, I had this weird feeling in my stomach I was missing some cosmic romantic sign. Turns out, the cosmos reckoned I needed a friend much more than I needed someone to test the bed springs with.

He mumbles something, and I cup my hand behind my ear. "What?"

"I need you to give Eunice this final report, and Lexi's not in her office. So you have to do it."

He hands me a health and safety report, and in the highlighted box, I see the number 99.

"For the love of Sonic ice, why are you being a chickenshit about giving Eunice a certificate with a ninety-nine on it? That's superb, isn't it?"

While his voice is deep, the grumble that comes out is unintelligible, and not because of decibel levels.

"Dude, seriously, what?"

"She's gonna take my balls back."

"It's a ninety-nine!"

"And I brought it up from the ninety-seven I had to give her last year that still provides me with a semiannual circumcision, but even you might notice the score is still only two digits."

"What's keeping her from a hundred?"

"You mean besides the fact that this castle is over a hundred and fifty years old, and it's damn near impossible, even with all the amazing improvements they've done?"

"So why don't you give her that last point for effort and call it good?"

He swings one of his legs over the arm of the chair and folds his arms over his chest. "Because as much as I love having a bat to go with my balls, I've never fudged a report, and I'm not starting now."

He offers his admirable explanation like it's a bad thing, and I shake my head. He's every bit his brother's twin in one regard. They might have spectrum-opposite personalities, but neither of the Hilton boys will bend so much as a gnat's hair on their integrity.

"Better man up and get it over with. She's downstairs getting ready for Cammie's bachelorette party tonight."

He tries to use puppy eyes on me, but all it gets him is a talk-to-the-hand palm response.

"No."

"Come on, Nee. She loves you."

"And she almost always loves you."

"'Almost always' will be my death, or at least render me anatomically inaccurate."

"Did you think to bring her a jug of her favorite protein powder? Or some energy bars? Or a sexy sweatband?"

"Sweatbands are sexy?"

"Do not ask the woman who grew up in the Richard-Simmons-slash-Jane-Fonda era of exercise if headbands are cool or not."

"Duly noted. Still doesn't help me."

"Not my job."

"You are a mean woman."

"Only when I won't help you wiggle out of your dilemma du jour."

His sigh could power a sailboat across Lake Maggie. "Then I'm not going to accidentally get caught kissing you to make Roy jealous."

He finger-quotes *accidentally*.

The tomcat has returned.

"Unlike some in the room, I don't play games with people's emotions."

"Not fair. I do have limits."

"Really? Who plows through women like a fifteen-pound bowling ball on free game night at Marty's Pins-N-Pints? Hmm…who could that be?"

"Not true. I'm merely willing to explore options, unlike my thick-headed brother. The relationship fairy plops his perfect person right in front of his face, and he's oblivious. And I'm a serial monogamist, by the way. It wounds me deeply you think I'm a use-'em-and-lose-'em kinda guy."

I don't feel guilty because I've seen his moves when I'm sober, and he's not, but he appears genuinely hurt by my accusation. "You're right, I was unfair. Still, there doesn't seem to be a whole lot of cooling-off time between episodes of your great girlfriend search."

"Look, there's either something there, or there's not. I'm not in the string-them-along-until-you-find-something-better club. Oh, damn, did I admit to having something in common with my blockheaded twin? Regardless, I may not have found the one, but I know love when I see it. I'm a bit of a love doctor, actually."

"If your PhD's in delusions. There's never been anything between Roy and me besides the plexiglass in the squad car, so you'd better check the return policy on that degree. Besides, there's a gulf between us we can't bridge, and it's called the past. I'm a changed person, but he's under no obligation to believe me or put faith in my recovery." For variety, I use my other hand to give him the crossing guard hold-up-there gesture. "Don't lecture, okay? It's healthier for me to be realistic than moon around like a lovestruck eighth grader."

"No one doubts you now. I still can't believe you've stayed in this town, where everyone knows all your warts. You don't have anything to prove."

He's right. I don't owe anyone but myself and the father who loved me when he should have booted me two counties over.

"That's the things about the MacInneses and this castle. They inspire me to be better. Be different. Dream. I'm comfortable with my choices, and I'm an open book. If Roy wants to give Bethanie 2.0 a try, I'm all in, but he's got a child to consider, not just his own heart."

"He got the book smarts, but I got the street ones. I can't seem to break him of overthinking everything. He seems to believe getting caught in Chloe's mother's snare way back means he can't trust himself, his judgment. At least as far as women are concerned."

"I can't fix that. I'm the last person who can judge another or tell someone how they should act. The fact is, the next move is your brother's. I'm not going to chase him, and I'm not going to beg."

His expression turns wistful, one I've not seen on the guy who hides the tender heart beating in his rock-solid chest with jokes. "I want you to be happy. You looked freaking amazing at the gala. I was hoping my dunderheaded twin would get a clue, but he's determined to punish himself."

I stare, unsure what to do about not receiving the flip response I expected.

Tears win out, hot and fast. If there's anything I'm good at, it's the art of being understanding to everyone but myself. "Damn it, stop being so thoughtful." I snatch a tissue and press my fingers to the bridge of my nose to stop any leaks. "A pretty dress doesn't make me a princess, bless Chloe's little heart. I'm more Birkenstock than glass slipper, so it's best he doesn't put stock into my rare dive into the glam zone."

"Roy has never been about appearances, but we both know you clean up real good." A goofy laugh escapes him, probably his attempt to stem my tears.

"Gee, thanks. And as much as I love dissecting my nonexistent dating life with you, I have work to do." I wiggle skedaddle fingers at him. "That was a hint, by the way."

He presses a hand to his chest. "My wounded heart takes yet another beating. It's so difficult being a doctor when your patients are insufferable." He hoists himself to his full height and walks toward my door like he's off to make his rounds.

I've known him too long, and I like this kind side of him, the side he'd snag the right woman with in a minute if he'd dare show it. "Thank you, Doctor. I'll make sure your Yelp rating's five stars, but you forgot your paperwork."

He looks at me over his shoulder, and I point at the chair beside his.

"It must have fallen from my lab coat."

"That thing covering the top of you is called a Henley."

I swear an army of five-year-olds could take lessons from this man on foot-dragging, but I don't relent until he's gathered his report and is back in the hallway.

"You're hilarious."

"Glad you agree. And close my door, please. I don't want my delicate ears to fall victim to your screams from downstairs as you're rendered batless."

He gives me his best snarl face but does as I ask, and I'm not sorry when silence engulfs my office again.

Why couldn't I have fallen in love with him instead of his identical-faced, opposite-everything-else brother? It would have made my life so much easier.

But no, I'm the fool pining for the one man on the face of the planet I can't have. You'd think I'd have gotten that through to myself by now.

Apparently, rigorous self-honesty applies to thick skulls but misses sore hearts.

CHAPTER TWENTY-FOUR

LEXI

CAMMIE'S HEN do turns out perfectly, but considering Bethanie was in charge of most of it, that's no surprise. I've not been to many bachelorette parties in my life, but in a way, that's made this one special. The bride-to-be is glowing, as is every bride's right, and it's pure delight to see how close the sisters are, their love and support of each other obvious with every joke, hug, and kissed cheek. As for me? There's an optimism, a glimmer of something I've not considered before, that I can have happily-ever-after, or at least chase the idea of one, pursue dreams I not thought to dare. Perhaps even have a gathering of female friends—and if the stars align, my sister—to share the same closeness these lovely ladies have.

Before, at home, I'd have labeled myself a right numpty or credited my outrageous thoughts to one pint too many.

Since I've come to America, I've started believing in miracles.

And I've been sharing my inclinations and my bed with a man who's kissed away the *im* in *impossible* in my wild notions.

I suggested the final setup of the tables and chairs on the huge veranda accommodating spillage from the ballroom, or in this case, serving as its own event space. The grand staircase down to the east lawn is the perfect set piece and makes the marble floor surrounded by balusters carved from the same veined white stone almost too beautiful to be real. Of course, the miniature dragon finials at the bottom of the stairs are the perfect touch. I can't imagine how many pictures have been staged on this deck and the iconic steps, but it's easy to understand why it's a favorite for photographers.

As I take in the fruits of my ideas, I pat my own back at the fine transition I've made from ordering copper piping to laying out party floor plans. The weather's pure barry, too, the temperate breeze dulling the melt-your-skin-off heat I'm still unsure how Texans survive year after year. Cammie orchestrated much of the details of the event her way. The start included all her female friends and the normal shenanigans. The second half has Trey and his buddies joining in, which made for eyebrow-raising fun with some of the bawdy mischief these men sometimes make after a wee bit too much ale.

All in all, it ends perfectly, but I'm more than ready to slip away when everyone starts their goodbyes. I head for one of my favorite spots on the estate, which is, of course, the balcony where I've had my coffee almost every morning of this trip.

Now, though, it's deep into the evening, and the moon is full and bright in the October sky. The air's crisp after a warm afternoon, and I'm glad I raced through my suite to grab my jumper and a tartan off the divan. I'm snuggly as I settle into one of the rocking chairs to enjoy the quiet.

I'm expecting it when the public door to the balcony opens and Bethanie and Bunny join me. We agreed to meet here, but I knew it'd take them longer to get away. They've snagged wraps from the couches in the family room, and I wave them to the chairs on either side of me.

"That was lovely. I'm grateful Cammie invited me."

Bethanie pops the top on a bottle of sparking water and pours it into the three glasses she thoughtfully brought along.

"Are you kidding? She's your number one fan after all you did to help ensure our hospital is going to be a fabulous success."

"Don't talk shite, Bethanie. I was the tiniest cog in this machine and came late in the game. 'All I did'—please note the air quotes—was make the lot of you look good, which was my job."

She hands me a glass and turns to Bunny. "Will you give it a shot? I honestly don't know what it'll take to get this woman to take a compliment."

"Don't put me in the middle of this, especially since you don't have a high score in the accepting-praise department yourself."

Bethanie huffs and sits back, tucking her lap blanket around her. "We're a trio, aren't we?"

Bunny raises her glass. "Indeed, and it breaks my heart we only have our intrepid Lex for another month."

My throat goes tight so fast I can't even swallow the sip I've taken. It takes three deep breaths before I manage to speak. "I can't believe my time here's passing so fast. This last year went by at a snail's pace."

"Then we'll have to make the most of it." Bethanie's the youngest of our trio, and despite her backstory, she's often the most positive.

Having become attuned to one another's moods, we go quiet, enjoying the soft wind coming off the lake and counting the slivers of clouds passing across the sky. Fall is my favorite time of year, although I'm reminded daily that the definition of the season varies greatly here. Still, the moonlight over the evergreens is beautiful, even if it can't rival the riot of color in the trees of home.

Bunny, to my surprise, is the one to break the quiet. "Do you gals want to talk about the respective flies in our glasses of sweet tea?"

I consider her question, because it's not flippant. The weeks since the gala have been so busy for all of us, we haven't had a deep conversation since we all confessed our man troubles over a new batch of shrubs late one night at the tavern. That's a good thing, as it's given us time to mull over what we want.

Bethanie raises her hand like she's in school, eliciting laughs from us all. "I'll begin, since there's not much to say in my case. I've been working with my sponsor, and one of the things she nailed me on was when she asked me if I've ever actually told Roy how I feel, or if I expect him to read my mind."

"Are you saying men don't know exactly what we want and need at any given moment?" My joke, albeit a bit lame, holds a kernel of truth. "I do hate it when someone points out the obvious, don't you?"

"My universe has thrown random curve balls at me for over a decade. This one hit hard, but my sponsor's right. I've always sworn that I hate games, and yet, I've been playing one for a while. So, I've spent the past couple of weeks digging into my journaling and had a session with my therapist to get myself straight before I made any moves."

"Good on ya, love."

"What it comes down to is spending some time by myself, and doing the work made me realize that this is the biggest shift I've had since I decided to get sober. I've been moping around, thinking I don't deserve someone like Roy, and that's bullshit. I'm far from perfect. Never was, never will be. But I have a lot going for me now, and while I confess I'm still working up my courage, I'm going to talk to Roy. If he can't take a chance with me, and I fully accept he has every right to be cautious, then I'll move on. But the answer's always no until you ask, so I'm asking."

Bunny lifts her glass again. "Bravo, my friend. Funny thing is, you can basically substitute my name into your story, and you've got mine."

I cock my head at her. "Do tell."

"You both know about the offer I got on Due West and Gene's reaction to it. Well, not long after, I got a second call from the rep at H-E-B about distributing my best-selling beer at all their stores across Texas. I asked for a meeting and pitched my shrubs, too. I've been waiting all day to tell you they accepted my counteroffer."

Squeals abound across the balcony, and we lose time to hugs and high fives until we finally settle. "Long story short, I did pretty much what Bethanie did. Lots of thinking, journaling, talking to my bestie, Dani." She holds up a hand. "Not that you crazy ladies aren't my BFFs, too."

Bethanie shoots her a look. "No ego-buffing necessary. Get on with it, will you?"

"My big revelation is I already have what I thought was lacking. It's nice and all, but I don't need any affirmation from these two crazy offers, because I've had it all along. Maybe my thick skull had to be bonked a couple of times for me to get it." Bunny winks. "Or maybe a few of the universe's throws went wide from Bethanie's world and struck mine."

"Och, aye. It's frustrating how we're so good at believing in other people and not ourselves. And how the universe's favorite fast pitch spares no one."

"I'm going to throw those suckers back to home plate this time. I'm determined to fix my confidence issue." Bunny squares her shoulder as she makes her pronouncement, helping make it final. "Anyway, I told you I grew up rich, and then I married an insanely wealthy man. People may think it's trite, but I can testify firsthand that money does not make you happy. Somehow, I got caught up in my old way of thinking and got stuck on the idea of showing the moneybags crowd I have enough gold to blind my ex and make my parents see me."

I reach over and give her arm a squeeze. "Then ricocheted from hiding from them to wanting to impress them."

"You got it. I had to get it, soul-deep, that I always had on my ruby slippers. I just never bothered to click the heels. I don't have anything to prove to anyone, including Gene. I really do love him, but I can't make my decisions about my life based on him."

Bethanie sits forward in her chair, as eager as I am to hear the finale. "And?"

"And after a lot of thought, I'm going to take the H-E-B offer, especially since they're finally expanding in this part of the state. I'm staying right here, where I have real family, the kind who chose me and I chose back. If things work out with Gene, fine. If they don't, I'll get over it and move on with my life. I'm not going to make any decisions based on someone else ever again. So, I'm going to buy the space next to the tavern, remodel it, and open the cocktail bar we talked about, Bethanie. Which means a lot more marketing work for you."

She whoops loud enough to echo off the turrets and does a little dance in her chair. I don't whoop, but I do smile.

"I knew you'd come to your senses." Bethanie polishes her nails on her shirt like this is entirely her idea.

All I can offer is an approving nod. "I'm so happy for you, love."

Bunny throws me a kiss. "Thank you. I am, too, but mostly because I didn't make this decision based on anything connected to Gene. I made it for me, for what I need, for what's best for Bunny West."

"As it should be." I wince internally, as if I'm some kind of authority on making healthy choices.

Bethanie seems to have cued in, because she gives me her take-no-nonsense look. "So what's up with you? You haven't mentioned Logan in quite a while."

I squirm, wishing I had a firm decision I could add to the night's good news. "There's nothing to say. He flat out told me he wants what's between us to go farther, but I already told you he has this fantastical idea I need to sow some wild oats, or more accurately, he thinks *I* think I need to do that. In the moment, can I honestly say he's wrong? It's put a block between us."

"Then sow already and see if it's the right answer." Bethanie's her usual blunt self, and I can't help but shift in my chair.

"I'm nae sure I'm a sowing kind of girl."

Bunny throws up the wait-a-minute finger. "Didn't you call DeWayne back? Make a date?"

I expect guilt to churn up at her question, but to my shock, I feel nothing of the sort. Neither elation nor like I'm going to boak. "I did. We're supposed to have dinner next week, before the Halloween party."

Bethanie nods in satisfaction. "There you go, then. Sowing doesn't have to mean sex with any man who looks your way, but then again, that's fine, too. It's like going in for a second opinion before major surgery, but in this case, third, fourth, and fifths."

"I still feel awkward about it. I didn't intend to fall into Logan's bed or into my feelings like I did, but it happened." And there it is again. The sense things are right. Balanced. Everything in its proper place. "It's wonderful. And strange. And confusing. And moving too damned fast."

"Fast isn't always bad."

"True, but I don't want to rehash old patterns. Still, you're rockets if you think I'm going on a dating spree."

Bunny give me a slow-your-roll side-eye. "We're not asking you to start notching your bedpost. What we want is for you to put Lexi at the top of the list."

"That's what my bestie back home said, so I guess it's unanimous."

"Are you asking Logan to the Halloween bash?" Bethanie's question isn't loaded, merely curious.

"I'm nae asking anyone at all. I need some time by myself." I pause, realizing what I've said. "I've been alone for a while now, but this is different. I cannae explain what happened when I said goodbye to Douglas, but it shifted everything."

Bunny points a decisive finger at me. "I know what you mean. I feel like I've finally cast off the last ropes I had tying me to my ex, for real this time. It's something you can't quantify, but you know. In here." She taps her heart.

"Aye, 'tis, and why I shouldn't rush anything, even though my time here is short. Hurting Logan would wreck me. He's wonderful, and my heart wants to see where this is leading, but I have to be sure. He deserves that."

"This isn't about what Logan deserves." Bethanie throws me a Eunice-worthy frown. "It's about what you deserve."

"Maybe, but there'll be nae stringing him along or playing with his emotions."

"I didn't say you were. I meant don't fall into your old ways of putting *his* feelings first. It's the Lexi Show, starring yourself and your feelings."

I can't reach Bethanie from where I'm sitting, so I hold up my hand in a promise. "I swear I'm the Beyoncé of my own life now."

She settles back and shoots me a smug smile. "Just making sure."

I look at my two fierce friends and feel bathed in love as bright as the beams of moonlight. I don't know what's going to happen with Logan. Bunny doesn't know what's going to happen with Gene. And Bethanie has no idea what will come of her decision about Roy.

No matter, though. In the end, with whatever comes, we'll handle it. Best of all, we have each other. A new sisterhood distance won't diminish. I never expected such a gift from my unexpected trip, and now I can't imagine my life without these amazing women in it. Add in the Grannies, the other MacInneses, and the mass of Magnolia Bloomians I've met. I'm going to need a bigger address book.

That's the greatest gift of all of these crazy weeks. Yes, Logan has his own special place in my new world, but knowing I've made forever friends, forever family, by choice, is priceless.

Bunny shrugs off her blanket, clearly planning to stand. "All right, you two. I've got to get some beauty sleep. Everyone have their outfits ready for the wedding?"

This almost earns a squeal from me. "I'm so excited about getting to go to a wedding in the chapel. Cammie's going to be impossibly lovely as the newest MacInnes to wed there."

"She will be, and it's going to be perfect, thanks to you two." Bunny game-show waves between me and Bethanie.

"After the gala, her wedding and reception were walks in the park." I was happy to take these chore off of Kiki's list, too, as my spreadsheet skills are now on point.

We all get to our feet and join in a group hug. I bask in this delightful companionship, this warmth I didn't realize I needed three months ago. Tomorrow will be lovely and another glorious day spent in the company of good friends.

I cross my fingers things work out in record time for my two new sisters of the heart. I keep my worries to myself this might be a win for only two out of three of us.

CHAPTER TWENTY-FIVE

BETHANIE

THE CHAPEL at Castle MacInnes is legendary for good reason. To date, the myth has stood the test of time. No one married in the small but beautiful space has gotten divorced. Cammie's about to put her and Trey's names on the roster, and while I might not be a MacInnes by blood, I'm as thrilled as anyone to witness the event.

Cammie's tea-length dress is a soft, petal-pink silk. Tiny rosebuds and a bit of baby's breath have been tucked into her loose chignon, blond wisps floating around her face, her head-to-toe elegance and beauty worthy of a magazine cover. She's holding simple ecru lilies, bound with a length of the magic lace I'd give anything to own.

Someday. Hopefully.

Trey's in a navy suit, his smile one of a man in love, his gaze locked on his bride as she walks gracefully down the aisle on her father's arm. His best friend from Lubbock stands beside him, and next to him is Roy. I knew he and Trey were friends, but I didn't know they were close enough that the object of my unending thoughts would be in my line of sight the whole ceremony. Thankfully, I'm way in the back and hopeful he's too busy being a groomsman to notice me. It doesn't hurt Chloe's an adorable flower girl, defying the adage never to have children or animals in weddings because they can steal the show. She's completed her appointed task, and now she sits like a perfect angel in the front row, where her daddy can keep an eye on her.

Thankfully, one more thing keeping his attention off me.

Cammie's matrons of honor are, of course, Ally and Bailey. The three sisters have been through so much, growing so close last year. All of us go misty-eyed when Cammie's dad kisses her cheek and hands her off to an anxious Trey.

Harville's deep voice jerks me out of my self-absorption, and I sit up straighter in my seat to pay attention.

"Thank you all, family and friends, for helping me do my favorite job. There's no greater honor than being asked to bless the union of two people beginning a new life together, and today I'm especially proud because I've known these two amazing people for a very long time. Since I was blessed to take my position at St. Andrews, I found more than a church home. I found a new family who mean as much to me as anyone by blood. All the heartstrings tying me to Magnolia Bloom, from the MacInnes and Greene families you see represented before me, to the Broders, the Steeles, and so many more, are testimonies to the unbreakable bonds that form when we're brave enough to work through the trying times that come to each and every one of us. To have the honor of bringing two more hearts together in this tradition means everything to me, and, Cammie and Trey, I thank you for letting me be a part of the start of the next phase of your journey."

Trey nods and smiles at Harville, and Cammie tosses him an air kiss. There's soft laughter in the congregation and more than one tear wiped away.

One of those is mine. Harville is spot-on about the ties binding all of us in Magnolia Bloom together, regardless of which part you hail from. There was a time when I hated everything about this town, or I thought I did. Back then, my pickled brain stewed on slights mostly imagined, the bottle keeping me blind to how many hands were waiting to help me, support me. And like the sexy pastor who got his own miracle, all I had to do was take the risk of accepting the love and support that were there all along.

Harville is perfect from word one to the moment he presents the newlyweds to the combined forty or so of us lucky enough to witness the short and sweet ceremony. The rest of the crowd's waiting downstairs in the ballroom, as half of the town wants to be in on the dancing and celebrating.

Despite my brave words to Bunny and Lexi yesterday on the balcony, the reception's more than half over before I find my nerve to look around for Roy.

I would have saved myself time if I'd checked the dance floor first, because he's there, holding Chloe, but acting as if she were the next Blackpool champion at seven years old. My heart about bursts with how beautiful the picture is, the big, tough police chief with a little girl in lavender chiffon in his arms, her slender arms wrapped around his neck and her face the picture of complete trust.

When the music fades, Chloe gives Roy a kiss on the cheek and races away to join the other kids in the crowd, completely unaware of the raw love in her father's eyes as he lets her go.

Which makes me hesitate. Do I really want to disturb such a tender moment?

Someone gently bumps my shoulder, and I look to see Cammie standing beside me. I didn't expect to convey more than my best wishes in the receiving line, much less have a chance to talk to her.

"What's the frown for? You're supposed to be enjoying the party."

I return her hug, being careful not to smudge her makeup any more than the evidence of the tears she's already shed. "I am. Everything's perfect."

"Thanks to you."

"Not hardly. I leaned on Lexi, a lot, but we're ecstatic everything came off."

"Flawlessly. But quit avoiding my question. What's up?"

I got to know the blushing bride from meetings to finalize details of the ceremony and after-party. Cammie's one of those people who seems to have an infinite capacity for caring, and she drew me into her orbit without hesitation. Trey helped me through my legal troubles, so she knows all my warts, but she didn't hesitate to extend a hand of friendship despite my rather ugly past.

She even got me to confess my secret-not-secret crush on Roy and didn't tease me. Well, a little, but only in the kindest way.

"I gave this big speech to Bunny and Lexi last night about how I've never actually told Roy how I feel, thinking he should somehow magically know. I've challenged myself to be open and vulnerable with him, but all I want to do is run home, put on pj's, and binge on *Downton Abbey* reruns."

"I get it. I nearly ran away, too. In fact, I was packing boxes, but look what I'd be missing if I had."

The fire arcing between her and Trey can probably be seen by the astronauts on the International Space Station. "Your situation was a little different."

She gives me her patented eyebrow lift and pursed lips, which is law-speak for *oh, really?* I can almost hear the words in an English accent. "I decided for Trey that I wasn't right for him. My arguments were rather convincing, if I do say so myself. Thankfully, the soft-spoken man over there has a pretty determined center."

"Lucky you."

"Damned right. I shiver when realize how closely I came to giving all this up."

"But—"

"No buts, Bethanie. You're right it's not fair to play games, especially once you know what you're doing. Put this out there, in the open. I can't promise you how it'll turn out, but if you don't try, you'll never know."

"I thought you did real estate, not brutal cross-examinations."

"Keeps my skills sharp. Point is, law practice aside, I'm one hundred percent MacInnes, and if there's one thing we know, it's stubborn. So quit being a ninnyhammer and go talk to him."

Someone calls her name, and she slips away to slide into Trey's embrace.

I unerringly find Roy at a table across the room from Chloe, watching her twirl herself dizzy with her pals, all engrossed in showing whose dress spins the best. He doesn't let her out of his sight. The only problem with my destination is Nathanial's sitting beside him, and they're obviously giving each other hell, as they always do.

Nathanial notices me and waves me closer. "Tell him, Bethanie. Tell this idiot I'm clearly the more handsome brother."

I give my head a despairing shake. "Really? This is what you two are arguing about over here?"

Roy grunts. "I'm not arguing about anything. My brother's in love with his own voice and won't shut up no matter how much I'd like to shove this napkin in his beak. All I want is to relax and have a beer since I'm off duty tonight."

Nathanial stands, gives me a quick hug, and heads off. "I'm going to go find someone who appreciates me."

Roy and I both sigh, but neither of us tries to stop him. "Can I join you?"

He nods to the empty chair. "Sure. Can I get you a soda? One of Bunny's shrubs?"

"I'm good." He starts to move his beer away, but I stop him. "You don't have to do that. I still have a lot of people to convince, but honestly, I'm not triggered being around alcohol."

Although reluctantly, he pulls the bottle back. "Good to know."

"Everyone's journey is different, but while I'd be lying if I said I never wonder about indulging again, it really doesn't have any appeal anymore. Not after everything I've been through, how much I nearly destroyed. And how good I feel to be free."

"Is that why you've been looking at me across the room all afternoon? You want to talk about your recovery?"

So much for me being sly and subtle. Or rather, points to the man for being equal parts police chief and detective. At least he doesn't tease me for being unable to take my eyes off of him in his cutaway, the jacket now draped over the back of his chair, his bow tie dangling from his collar. I swear there's nothing sexier than a man in a Texas tuxedo, and there's no one in the room who looks better in black Wranglers and spit-shined boots. There were plenty at the gala, but Roy was in his uniform then. Now it's my turn to ogle a handsome cowboy instead of a lawman. Or maybe a handsome cowboy lawman.

However you cut it, he's mouthwatering.

"My journey from hell to here isn't what's on my mind, although it may be part of what I need to say to you."

That makes him straighten in his seat. "Okay. This sounds serious."

"It is. For me, anyway." I let my breath go in a soft whoosh and suck in fresh air for courage. "Roy, I like you. And not as a friend, although we are, in a weird sort of way. I like you romantically, and I've never had the guts to tell you. I thought somewhere along the line I was sending you signals, and you weren't interested, but the fact is, I'm not sure you know how I really feel, and I'm sorry I expected you to read my mind."

He slams a mouthful of beer, and I try not to explode into flames as he processes what I've said.

"Bethanie, I—"

"Don't feel like you have to say anything. I needed to tell you and say I'm sorry, but honestly, I wasn't playing games, at least intentionally. I didn't know how to say it, so I finally decided to blurt it out. It seemed easier to tear off the bandage, as it were, but honestly? I've reached a place where I really like me. Just as I am, flaws and all. And you know what else? I'm only going to get better. I needed to tell you because I'm a little tired of people watching me, waiting for me to break."

A shriek turns into a wail, and Roy bolts to his feet, his eyes already on Chloe, who's headed this way, clutching a hand against her chest.

I don't need him to speak. He's been diverted into dad mode, as he should be. His child is hurt, and that takes priority, so I back away as Chloe launches herself into her father's arms. She gasps out that one of the boys stepped on her fingers, and it hurts, and she wants to go home.

I leave Roy to attend the histrionics with his gravelly voice going soft as he reassures his little girl she's not maimed for life.

Although I wish we'd had a chance to say more, maybe it's better this way. He was saved from having to come up with something to ease the awkward moment, and I'm saved from melting in embarrassment.

I did what I said I'd do, and in the most insane way, I feel lighter than I've felt since I took my last drink. Yes, I'm struggling with awkwardness, but the bigger part of me knows if I can risk myself this boldly, this completely, and not want to run like hell for a bottle of vodka, I'm going to be okay.

Good or bad, it's all out there now, and he can do with the information what he will. My conscience is clear, even if my heart is pounding.

And now it's time for me to get on with my life without silly fantasies getting in the way.

CHAPTER TWENTY-SIX

LEXI

IT TURNS out my thoughts about high heels the first time I met Logan are correct. For the wedding, I have on lovely, sparkly wedges I found during an impromptu shopping trip with Bethanie and Bunny. We all netted super-cute outfits from Traycee's Emporium and wedding-worthy cocktail dresses at Marissa's. In my case, as I suspected, the heel height puts my nose right in the hollow of his throat, where there's a hint of delicious cologne, and it doesn't take more than the slightest stretch for me to kiss his perfect lips.

He sets me away, and I execute a graceful turn, then he pulls me back into the center of his embrace. We're a little too close to be in dance frame, and I couldn't possibly care less about the technicality as long as I get another hit of the leathery, cedary aroma made better by blending with the warmth radiating off of him like sunshine in summer.

These last few weeks have been nothing short of confusing and utterly wonderful at the same time. After our talk, I was afraid he'd avoid me, or ignore me, but nothing of the sort happened. Things changed a bit, but it's mostly because of me. We still see each other, but we've pulled back to what I guess is considered normal dating, not the inferno we jumped into after the gala. We don't see each other every day, but we go out a lot, sometimes ending up snuggled in his bed or mine, but not always. He's taken me to movies and small-venue concerts. We went to Dallas for the ballet, Atlanta to a clogging exhibition, Fort Worth to the botanical gardens. It's been…lovely.

When the song ends, I grumble, "That wasn't long enough."

"We danced three songs in a row."

I look up at him, my frown only half pretend. "See? You agree with me."

He drops a kiss onto my waiting lips. "I'll always agree with you."

"Liar." Of course I'm teasing, and I let him lead me back to the table. I'm sure pouting isn't a good look on a grown woman, so I pretend I don't mind when someone I haven't been introduced to asks Logan for a turn. He give me an *is it okay?* look, but even though I want to be a total cow and claim every song, I know I can't. I hide my sigh and nod, acting like it doesn't bother me.

It bothers me. A lot. But I spend the time he's away chatting with Bethanie, who's surprisingly lighthearted after her confession to Roy. I'm not sure I'd be quite so centered if I'd made such a vulnerable speech and had nothing to go on by way of reaction. Roy left the ballroom, but whatever he did clearly pleases Chloe, who's back with her cadre of friends, all doing serious damage to massive pieces of wedding cake. I've seen Roy glance this way several times, but Bethanie seems content to give him space. She seems determined to dance the night away, saying yes to one and all who ask her.

I'm terribly happy for her. Her heart will be sore if Roy can't, or won't, give her a chance, but I find her maturity comforting and hopeful. I've never been in her position, so I wouldn't dream of judging, other than being firmly on Team Bethanie and having pompoms ready if things go well and tissues if they don't.

A touch on my arm makes me jump. I didn't realize I was so far in my head, but my ready smile for Logan fades when I see his expression. "What's wrong?"

He sits next to me and takes my hand, kissing my knuckles. "My brother's manager called. He's been hurt on the set of his new film. I've got to fly to Los Angeles. It's pretty bad."

"I'm so sorry. Is there anything I can do? While trite, I mean it."

"Thank you, but I've got to race to my place and throw a bag together. I can get a flight out of DFW tonight if I hurry."

"Do you want me to take you? Even if you eejits over here drive on the wrong side of the road, I can get you there, I'm sure."

He laughs, the strain on his face easing ever so slightly. "I appreciate the offer, but I'm good." He pauses, looking down at the floor and licking his top lip. I've not seen him nervous before, so I chalk it up to worry. "Lexi, there's something I'd like to ask you."

"Anything. Tell me."

"Would you stay? There's so much more we need to talk about, but I have to go."

"Of course you do. He's your brother."

His laugh contains a wealth of sadness. "We're not close, as I've told you, but I need to do this. For me and for him. But I don't want you to go back to Scotland before we have a chance to work out... whatever this is between us. It's asking a lot, but would you?"

I have plenty of time, legally, before I risk the ire of the authorities. The Customs officers explained I can stay for six months as a visitor without any problems, and I could extend my time with a more complicated visa, but the thought of staying beyond six months didn't even enter my mind at the time.

"Yes, I will. I'll have to go home eventually, but if it'll give you peace of mind, I'll work things out for a while."

His whole demeanor shifts, as if I've pulled a weight off of him. It touches me he's so concerned about the moment, when his focus should be entirely on his brother.

"I'll keep in touch and let you know how everything's going."

"Please do. I'll be worried. About you both."

Leaning toward me, he kisses me quickly, but deeply, and I blush at the public display. I push my chagrin aside as he stands, brushing his thumb over my cheek as he walks away.

All the lovely gentlemen I've met over the weeks seem as determined to keep me on the dance floor as Bethanie, and I'm grateful for the distraction, because if left to my own devices, I'd be inside my own head and coming up with ten thousand scenarios about what Logan meant by working out *whatever this is between us.*

The rest of the reception goes off flawlessly, but I'm ready to go to my little apartment one floor up and get out of my pretty shoes and my pretty dress, since the one person I wanted to see me in it is gone.

The feeling of loss stays with me for days, and I throw myself into work. When Kiki finally goes into labor, it's the perfect way to end my moping because I'm too busy obsessively checking my phone for texts from Logan and updates from Harville on the family group chat. I'm put out of my waiting tension when Kiki, with her usual efficiency, brings a beautiful seven-pound, six-ounce little girl into the world a mere eight hours after she headed to the hospital.

No one wants to hear baby stories, but Travis took eighteen hours and Sadie twenty-three. But who's counting?

I join the family in a quick visit to the hospital, and I didn't plan on interjecting myself into Kiki's room, as every new mother needs rest, so when she asks for me personally, I go. Still, I feel awkward and hesitant.

She's glowing, of course, and little Mia Olivia MacInnes-Crowder is angelically asleep in her bassinette.

Kiki reaches for me, and I take her hand. "You don't need me to tell you how beautiful she is, but…."

"Oh, you can tell me. The truth never hurts."

Harville's practically levitating off his perch on the bed beside her. There's no need to ask his opinion of his new beauty or his radiant wife.

I let her go and step back, wanting to give the new family space. "What can I do for you, love? I'm thrilled you asked to see me, but I'm a bit surprised."

"I wanted to ask you a huge favor. It's not fair, really. I'm being totally selfish, but I don't want to come back to work yet."

"Stars above, Kiki, you gave birth five hours ago. You can put this off a wee bit."

Harville does a very good imitation of Roy's growl. "I cannot get her to let it go. I'm not sure why I've been blessed with such a stubborn, opinionated—"

"Enough already." Kiki's frown is all bluster, and we know it.

I haven't told anyone about my promise to Logan, as I'm not sure how long it will even be in effect, but I'm glad I can reassure her. "I'm happy to stay. I've only been here a little under three months, so I easily have three more to figure things out."

"That's the thing. I don't want to come back full time for much longer than that. I'm fine working from home, maybe coming into the office a few hours a week, but I can't—"

She breaks off, tears streaming down her face. Harville jumps like a man scorched and races to grab the box of tissues a few feet out of his reach.

She gives me a watery smile. "I hate this. I never cry, but for the last few weeks, bam, the waterworks hit me out of the frickin' blue."

I pat her arm, adding a warm squeeze. "It's the hormones, lovey. It won't stop for a while, sorry to say."

"So my doctor says. I don't like it."

I look at my work compatriot and now dear friend. "Welcome to motherhood."

I want to tell her, *Wait until your milk comes in*, but she'll find out soon enough. I think I cried more than Travis and Sadie for the first six months each.

"I'm a mess, but I'm trying to be logical, too. I don't want to give up being chatelaine. I know it's my calling. But I can't leave Mia. I just can't."

"Sweetie, this is the new age. We'll figure this out. All you need to worry about is your new precious bundle and that big hunk hovering over you like an avenging angel."

She rolls her head toward Harville, and he brushes her hair back with a touch so gentle it makes me sigh.

"Forgive me for being silly, Lexi. It's not like me."

I rush to reassure her, remembering keenly the mental ups and downs after giving birth. "Put all this worry away. Bethanie and I will keep things shipshape, and all you need to do is worry about this beautiful little girl, aye?"

She nods, and it's clear her postpartum euphoria is all used up. "Yes, ma'am. Thank you."

"Nonsense. I'm the one grateful to you, but enough, aye? You need to rest. You're exhausted."

Harville escorts me to the door, pulling me in for a crushing hug. "You're a doll, Lexi. Thank—"

"Wheesht, man. I'm happy to be here for all of you. You take care of your sweet wife and precious bairn, and dinnae fash yourselves one more second. I'll ring the lot of you next week when you're home and settled."

I leave the hospital in a bit of a fog, wondering what is going on, but it seems the universe is conspiring to keep me in Magnolia Bloom. I can't parse my feelings as they ping from excited at the prospect, to uncertain I'm not setting myself up for some serious heartache when the day comes that I have to fly back across the Atlantic to the only home I've ever known.

The home that now seems not only a continent away, but a lifetime away.

CHAPTER TWENTY-SEVEN

BUNNY

DANCING WITH GENE at Cammie's reception was delightful, but we kept things light. Like Bethanie, I'm not playing games with Gene. We haven't had our "talk" yet, somehow mutually agreeing to enjoy the night without any strain between us.

I'm the one who asked him on a date, at the time feeling confident and full-on girl boss. Now, as I pile the fifth outfit onto the chaise in my bedroom, I've completely destroyed my hair and am doing everything in my power to not cry and ruin my makeup, too.

My doorbell rings, and I wish the dang delivery man would leave the box without a signature, whatever it is. I can't remember what I ordered, but at the moment, I don't care if it's ice cream and will ruin if I don't get it.

A second, more impatient ring makes me scream in frustration, throw on a robe, and hold it shut as I stomp across the house. I throw open the door, ready to sign and get on with my business, but stop short because it's not the UPS man. It's my art man.

"Emmett?"

"Do you need me to show proof of ID?"

"Shut up and come in."

He sigh is laconic and utterly Emmett, and he side-eyes my robe and hairstyle, which defies a succinct description, unless *ohmygod* is now in the dictionary.

"Shut up."

"You already said that."

"You're making me repeat myself."

"You can't blame any of this," he does an up-down wave of his hand, "on me."

That does it. I snap, and my attempt at a witty reply becomes a sob. I collapse into my armchair and hide my face in my hands.

A warm hand is instantly on my back, then pushes the scraggly bits of hair back from my forehead. "Hey now, overreaction much? It's all fixable."

"Go away and let me be a pathetic mess in peace."

"Nah, can't. I brought you a present, and I can't leave until you squeal and hug me, but there'll be none of that until you wipe your face. Got it?"

"I'm well aware of your aversion to snot." I sniff and lift my head, looking for the box of tissue around here somewhere, but instead I see a pristine white handkerchief with the elegantly embroidered initials EQE in the corner.

I wipe, getting base and mascara and eyeliner all over it. I laugh at his pained frown, as we both know it'll never come out completely.

I try to return it, but he backpedals three feet. "You keep it. I've got more."

My smile is wicked but thankful. "Do I know what the Q stands for?"

"Quillan, after my dad, who is Quinton Everson's brother, which makes for a crapton of confusion at family reunions, and no, you shouldn't know as I never talk about him."

"Clear as mud, but I plead exigent circumstances. My head's mince, as Lexi is wont to say."

"No argument from me. Now, give that mess another swipe and open your present."

I obey and sit back as a box lands in my lap, wrapped in white and silver paper and bound with a ribbon probably costing as much as my last purse.

"It's too pretty to open." He starts to take it back, but I pull it out of his reach. "All right, all right. Sheesh, try to give a guy a compliment."

I do take care, though, to cause as little damage as possible. It's a bonus, because Emmett's almost dancing in his seat on the couch. As he knows darn well, I gasp when the wrapping paper reveals the logo on the box.

"Are these...?"

"This season's Louboutins? Why yes, they are."

I lift the lid slowly, enjoying the anticipation.

Hot pink. Ankle strap. Loubigirls. I may or may not have touched the screen, whimpering during a self-torture session on the website. I scrolled, knowing it will be a long time—new contract or not—before I can afford anything even from the clearance page. I wonder if, maybe, I'm past being that shallow.

I look at the shoes and stroke one of the heels.

Nope. Not past it at all.

A hoarse chuckle escapes. "I'm not sure I remember how to walk in heels this high."

"Well, you better figure it the hell out, because I bought these so with every step you take tonight, you know I got you."

The tears are back, and I surge from my chair and attack him, not giving a flying flip if I get snot or mascara or anything else on his shirt.

"Girl—"

"Shut up. Shut. Up." I nearly strangle him in a hug. "I love you so much."

"I love you, too. I do wish, though, you weren't intent on destroying everything I own right now."

"Whatever. Buy a new shirt." I pull back and make a pretense of smoothing his collar. "Thank you." Every bit of my heart's poured into my soft words.

Emmett Everson's the closest male friend I've ever had, and he gets me. In a way no one else ever has. Not other girlfriends. Not my ex. Or my family. He's the brother I didn't know I needed, and someone I can't imagine living without.

"You're welcome, Bun. I'll always have your back." He looks down. "Or your feet. Whatever."

He jokes, but he means it. Emmett would wade through mosquito-infested swamps to get to me if I needed him, or worse, the five a.m. crowd on Black Friday. His devotion isn't lost on me, nor is the peace of having someone like him in my life, at the ready, for wallowing and wine, or to give me an Italian-loafed swift kick in the butt if I need it.

I smile through the cleanup of my face, thinking of the times I've commiserated with him, or told him to buck up and deal with it as our friendship isn't one-sided.

"I guess I'm starting over." I examine the now-drenched, makeup-stained handkerchief, then give up.

"Damn skippy, you are. Let's get to your room and see what we can pull together to showcase these masterpieces, shall we?"

I gladly let him pick out my new ensemble as I fix my face and manage to tame my rat's-nest hair into a once-again sleek coil. The style's not hard to do, or isn't with as much practice as I've had over the years. By the time I'm presentable again from the neck up, he's chosen a simple, solid black, turtleneck sweater dress, a long gold tassel necklace, and my favorite earrings—drop chains ending in pink crystals.

I take the dress into the bathroom, using the silk scarf trick to get it over my head and save my makeup, and need only a smoothing swipe of my hand to get my hair back in place. I'm putting the last earring in as I walk out, and he's holding my new shoes toward me like they're gifts from royalty. They're probably worth an earring in the queen's crown jewels in actual dollars, but in heart dollars, they're priceless.

Once I'm strapped in, I give a *whoops*, as I'm a little wobbly, then muscle memory kicks in, and I do a runway walk and turn, and earn a round of applause. We decide on Perfect Passion Pink for my lipstick, and I swear I can hear strains of the score to *Cinderella* playing in the background.

"Damn, girl. You are going to give the man a coronary."

"I sure hope not. I'd like to spend the night in his bed, not the emergency room."

He pretends to fix an errant strand of hair, but we both know I'm ready. "If you don't end up on his Tempur-Pedic, the man's too far gone to save."

I air-kiss his cheek. "Thank you, love. You've saved the day."

He tucks in his shirt and does the pretend-run-his-hand-through-his-hair. "It's what I do. Call me later." He shakes his head decisively. "No, call me tomorrow when you're recovered from a night of about-damn-time sex."

He's out the door before I can confirm or deny I'll obey, but we both know I will. Not with salacious details because, for all his bluster, Emmett's all innuendo. He's never told me an inappropriate thing about his life, and I've never offered any about mine. But as I look down and wiggle my toes, I'm sure of one thing. He's a true friend. And he's had my back—and my feet—for years now.

And the time has come to find my black suede clutch and wait for Gene. I might have asked him out on this date, but he's old-school and insists on picking me up. A glance at the clock relieves my worry I'm going to pace the taps off my heels. I have absolute certainty he'll be on time, so only fifteen more minutes of agony.

I don't play games. As soon as I hear his car pull up, I head out my front door and wait on the porch until he stops and gets out. I'm gratified when he rounds the front of his car and stops dead in his tracks.

Fidgeting isn't ladylike, but what's a girl to do when a man looks at her like the world has stopped revolving, and she's the center of gravity?

He recovers and joins me on the porch, looking effortlessly put together in navy slacks and a white button-down, and I do my own can't-find-air moment at his perfectly fitted windowpane sports coat. He's also seen the barber, because his salt-and-pepper hair I want to touch is neatly trimmed and slicked back with the perfect hint of product. It may be a part of my snob holdover, but I do love a well-dressed man, and Gene earns the title hands down tonight.

"Bunny, I...wow."

I drop my eyes, not for effect, but because his reaction has made every bit of the torture of the last few hours worth it. I look back up and into his emerald green and nearly drown.

"Back at you, mister." I don't say it, but I sure think it that George Clooney ain't got nothin' on Buddy Gene Autry.

He offers me a simple bouquet of wildflowers, and my heart nearly melts. I've been given vases of hothouse flowers costing veritable fortunes, but the bunch I'm holding means more to me than any of them ever did put together. It's one more notch in the how-much-I-love-him tally that he knows this about me, as I'm sure I've never told him.

He extends his elbow, and I take his arm with pleasure, enjoying every bit of his gentlemanly courtesy, from helping me into the car to assisting me at the restaurant by pulling my chair out and waiting until I'm comfortable before taking his own seat.

We've got the premier table at the new upscale establishment adding its name to the business association roster. The enormous fireplace is roaring, but we're the perfect distance away so we can enjoy both the heat and the blaze, but not roast ourselves like hunks of meat on a spit. A cold snap made choosing an outdoor option unwise, but after I put my flowers in the center of the table, I decide the spot couldn't be any better.

If the evening had started beautifully, it only gets better from there. Superb service, amazing food, and a perfect dinner partner make the night something out of a dream. Except I'm the one who started this, and I haven't found the gumption to tell him what I need to. As the waiter pours our after-dinner coffees, my time has come. I desperately wanted to order a digestif, but even though Gene doesn't have a problem with people drinking around him—he owns a dance hall, for goodness's sake—I want him to see I don't need false courage to talk to him.

I lift my cup in a toast. "Thank you for a wonderful evening."

"I hope it's not over."

I feel my face flush, damning the blush, but nodding. "Me, too."

In his maddening, sweet way, he waits.

It takes all I have to stay still in my seat. No more itchy wiggling.

"I've been doing nothing but thinking since we talked about the offer I received on the tavern. Since then, I've gotten another one, the details of which aren't important right now. What I need to tell you is, I'm not going to leave Magnolia Bloom."

His smile is as gratifying as the stopped-in-his-tracks expression earlier. "I'm really glad."

I give a short nod and plow forward. "But you need to know, I'm not staying because of you."

The smile fades, then disappears into a frown. "I'm not sure I was thinking that."

"Maybe not, but you have to understand I'm doing this for me. Not 'for' you or to 'get' you. For me."

I didn't mean to be quite so blunt, but it's out, and I can't take it back.

"I'm even happier, then." He takes a sip of coffee. "Now, it's my turn. It's no secret I don't want you to leave, but what I want is for you to be happy. If you need to grab the brass ring being offered, I'm the last person who would judge. I would've been sad, but your happiness would have made it bearable."

"Oh." *Gee, Bunny.* Time to apply for that Mensa certification.

I clear my throat so I can get out the parts I haven't covered yet. "I'm going to buy the space next to the tavern and open the cocktail lounge I talked about. Bethanie is going to help me, as it will be a whole new venture."

"That's fantastic, but there's a problem."

I look around the room. "There is?"

"I heard someone talking at the last chamber meeting. You weren't at that one. They were talking about buying it before all the investors at the gala wise up and start eating up the retail space in town. A crotchety old man reached out to the realtor and snatched it up. You might be able to negotiate it away, but I don't know."

I put my cup down as my hand starts to wobble, and I sit back, devastated.

I can't count the hours I put into thinking about this, the pages of notebook paper I've covered with notes and sketches and figures, the dreams I've had as my imagination took flight.

Gene reaches into his coat and pulls a folded paper from his pocket and slides it over to me. I open it, wondering who I was going to have to sell my soul to now.

The words are all a blur. *General Warranty Deed. Grantor...* Some business entity I've never heard of. *Grantee...*

Buddy Gene Autry.

Wait, he's the crotchety old guy?

I read it again, note the seal from the county records office.

"Look at the next page."

I flip the one in back to the front, and it's an almost identical form, except this one doesn't have a seal on it. The grantor is Buddy Gene Autry.

The grantee is Bunny Eliza West.

Consideration: Ten dollars and other good and valuable considera-tion, the receipt of which is hereby acknowledged.

The grantor's signature is filled in with Gene's name and notarized. The grantee's spot is blank, although my name is typed underneath.

I'm not sure how long it takes to sink in, but when I look up and dash a tear away, I'm a little mad, too.

"That was mean."

"Yeah, a little."

"Why would you do this?"

"Because Magnolia Bloom's growing too quickly, and I didn't want to take the chance someone might buy the place out from under you... if you ever decided you wanted it."

I look at the deed again, gobsmacked. "Gene, you can't give me a piece of property worth tens of thousands of dollars."

"Well, I can, but I'd prefer you married me, and it was part of our joint estate."

My eyes jerk to his so fast the room spins.

Gene reaches across the table, takes the papers from me, and clasps my fingers in his. "I've been doing a lot of thinking, too, and I know one thing. I've wasted a lot of time in my life, and nearly losing you made me go half crazy. I wanted to believe you were interested in me, but I couldn't get past my certainty I'm a little too used up for someone as talented, beautiful, and savvy as you. Then you scared me half to death, talking about leaving, and it woke me up."

Something garbled comes out of my throat, but neither one of us can make it out.

"I love you, Bunny. I have for a long time, but was too damned scared to admit it to myself and utterly terrified of you finding out. But here it is. My soul laid bare. If it's what you want, what you need, I'll go to Dallas with you. I'll give you babies. I'll help you build orphanages in any Baltic country of your choosing. Anything. If you don't feel the same way, it doesn't change one word of that deed. It's yours. But...."

He stands and walks the short distance to kneel beside me, reaching into his pocket again, this time pulling out a little velvet box. The space in front of my eyes goes sparkly, and desperation makes me take in a sadly unladylike gasp of air. When my vision clears, there's a round brilliant diamond in a classic platinum setting in his hand, winking at me in the candlelight.

Simple. Elegant. Stunning.

"Will you marry me?"

My one previous experience with proposals is a distant and sad memory. This moment, this beautiful, beautiful man looking at me with his heart on his sleeve, is more than I've ever imagined. Ever hoped for.

All I've ever wanted.

"Yes." I can't get out more than a choked whisper, but all the love I've been holding on to is there. He takes my hand and slips the ring onto my finger, and I throw my arms around his neck. He stands, bringing me with him, and the room explodes in applause. I honestly wasn't aware we were the stars of the evening because all that mattered, all I was looking at, was him.

Like everything about this evening, his kiss is perfect, sending my pulse soaring and filling all the empty places, pouring gold into all my cracks, making them beautiful.

I pull back, grazing my fingertips along his jaw and then back through the hair I've been dying to touch all night. "Gene?"

"Hmmm?"

"Come home. With me."

Joy lights him from the inside, and we can't get the bill paid fast enough. I remember at the last second to hurry back for my flowers, and the lady one table over smiles at me. "Be happy, honey."

I nod. "I will."

In fact, in about thirty minutes, I'll be delirious....

CHAPTER TWENTY-EIGHT

LEXI

I ASSUMED I'd be a fluttery mess getting ready for my date with DeWayne. I was wrong.

I step into the living room to do a little twirl in front of my dream team. Bunny was in charge of hair and makeup, Bethanie moral support. We've had to tie anvils to Bunny's ankles to keep her on planet Earth, and Bethanie's wonderfully okay with being in limbo where Roy is concerned. I'm proud of her, ecstatic she can be centered in uncertainty. I'm not so good there, but she's doing fine.

Bunny lifts her flute of rosé in my direction. "Perfect."

Bethanie golf-claps, and I chuckle. "We've made a good Texan of you after all."

I can't argue, seeing as how I'm wearing blinged jeans from Traycee's, a boxy royal blue long-sleeved shirt tied at my waist, refurbished and painted boots from Henry's on Second Street, and a crimson felt fedora I snagged on opening day at the new-to-me shop next to Henry's. Bunny decided all my hair needs is a simple pullback with a herringbone braid pulled over one shoulder. She assures me I won't have hat hair this way.

I take my fashionista friend's word.

"I can honestly say the only thing on my body I've never worn before is my knickers."

"I hope you put on a super-sexy set for tonight, for good measure. Lots of lace. Little satin straps. Easy to unhook." Bethanie wags her brows at me, and I wrinkle my nose.

She hasn't given up her support of the sow-wild-oats theory. I haven't shut down all consideration in that direction, but neither am I determined to go there, either. "You're nae gonna stop, are you."

It's not a question.

"Nope."

I know my makeup's on point, subtle but interesting. I got into a habit of doing only the mascara-blush-lip-shine minimum and didn't realize how much I missed my old routine. Now, thanks to my new cadre of stylists, I've upped my game significantly. And I like it.

It all culminates in my two B's seals of approval, and by the time I'm gliding down the front steps to meet DeWayne to introduce him to Penny, I wonder who this woman is who feels like she's shed ten years, like her feet have little wings. Like her soul might willing to come out of the sad, dark place it's been hiding.

I'm a bit giddy as DeWayne gives me a hug.

"You look incredible. I've nearly worn holes in my boots waiting for today."

He kisses my cheek, a gesture I'm starting to get used to and one I absolutely approve of.

"DeWayne, this is Penny the Dragon."

He gives her snout a rub and smiles at me. "I've met the beautiful Penny before, when I came for the games. Even have a picture with her on a roll of film somewhere, which tells you how long ago that was. I'm delighted to remake her acquaintance, though."

Talk of the amazing pink granite statue fills our drive to Atlanta, where he's taking me to dinner at a quaint Italian restaurant. One of the best kind—out of the way and known only to locals.

"If it's a local place, how do you know about it?" My tone's teasing, but I am curious.

"It's a place my ex-wife and I would come, back in the good times. Her folks are from this area, so I know quite a few good spots."

He must have seen something on my face, even though his revelation doesn't bother me. Or I thought it didn't.

"Should I have picked someplace else? I didn't think about my ex when I chose it, I promise. Now, in hindsight, I feel like a dolt."

I hurry to reassure him. "Please don't. It clearly has good memories for you."

"It does, and I guess it's as good an opening as any to get the obvious questions out of the way, but rest assured, I don't want to talk about my ex for the rest of our first date."

I get a little bubbly feeling with the implication *first* doesn't mean *last*, but it's not euphoria. Just a nice lightness that his thoughts run in such a direction.

He waits until we're seated and the waiter has taken our orders before jumping in. "I was married sixteen years to my high school sweetheart, but the sad truth is, military life is hard on families. One too many TDYs and remote tours had her throwing in the towel. I can't blame her."

"TDY?"

"Sorry, military jargon for temporary duty. I'm in the Air Force, which is generally considered the branch that's easier on families, but it's by no means easy no matter where you serve. Anyway, initially I was devastated, but we've managed to become friends again and co-parent really well, if I do say so myself. My son is a junior at UT, and my daughter, being a pure contrarian, started at A&M."

"Ah, the big rivals. I've picked up a bit of the local rules about colors and such. So maybe I shouldn't have worn a maroon hat?"

He gives me a huff-laugh and a big smile. "Are you kidding? You look amazing, although I've mentioned that already."

I duck my head. "You did, thank you."

"I have plenty more compliments where those came from, but I'm trying not to sound like a starstruck teenager."

"Haud yer wheesht, man. No bammin' me now."

"I promise you, I'm sincere. But to your point, I've accepted I'm now part of a house divided, but as long as I don't have to choose on game day, I'm good."

The rest of dinner is equally as easy as we switch topics from American traditions to Scottish ones, me explaining our own rivalries over our football, which I point out is the *real* football, and my Douglas's beloved cricket. I tell him about Travis and Sadie, my transition through grief to where I am now after losing Douglas, and even more lighthearted things as we compare the mad things people in both our countries do. Every moment, from our last sip of Chianti to the drive home to now standing in front of Penny again, has been fun. Genuinely nice.

When he bends his head to kiss me, I'm ready. I lean in, champagne-in-the-veins tingling through my body. His lips are warm and firm, his hands strong and confident as he slips his arms around me and pulls me in, his hair soft under my fingertips as I put my arms around his neck. I don't have any reservation, embracing the excitement fluttering my stomach.

He takes my hat off and strokes my hair, running my braid through his fingers without breaking our connection. It's one of the most sensuous things I've ever felt. So innocent seeming, but so seductive in actuality.

My pulse rises. With my hand on his neck, I can testify his has soared, too. The low rumble in his throat makes me smile underneath his mouth, and I feel his lips curve, too.

One thing is sure, Lieutenant Colonel DeWayne Tomlinson deserves one of those fancy medals for kissing. Minutes pass, how long doesn't matter, before he pulls back, his body screaming, *Not yet*, if the tension in his arms is any indicator.

"Wow." He taps my nose. "I seem to say that a lot around you."

I feel my cheeks flush. I don't know what I was expecting him to say, but that one word is a balm to a spot in my heart I didn't know was sore.

And in a flash of lightning, I get it.

I get what Bethanie and Bunny, and even Logan, meant when they urged me to sow my oats.

I press my cheek against DeWayne's chest, and in the shadow of Penny's giant wings, the soft breeze rippling my shirt, the moon high and big and bright, I understand what I thought I was missing in my life isn't blazing passion in countless bedrooms. What I actually need is the feeling of being courted. Wanted.

Desired.

It's not that Douglas didn't desire me. He did, and I felt the same for him. But he was a boy, and I was a girl, and neither of us knew shite all about what we were doing. We hung on and kept forging through. And in the arms of this delightful man from Dallas, I know I've been completely truthful with Logan. I never would have left Douglas, because I wasn't miserable and didn't begrudge my quiet, comfortable life.

But my life inexorably changed after he died. It doesn't matter how obvious the statement might seem. I wasn't looking for change. I was looking forward to a different phase of our lives together, but those plans were ripped right out of my arms when I let go of Douglas's hand and let the doctors turn off the machines giving everyone false hope.

Especially me.

And I was lost and scared and alone for literally the first time in my life. I went from girl to young woman to wife without ever doing the transitions most people do. I didn't go to uni to live in dorms or crowded, shared apartments, building a life without my parents hovering nearby. Instead, I went from my parents' house to a tiny apartment with Douglas, getting pregnant not long after and starting a life completely different than I imagined. And now, I'm in the same position. I'm facing a future that's turning out nothing at all as I imagined, and yet I'm finding this new way isn't bad. Simply different.

I didn't want this new life. I didn't pray for it or ask for it or yearn for it, but I wasn't given an option, and now, after a year of mourning and finally saying goodbye, I realize there is a treasure in even the most painful of circumstances, a prize I've been blind to while the wounds were fresh, tender, and weeping.

In what's become an unconscious habit, I reach up and touch the cairngorm hidden in my cleavage. I suppose it's one more sign the stone is warm only from my body heat, not from the mystical signal it gives me from time to time.

I wasn't looking for a present, a surprise, when I took the unexpected invitation to come halfway around the world from where I've spent my entire life. Yet I was given presents, plural, from the moment I set foot on Texas soil. From the MacInnes magic to my Magnolia Bloom friends and newly formed heart family, to an incredible man who is confident enough to give me room to figure all this out on my own.

And of all the things and people I didn't expect and am not entirely sure I deserve, I got DeWayne Tomlinson. A funny, intelligent, handsome, amazing man. A rare gem all on his own.

For some other very lucky woman.

DeWayne uses a gentle knuckle to get me to lift my chin and look at him. "What's going on in that pretty head of yours?"

I let the flattery sink in, holding it to my heart like the gift it is. "I was thinking this has all been lovely."

He winces and sets me away from him enough so we can step back to take a seat on Penny's retaining wall. "Lovely, huh? Ouch."

I bite my lip, wishing I could say the words he wants to hear. "Aye, it's been brilliant."

He gives a sardonic lift of one side of his sexy mouth. "You left out the silent 'but.'"

I take his hand and use my other to stroke the long, tanned, capable, and yes, lovely fingers. We don't use that word for men enough, even when it applies so perfectly.

He squeezes. "Let's see if I have a handle on this. If I ask if you'd like to go for a nightcap, or even better, if you'd like to go out again, you're going to say no."

"DeWayne, I'm—"

"Please, whatever you need to say, don't say sorry. I had a wonderful time tonight, especially the last ten minutes."

My chin wobbles, but I meet his eyes, as he deserves that. "Is that how long it's been? It felt like forever and not long enough."

He reaches over to brush back the stray hair the wind is blowing in my face. "Thank you for that patch on my wounded heart."

I scoot closer and put my head on his shoulder. "You are a wonderful man, DeWayne."

"But...."

"Blast, I hate that word."

"Not more than me right now, I assure you."

His arm braces behind my back, and it's warm and solid. "I wish I could say the words you want to hear. This has truly been a lovely evening. And it isnae fair, but you have no idea what it's done to help *me* understand *me*. I won't bore you with the whole story, but I've never felt especially pretty or wanted, and I like this being-courted thing. It's new, but I could get used to it. Mostly, since I came to America, I've discovered I'm nae so bad."

He rears away, forcing me to drop my head back so I can see his face. "Forgive me for using this language with a lady, but that's the damn dumbest thing I've ever heard. You're beautiful, Lexi. Gorgeous. Funny. Vibrant. Sexy."

I put a fingertip to his lips. "Stop, you silly man. I wasnae digging for compliments. I was trying to tell you that you make me feel all those things, and I have nae words sufficient to thank you."

"But I'm not the man you want to hear them from for the rest of your life."

I close my eyes, and when I open them, a tear falls down my cheek. "I'm sorry." My whisper is a croak, and he saves me by putting his cheek on top of my head and simply holding me.

"I am, too."

His whisper's a little more stable, and I hate the hurt I hear in what he doesn't say. We move apart, but he keeps a hold of my hand for another minute.

I clear my throat and try for a normal voice. "I feel I should ask you inside for coffee or that nightcap."

He kisses my knuckles and lets go. "Thank you, but I'll head back."

"When do you return to Lakenheath?"

"Not for another week, but I'm afraid I'll have to scrap the wish list I started on my computer. I had the days chock full, but they all included you."

I stand, and he follows, giving me a full, double-arm hug before he turns to go. Then he stops, twisting around, and gives me a smile I'll remember forever. "Be happy, Lexi. You deserve it."

"You, too, DeWayne. You'll find someone worthy of the incredible man that is you."

His smile is wry. "I thought I'd found her."

He doesn't wait for me to come up with an amazingly erudite reply, for which I'm grateful. I couldn't have found those words if annual rainfall in East Texas depended on it.

I wait until he's in his car and pulling away before I offer a final wave and move up the castle steps. Everything inside is quiet, still. There aren't any in-house guests tonight, so I'm in no danger of anyone seeing the tearstains on my cheeks and wondering what's up, or worse, asking me if I'm all right.

I'm not sobbing. It's not those kinds of tears. They're sad, yes. He really is a lovely, lovely man, but I made the right call.

As I think the words, my phone rings, and I pull it out of my pocket, quickly swiping to accept when I see the ID.

"Hallo, Travis. Why're calling so late?"

"It's not late out here in California. And what do you mean late? Isn't it six-ish there? I figured you'd be in the kitchen starting coffee."

In a flash, the calls from Sadie and my sister flash through my head. Not a single member of my family's given the slightest notice to my careful dissemination of my itinerary, complete with contact numbers and all the other bits I felt they'd need while I was gone.

If the universe wanted to send me a sign that no one is sitting around waiting on me, I've got it. In another time, I might have been hurt to realize I put this all on myself, but tonight, I can honestly say thank you.

"Mum?"

"Sorry, love, got lost for a second. The thing is, I'm in Texas, visiting our MacInnes kin."

"You are? Oh, yeah. I was supposed to call you to see if we could get together, wasn't I?"

"It's all right. I've been busy."

"Glad to hear it."

I let him prattle on about what's happening out on the sunny West Coast, and once again, I'm reminded I can be a tad dense sometimes.

"Come to think of it, Travis, we might be able to meet up after all. I'm going to come out to Los Angeles. Is it awfully far from where you are?"

"Pasadena's only a few miles away. Traffic is beyond shite, but I can come see you, or you could come out here, and I'll show you around the campus and my office."

"Sounds brilliant."

"What's bringing you this way?"

I can't tell my son it's the most beautiful man I've ever seen who's also the most glorious lover a woman could want in a thousand lifetimes.

"Catching up with a friend."

"Let me know when, and I'll make some plans."

Plans. Something I'm good at, and here I stand, in front of the door to a beautiful little apartment I'm about to rush into, pack a bag faster than my barmy brothers-in-law can drain a pint, and race pell-mell to the airport to be there first thing in the morning. I'll beg, borrow, or steal to be on the fastest flight on the schedule.

And hope with all my strength that the man who made it abundantly clear he wanted me before wants me still.

CHAPTER TWENTY-NINE

BETHANIE

MY JOB for Halloween at the castle this year was ticket taker for the dunking booth, but the sun's gone down, and the wind's too chilly for anyone to walk around drenched, which means I'm free for the evening.

I'm slugging down a needed glass of lemonade when I hear my name and turn. Squealing with delight, I race toward Lexi and swallow her in a hug.

"When did you get back? How's Logan? How's his brother? Did you get to see your son, and by the way, you left without telling me about DeWayne."

She fans me with her fedora, black this time and her new favorite accessory. "Slow down, you silly hen. You'll hyperventilate."

We hook arms and head for one of the many picnic tables stationed around the food and drink carts. I let her get completely seated before giving her the stink eye to hurry up.

"In order, I got back about three hours ago, but needed a shower and a quick nap. Logan is wonderful. Amazing. Impossibly beautiful.

His brother is fine. He's supposed to be out of ICU today, and Logan says when he's stable, he'll head home. I did see Travis. He drove up from Pasadena, and we had a marvelous couple of days with him playing tour guide."

I wait, then tap the table with a fingernail. "You missed one line item."

She gives me the wicked smile she keeps tucked in her superpower toolbox, though I'm certain she's employed it more recently than she has in the past few decades combined.

"My date with DeWayne was lovely, which I texted you from the airport."

"Yes, you sent me those six words and not a scintilla more, you mean thing."

"I wasn't being cagey. I was distracted and exhausted, then busy with Logan."

I wiggle my eyebrows. "Busy, huh?"

She returns an eye roll. "Very busy, in fact, but he was also distracted, which I understood. He needs to stay focused on his brother, so we had a quiet three days together, and then I spent time with Travis. I offered to stay with him—Logan, not Travis—but he disliked the idea of me sitting in a hospital for days on end."

"That's Logan, thinking of you, not himself."

"I'll have to get used to it, but I'm willing to give it a go."

"What made you bust a move and leave for California without hardly a word of warning? I've wanted to text or call you from the minute I heard you left, but managed to keep my nosy self in line. I hope you appreciate the level of restraint here."

"Aye, doll, I do. The abridged edition is this. DeWayne's an amazing man and a fabulous kisser."

"Ohh, so there were some oats sowed, then."

"A few flung about, but not the whole bowl, if you catch my meaning. He's going to make some woman a great partner someday, just nae me. There's a tiny piece of me sad about that."

I give her a shocked brow.

"A tiny piece, ye mad hen. Anyway, after our date, I got a call from Travis, and like my Sadie and my sister, I realized no one, literally no one, noticed I'm not in Scotland. I haven't even heard from my parents other than a text saying they were off to the Isle of Skye for a big holiday. For a minute, I was disappointed, but I realize there's no one tying me to Bearsden anymore. I mean, it'll always be home, right? But there's nothing I *have* to go back for."

"Wow, that's a lot to get from one date and a kiss."

"It wasnae all from the date, but aye. I thought such a realization would devastate me, gut me, but I never expected it to free me."

"So you freed yourself right on over to LA and told that big hunk of man you were his?"

"In those words exactly? Nae, but we've agreed to see where things go."

"Like straight down the hall of his house to the big bedroom on the left?"

She slaps my hand. "Possibly." She stops and frowns. "How do you know where his bedroom is?"

I laugh. Loudly. "He had a big Christmas bash there one year. I got the nickel tour."

Her expression clears but goes sheepish. "Blast, but I sounded like a jealous harpy, didn't I?"

"Proves what I already knew. You're crazy about him."

"Yeah, right, that's hardly a big secret, aye?"

"No, but it's fun to tease you."

I look around the busy lawn, ecstatic that yet another event has gone off without a hitch. I don't want to risk jinxing anything, so I cross my fingers under the table where she can't see my silliness. A movement catches both our attention, and we throw identical smiles as Bunny's laughter peals across the grass as she and Gene approach the Hi Striker. We watch with interest as he swings the mallet, adding a hefty grunt, sending the puck sailing upward, and giving the bell a decisive ring. The midway barker, being played by Trey Greene, hands Bunny a— wait for it—bunny, and the two walk off, oblivious to their audience.

Lexi's eyes go mellow with happiness, and I'm sure mine are equally moist.

"Och, now there's a happy ending I'm overjoyed to witness. And did you see the size of the rock on her finger?"

"I'm still experiencing temporary blindness from when the sun hit it."

We both know Bunny would have been equally happy with a ring tab from a soda can, but we're glad she didn't have to settle.

"Now that we've got you and Logan squared away, too, the world's all put back in its proper orbit."

Lexi looks at me, and I feel the nailed-to-the-floor thing usually reserved for Eunice or one of the other Grannies. "That isnae quite true, though, is it, love? I see a certain lack of texts about Roy while I was away."

"That's because there was nothing to text you about. He's been busy with work, and while he doesn't exactly avoid me, he also hasn't sought me out, either."

Lexi, being Lexi, takes my hand and pats my wrist. "And how're you about that, then?"

"I'm okay." I pat back when it appears she doesn't believe me. "I'm serious. I've even surprised myself how okay I am with it, with him. With me. I'm not lying. I'll be really sad if he doesn't at least want to go on a date, but I'll heal, and I'll move on."

"Good on ya. And I mean it. You're a different person than even the strong woman I met nearly three months ago." Surprise makes her pull her head back. "Three months. I still blink fast when I realize how long it's been and how fast it's gone."

I snap my fingers, startling her. "Sorry, I forgot to tell you about Gene's son, who I now know is named William."

"I thought they haven't seen each other in a long time."

"They haven't—or, more accurately, they hadn't—but Bunny convinced Gene to call William, and it turns out his mother had him believing all this time Gene didn't want him, and of course, Gene believed William wanted nothing to do with him. Anyway, William has agreed to consider coming out some time for a visit. Nothing in stone yet, but it's another miracle we can add to the books."

"Damn, but that's good to hear."

The sound of a horse snuffling and an increase in the decibels of kids screaming have us turning toward the staging area for the hayride.

"Look who's in line." As if I needed her to, Lexi points to the space behind me.

I don't need to look. My Roy Radar goes off if he's anywhere within spitting distance. He's not in uniform tonight, making him mouth-watering in jeans and a navy Henley. I can't fault him for not wearing a costume. I'm not, either, but Chloe's adorable in a pink genie outfit, complete with pillbox hat and scarf draped under her chin.

"Go." Lexi's voice is deep and urgent. "Go take the hayride with him and Chloe. Let him know you're still waiting."

I shake my head. "I don't want to look desperate."

I'm sure I didn't speak loud enough for her to hear me, but Chloe turns and sees me, then makes a beeline for the table, her father following at a far more decorous pace.

"Hi, Miss Bethanie. Hi, Miss Lexie."

"Are you having a good time?" I keep my attention fixed on the little minx instead of the all-too-distracting man who's now a mere two feet away.

"I have so much candy. Look." She holds out her jack-o'-lantern, and she's correct. That is a lot of sweets.

"You won't have to go to the market for candy for ages now."

She frowns at the thought. "I don't like that. Maybe—"

"You can worry about it next week, honey." Lexi, ever the water smoother, covers my gaff.

"Are you having a good time, Miss Lexi?" I'm stunned at this child's courtesy. Granted, I'm not around kids a lot, but she never fails to blow me away with how comfortable she is with adults.

Lexi, now in mother mode, fixes the left-leaning tilt of Chloe's hat. "I'm having a grand time, but I'm a little sad."

Concern morphs Chloe's face in a snap. "Oh no, why?"

"Well, I wanted to go on the hayride, but I don't have anyone to go with me."

In the next breath, Chloe's face is bright again. "You can come with me and Daddy."

Lexi gives me a wink while the child's attention has momentarily gone to the stone-faced man looking at Lexi with a clear *What are you doing?* in his expression. She doesn't let it phase her. "Not allowed. Two people at a time, I'm almost certain."

Chloe looks at the adults around her. "Come on, Miss Lexi. Daddy can stay here with Miss Bethanie and hold my candy. You come with me."

The little girl is practically dragging Lexi from her seat. "I'll be right back, Daddy. You stay right here, okay?"

She doesn't give him the opportunity to argue as she and Lexi are off, hurrying to reach the end of the line getting ready to board.

Roy grunts. I'm not far off in the same assessment.

"Sorry, Roy. I had no idea she was going to do that."

"Lexi or Chloe?"

"Either, I guess, but we both know Lexi is the mischief maker here."

His response is a little more growl than grunt this time. He watches the horse go into motion, Chloe happily ensconced on Lexi's lap, and turns back to me.

He stuffs his free hand into his pocket. "They're going to be gone fifteen minutes. Would you like to get some hot chocolate?"

The weather's cool, just nipping into cold, but that's not the reason I say, "Sounds great."

The painfully obvious one is I'll take any stolen minutes alone with him.

There's something adorable about the tall, silent Roy holding an orange tub of candy as he escorts me over to the hot-beverage booth. The line moves quickly, and we have plenty of time left in our quarter-hour date as we take a seat among the relatively quiet benches under the pecan trees.

I'm holding my cup with both hands and blowing on the steaming-hot drink, forcing myself not to gulp it and burn a layer of taste buds off my tongue. It at least lets me pretend I have something to focus on instead of my heartbeat, which might need the defibrillator we have ready at the first-aid station.

It appears Roy doesn't have my cool control as he sips, barks a, "Damn," and puts his cup down on the seat beside him.

Then he shocks me even closer to coronary failure by touching my knee so I'll look at him—as if there's any other reaction I could have to him touching me—and angling his body so he's the only thing I can see.

"I hope you know I've haven't had a single full night's sleep since Cammie and Trey's wedding."

Would it make me a terrible person if I let a big ol' goofy smile burst across my face? Just in time, I turn it into what, I hope, is merely a quizzical one. "Really? Insomnia run in your family?"

He growls, but only a little. "No, it does not. My problem sleeping is caused by one certain captivating, frustrating, beautiful woman who threw a gauntlet at my feet and then walked away."

"It's been a fair bit since the reception in question. You could have responded at any time."

"No, I couldn't, since I had to do a hell of a lot of thinking."

I risk a sip of my cocoa to moisten a suddenly dry mouth. "And did you come to any conclusions?"

"I did."

I wait five complete seconds before I break. "Care to share the big news?"

He takes my cup and sets it next to his, then puts his hand in my now-empty one. "Yeah, I think so."

I last only three seconds this time. "You're killing me here."

He uses his free fingers to sweep my hair over my shoulder. "I'm sorry. I'm not trying to be a jerk. I'm trying to get all the words and feelings swirling inside me in order. If this was a report for the mayor, I'd be golden. This stuff? Scares the crap out of me."

"Would it make it any easier if I told you I was scared crapless, too?"

"Not really. So I guess I need to get on with it." He takes a deep breath and looks me straight in the eye, making my knees, and every other muscle and joint, melt. "I like you, Bethanie. And in a romantic way. We've known each other a long time, and yeah, your past caused me some reservations. But that was because I knew what an incredible person was locked inside your cage. When you broke yourself out, it scared me to even think of you as anything more."

"I understand, especially when you found out about Chloe and her mom."

He stops me with a surprising shake of his head. "I'm not painting you with the same brush as her. Chloe's mom and I were an impulsive night when I was no teetotaler myself, so I have no glass house, I assure you. But I don't want to talk about her. I want to talk about how amazing you are and how impressed I am with what you've done with your life."

I try for a smile, but my mouth wobbles. "I don't think I've ever heard you say that many words in a row to me, not counting the time you read me my Miranda rights."

We can't change that fateful night, but we can make it funny now. Enough time has passed, and it's better to make it our friend than let it lurk in the background.

"I'll ask Tawny to do a word count when I go to work tomorrow." Which will confuse the heck out of his secretary, but I appreciate him leaning into my lame joke. "But listen, the point is, I'm done thinking. I'm sorry I took so long."

"I had to come to some decisions about me, things I've been hiding from, so maybe it's a good thing you and I haven't gotten together before now. Not that we're together. Shit. I'm shutting up now."

When he laughs, his face is transformed. Like his eyes, the sound is something I could hear every day and never tire of. "If you're determined not to talk, I have another idea."

Okay, now I'm really confused. "Come again?"

He reaches down and grabs Chloe's bucket. "There's no mistletoe around yet, but how about we use this as a substitute?"

He holds the jack-o'-lantern over my head, and I burst out laughing. Delighted laughing. Startled laughing.

Oh-yes-please laughing.

After I nod, unable to vocalize my plea, he sets the candy aside. Both of his hands cup my face, and he pulls me, with exquisite slowness, toward him. He meets me halfway, and I find out Roy Hilton may be the number one marksman in this county, but he's also, for damn sure, the number one kisser in the entire state. Of course, I don't have quite so much experience, but I'm completely certain I'm correct.

When we come up for air, which is much too soon, I'm literally dizzy and don't hesitate for a nanosecond to scooch over and settle into the circle of his arm.

"We should head back to the picnic table. You're under explicit orders, you know." It kills me to say the words, as I'd much rather slip off into the concealing darkness of the magnolia grove and engage in a session of heavy petting that would light the gossip fires of this town.

He sighs and lays his cheek against the top of my head. "You're probably right."

"I am, and it begs the question, what do you want to tell Chloe? I understand if you're hesitant."

His laugh rumbles against my ear. "You don't think Chloe going off so easily with Lexi is happenstance, do you?"

I move away so I can see him. "Chloe couldn't have known what Lexi was up to."

"No, but seeing as how I already told Chloe I like you, and she's been beside herself not saying anything, the little stinker saw a chance to play junior matchmaker. She's pretty smart for her age."

"I've always known she's special."

"True."

I scratch at my neck at a sudden burst of uncertainty. "So she's okay with this? Us?"

"She said, and I quote, 'Miss Bethanie is the best, and she's really pretty, and she could be a real princess, and can I be a flower girl again?'"

"All in one breath? I'm impressed."

"I told her not to get ahead of herself on the flower girl thing, and she said she understands old people have to do things slowly sometimes."

"Ouch."

But I'm really, really glad he slipped in the pause button on things going serious too quickly. I'm more than willing to consider picking out a new shade of chiffon for a dress for Chloe, but not yet. It's a future I'd like to leave as an option, but Roy and I need to spend some time together, learn about each other as mature, healthy adults.

"Is it okay?" Roy strokes my chin with the pad of his thumb, and I forget how to breathe. "If we act like old people for a second?"

"Yes, it is. I'd like to date, like a normal person, without a vodka haze blurring every stinking minute. I've never had that before, and it's something I'd like to experience."

"Me, too."

We grab one last long, hot, melting kiss before we take our cups and head back to our post, arriving as the wagon returns, and Chloe and Lexi are headed this way.

Lexi gives me a wink, and I want to act stern, but I'm too euphoric to pretend. She excuses herself to go make a round of the booths she hasn't gotten to yet, and I'm left with Roy and Chloe, feeling a flash of awkwardness and uncertainty returning. I'll get over this tendency to doubt. I'll make myself get over it, but it's a work in progress.

Leave it to a seven-year-old to fix it. With her childlike innocence, Chloe slips one hand in her father's and the other in mine and starts tugging. "Come on. There's a cakewalk, and Miss Eunice said I have to try to win her coconut cream pie." She comes to a screeching halt and looks around to be sure no one can hear and whispers, "She said she'll make me another one if I don't get it, but you can't tell anyone."

Roy and I nod solemnly, both of us crossing our hearts.

When we start walking again, he looks at me over her head, and I wonder if it's possible to faint from happiness. I'd almost convinced myself, as the days went on, I'd been a fool and reached for an apple too high in the tree.

He winks at me and reaches down, midstride, to pull Chloe into the circle of his left arm.

Which is when I realize he did it to free his right arm to twine around my waist and tuck me in close.

I revel in the warmth of his ribs against mine and how safe I feel as I snuggle as close as I can and not inhibit his long legs. I'm certain it will take time, but things are going to work out perfectly.

For all three of us.

CHAPTER THIRTY

EPILOGUE – LEXI

BUNNY AND GENE decided on the simplest of ceremonies. They chose to stand before Harville with no attendants, but the chapel's packed with all of us acting as witnesses and wanting to see the moment we've been waiting for.

Bethanie and Roy sit to the left of Logan and me in the front row, all of us bursting with happiness for our friends. Emmett and Wyatt are on the other side, and I nearly snort-laugh when I see Emmett trying to hide the tears in his eyes, batting away Wyatt's arm when he tries to hand over a tissue.

I listen with half an ear to Harville's sweet words joining Bunny and Gene forever, ashamed of myself for being lost in my own thoughts at such a time, but I'm getting antsy with how fast time is passing.

Logan and I had to talk about me going home. It's not a matter of me wanting to go, although he understands I can't stay away from Scotland forever for the sake of my heart, not the law. He said he'd love to come with me and test the visitor limits on himself this time.

Goodness, I love this man.

Cammie's knee-deep in the papers to get me a work visa for an extended stay, which will get us over the biggest hurdle now that I've agreed to be the assistant chatelaine until Kiki's ready to come back. I'll stay on full time, and with Bethanie already miles ahead of me, we'll keep things covered. Once Kiki's back and I return her cairngorm and her turret, we'll be an unstoppable trio making Castle MacInnes chug along like the steam train over the Glenfinnan Viaduct.

I'm so caught up in my own head, I almost miss the kiss and presentation. Thankfully, Logan is in control of his faculties and gives my hand, which he has wrapped in his, a little jostle. After all the kisses and hugs, he leads me down the east steps and into the shadows of the tree line before I wake myself up. I'm more than happy to come back to my senses when he kisses me, crushing me to him in the most exquisite way.

"I love you, Lexi. I hope you know that by now."

"Aye, I do, and I love you, too. I'm still in shock. I'm having a hard time believing it sometimes. I never dreamed I'd find love again. In America. With a man who makes me drool every time I look at him."

"I can deal with drool, since it means you're highly susceptible to my charms."

The moon comes back from hiding behind the clouds, and I can all but feel the beams bathing us in light.

He traces my collarbone with fingers that have given me unending hours of pleasure, whether from massages rendering me boneless, to sex leaving me breathless, to the way he twines his fingers with mine and holds my hand as though it's precious. When he follows the vee of my blouse, I nearly melt.

"I loved you before then, but when you wore that dress the night of the gala, making you look like a goddess in liquid silver, I was hooked."

"I was, too, but it took my head a little longer to listen to my heart."

"That's all right. It's listening now."

"Aye, you can be sure."

He lets me go and snuggles me against him, leading me to the magnolia grove that's supposed to be nigh onto as magical as the chapel. There, he proceeds to show me with lips and tongue and hands I affect him as much as he affects me.

When things are in danger of going too far, we break away by mutual, reluctant agreement and head back toward the festivities in full swing in the ballroom.

"It'll kill me to wait until the party's over to get you home."

Home. There it is again. I have a home in Bearsden. It's full of happy memories and sad ones that are healing. But I'm building a new one now, and the important thing is, I don't have to rush. We have all the time in the world.

"Anticipation will make things more grand, aye?"

"I'm not so sure."

"Och, don't be a grump. Come dance with me and get your mind out of your knickers. You only have to behave for another hour or so."

He teases the nape of my neck. "That's forever."

I stop and turn, taking his beautiful face in my hands and placing a kiss on his perfect lips. "I'll make it up to you tonight and for the rest of eternity."

"Promise?"

"Promise."

He slips back beside me, and the moonbeams fold into the glow from the party lanterns, the quiet of the grove into the laughter of the crowd.

I'm sure life will throw me more curve balls. That's the game. But I'll survive it all with family, both old and new, friends, and a man who's the other half of my soul.

As long as I have moonlight and magnolias, I can always find my way home.

Thank you for joining me in Magnolia Bloom. Be sure to catch up on any titles you missed so you're ready for *SWEET DREAMS IN MAGNOLIA BLOOM* coming March, 2022

ABOUT THE AUTHOR

Paula Adler is a born and bred Texan, and she doesn't care what the DNA test says, she's way more than 12.6% Scottish. If she's not writing, you can find her dancing or SCUBA diving. Contact her at paula@paulaadler.com or via her website www.paulaadler.com

Made in the USA
Coppell, TX
13 October 2021

64028225R00142